While Athena tries to decide whether to take her relationship with Kas Skoros to another level, she encounters two dangerous villains, a cunning murderer and a child trafficker.

After Detective Ochoa's cousin, Detective Inspector Villalobos, persuades Athena to help him with this baffling case, she realizes a truth that horrifies her and threatens both her and Kas. While at a crowded Christmas festival in the Sierra foothill town of Grass Valley, they encounter a man who attempts to kidnap Kas's nephew. It was Athena's lapse of attention which nearly causes this tragedy and threatens to destroy her relationship with Kas. Only their seeking of justice can right this wrong, and they risk their lives to do so.

Athena's Dilemma
Copyright © 2020 Donna Del Oro
ISBN: 978-1-4874-2536-4
Cover art by Martine Jardin

Published by eXtasy Books Inc or
Devine Destinies, an imprint of eXtasy Books Inc

Look for us online at:
www.eXtasybooks.com or www.devinedestinies.com

Athena's Dilemma
The Delphi Bloodline Series
Book 3

By

Donna Del Oro

DEDICATION

I dedicate this book to my husband, son and daughter, who have been very supportive of all my writing endeavors.

CHAPTER ONE

Bloody hell.

Athena closed her eyes momentarily against the bright sunlight glittering off the San Francisco Bay waters. She inhaled a whiff of briny scent spiced with a hint of pine from nearby trees. With a little more effort, she made another attempt to shut off the mental channel through which her strangely gifted mind often surged. The ebb and flow of too many people and their thoughts caused her head to ache like the bloody devil. Like turning off a spigot and thank god her mother had taught her how to do this. Only this morning, walking amid the crowds along the Embarcadero, she was having difficulty.

One middle-aged man, pulling two rolling suitcases towards a yellow cab, whipped around. Anger creased his face as the woman by his side opened the cab's passenger door and climbed in.

So much for this damned cruise! Nothing can save this rotten marriage. Dead as a doornail! Good riddance to it!

The man disappeared inside the cab but not before Athena had glimpsed a private look into their doomed marriage.

With a slight, sad shake of her head, she tried to shut off the Flow channel again. The noisy crowds disembarking from the cruise ship terminal at Pier twenty-nine jostled her as she stepped around rolling suitcases and the slow-moving elderly. She continued walking briskly along the Embarcadero southward.

Too much human noise.

Hurrying up, she retraced her steps on this morning constitutional, as her British father called it. This morning walk had become a habit, first initiated by her father years ago, and she'd looked forward to accompanying him on these walks as a schoolgirl in London and wherever else the Foreign Service had taken them. Her thoughts traveled to her parents in Milan, where her staunchly patriotic father served as British Consul General and where her clairvoyant, Italian-born mother served the local carabinieri and polizia di stato as an investigatory consultant. Her mother had taught her the importance of helping law enforcement in any way she could. Athena still questioned the wisdom of using their gift in that way. In her experience, that kind of association always backfired.

At any rate, she would make plans to visit them at Christmas time. How she missed them!

That is, if Kas didn't need her at the gallery. Christmas was a little more than six weeks away and she hadn't yet booked her flight. She'd moved to San Francisco only two months ago, and as agreed, had taken over management of the Stargazer Tower's art gallery, situated at street level on the southwest corner of the forty-floor building. Kas—Keriakos Alexander Skoros—had begged her to join him at the Stargazer and well, didn't love take precedence over all other concerns?

Lately, it seemed to. Falling in love again, rather never falling out of it, seemed to have a physical effect she had no control over. Call it a flood of endorphins in the brain, but she was its helpless captive.

Je m'en fou. Sono pazzo.

Being able to say, I'm crazy, in two foreign languages didn't change her situation one tad.

She opened her eyes and glanced to the right. After two months in the city by the bay, she had already developed a kind of mental map of the area. Lombard Street, that famously crooked street, emptied into the bay at this point, just before Green Street. The local TV stations transmitted from the red brick building across the boulevard that ran parallel to the Embarcadero and the piers. The Exploratorium was on her left, a delightful techie museum that she'd already explored with Kas. Broadway came up next, she reminded herself, part of her city-map self-quiz. San Francisco was a small city compared to London, barely one million inhabitants eclipsed by her hometown's eight-point-eight million in central London and twenty-six million in greater Metro London. Still, San Francisco was new to her and she was doing her best to sort it all out.

The Waterfront restaurant next to the Pier five building, where Kas had taken her to dine numerous times, was open even now, eight o'clock in the morning, but her favorite breakfast place was the Marketplace at the Ferry Building. Inside were restaurants, food booths, boutiques, all housed in a hundred-year-old building that had miraculously survived the 1906 earthquake. Fifty yards away, she caught the wafting of aromas from inside the Marketplace.

Ah, her favorite stop!

Then, like the darkness from a grisly underworld, she looked across the bustling boulevard at Washington Park. A water sculpture that looked like carved, gray granite blocks arose from the green grass. It was a place she avoided since her first walk through the park, as the mad and drug-induced ramblings of the homeless scattered about in sleeping bags and under makeshift cardboard covers and ratty tents bombarded her mind and caused her excruciating mental pain.

Help me, Mommy! They're crawling all over me, help me.

I'm gonna kill that bitch . . . next time she comes to suck my dick . . . ain't givin' her no ten bucks! Gotta kill her before she kills me . . .

Athena quickened her step as a man in rags left his tent, stood up and screamed at her from across the street. He raised his fist in a threatening gesture.

Hey, bitch! Whatcha lookin' at?

A woman of indeterminate age emerged from her cardboard hovel, orange hair all askew, her dirty pants and flannel shirt hanging off her gaunt frame like a discarded garment on a clothes hanger. She wept into her raised arm, spotted Athena and turned away, her sobs now audible.

What could Athena do in the face of this open human misery? Nothing. And the lingering guilt she felt added to her fear and pain.

On impulse, she ran across the street, dug a twenty-dollar bill out of her jacket pocket and handed it to the woman. Suspicious reddened eyes met Athena's even as the woman grabbed the money from her outreached hand. A spark of communication passed to Athena via her Flow channel, more information than she wanted. A pretty house, light brown with white trim, a husband-a steady wage earner whose growing disappointment had soured her for him. Three small children whose innocent eyes had turned fearful and sad. The woman's steady decline into deep depression, abuse of booze, drugs. A deceitful drug-peddling boyfriend who lured her away from her family and stole what little money she'd inherited from a relative before disappearing. And so here she was, the woman who'd made a series of horrible choices, had lost everything and now had something truly to be depressed about.

What could Athena do? Nothing. Knowing the dark secrets of these pathetic souls served no purpose.

Athena fled Washington Park and recrossed the boulevard, shutting her Flow channel with a bang. If nothing else, she hoped some of her city sales taxes would go to helping these people. After all, they were still human beings.

So what made her, her mother, and Lorena Skoros different from mental cases like some of those in that homeless encampment? Addiction and looney-tunes free but carrying a cumbersome burden since the age of nine, she regarded herself as truly sane. And there it was. She and the other Delphi descendants were lucky. Or maybe this was the tradeoff.

Sanity but a strange, sometimes disturbing connection to the minds of others? Her wise and loving parents had played a part, no doubt, in keeping her sane. Nature and nurture both held sway, after all. No one she knew from the Delphi bloodline had succumbed to mind-numbing chemicals to escape or ease their psychic pain.

Besides, what could she do? A twenty-three-year-old British citizen with a temporary work visa? Unsure of her future, vacillating from day to day, she felt in a way paralyzed with indecision. Should she set up an art business in Milan, where her parents now lived? Should she enjoy her sojourn in San Francisco with Kas and maybe carve out a more settled future with her handsome American boyfriend? Return to London, where the few British friends she'd stayed in touch with now lived and worked? Give up her art career and give in to wanderlust? Surrender to her psychic abilities and sell her clairvoyance to the public, like some kind of wizard-in-a-booth?

Some problems in the world, even she and the other gifted descendants of the Delphi bloodline couldn't begin to understand or attempt to solve. After all, she wasn't Wonder Woman, just a Delphi clairvoyant, one of several who found themselves anomalies in a hapless world over which they had no control.

Suddenly overcome with hunger and with relief, she ramped up her walk through the Marketplace as a mixture of aromas assaulted her. She paused at a few food booths but ultimately found the bakery with the delicious berry scones, bought a half-dozen, chatted briefly with the British owner about the upcoming Brexit vote, and then scurried out. She noticed the playbill flags on lamp posts she passed under, made a mental note to tell Kas about this musical play based on a De Niro movie — A Bronx Tale at the Golden Gate Theater. Maybe they could go one night.

Athena walked past Perry's Restaurant, where Kas had proposed to her a month ago, an unexpected proposal she'd declined gently. She recalled all too clearly the scene. A candlelit dinner, soft piano tinklings, a slight buzz from the excellent wine. Lucky for them both, he didn't get down on one knee and create a Hallmark movie moment. He'd quietly asked her in his usual pragmatic way, "Are you ready for marriage, Thena?" and showed her the jewelry box, all black satin and blinding diamonds. Not a solitaire but a bouquet of diamonds surrounding a large, center round-cut one.

He'd prefaced the proposal with a little speech.

"Thena, my father once told me, there are many people you can live with. There's only one person you can't live without."

After hearing what he added in a very quiet voice, she'd almost said yes. "I'm finding, much to my surprise, that I can't live without you. I don't want to live without you. How's that for a declaration of love from a longtime cynic?"

Her heart was close to breaking. But such a commitment was too soon for her, she'd told him, staring at the diamonds instead of his hurt expression. His dark blue eyes had pierced her, his voice, a little hoarse.

"I've found these past two, three years that I don't want to lose you. But I don't want to scare you off, either. We're just getting to know each other again." He shrugged one shoulder, apparently to minimize his pain, and looked down at the box. "Thought it couldn't hurt to ask."

But it did hurt him to ask and get turned down. Nevertheless, something deep inside her twanged a warning.

Too soon, too soon. I love you, you know I do. But it's too soon for me.

Her halting reply, "Your home is here. My home is . . . well, I don't know where my home is anymore. Milan? London?"

In hindsight, her reason sounded pathetic, even trite. Still,

6

she'd meant every word.

Anyway, he'd tucked the box into his sports jacket pocket and didn't utter another word about the subject.

Nor since then.

Now she was carrying a bag of his favorite four-berry scones to him. Trying to please him, trying to make a success of his art gallery while earning some money, testing whether their relationship could make a go of it long-term. Practicing her art on the other side of the world from her home country, from her parents, from the careful, cautious British way of seeing and doing things. Not leaping ahead, the impetuous, brazen American way, but treading with great care. Her English father called her headstrong and impulsive, but she really wasn't. Adventurous, yes, but not impulsive.

The high-rises on Howard Street loomed, throwing long shadows along her way, reducing the vast, bright blue sky into narrow strips of light. Her reverie broken, she turned up Folsom and increased her pace, eager to see Kas and share her morning cup of coffee and scones with him. A flutter of heartbeats reminded her how mad she was about him. What could she do about that? Cut out her heart and run her life like an automaton's, all brain and logic and gigabyte data?

The Stargazer Tower rose up before her on the corner of Folsom and Main, forty floors of green glass and steel, reminding her of The Shard in London. Barely one-year-old, it sat right in the midst of earthquake country, as her father had declared in full paternal concern during one phone call. Yes, yes, she knew San Francisco was at the confluence of several seismic fault lines.

The city by the bay was also a study of contrasts, the rich living cheek-by-jowl with the scraggly homeless. At night, addicts shot up and prostitutes plied their johns on Market Street while police avoided the area, leaving the tourists shocked and scratching their heads at the unbridled lawlessness before them. Residents wisely stayed indoors or picked their way among the nighttime detritus in cabs or Uber cars. As she reminded her father, London had the same worldly problems. Maybe not so in-your-face as San Francisco but still there.

Despite all, the city was a painter's canvas, all sparkling water, lustrous skies-when the fog banks cleared-and rolling hills. Architectural sights to behold no matter where you walked or drove. Exciting, sensational views. A majestic, orangish-gold suspension bridge pointing north and south, one that huge cargo ships from Asia sailed under. Another august bridge spanning the bay and taking travelers east and west. A dynamic, bustling small city, the gem of Northern California.

But increasingly dangerous, its throw-away human misfits-like denizens of the underworld-reminding one of their dark, hopeless lives.

On the bright side, and most importantly to Athena, this was the city where Kas now lived and worked.

CHAPTER TWO

"Good morning, Mr. Andrews," she called out to the day manager behind the lobby's Front Desk.

"Morning, Miss Butler." The African American man was in his thirties at most, broad-shouldered, carried an erect military bearing. Kas liked to hire vets, like him. "I see you've been to the Marketplace."

"Tomorrow, if you like, I'll get you a bakery item. What's your fancy?"

He smiled, showing a row of white, upper teeth. Athena was struck again for the hundredth time at the difference in the teeth of the English and Americans, a telltale sign that gave many tourists in London away.

"This time of year, I'd have to say, pumpkin spice muffins or scones."

"Okay, tomorrow morning then."

Even now, as Athena strode through the Stargazer's black-marbled lobby, she could decipher Kas's thoughts. Her mind automatically opened to his although she could turn the Flow off whenever she wanted or during the rare occasions when Kas insisted on privacy. He'd grown accustomed to Athena's mind invasions since his mother was also clairvoyant. Still, to people who lacked the gift of the *third eye*, as Lorena Skoros called their unique abilities, the intrusion was sometimes disturbing, to say the least.

Dammit, man, get to the point. How much, how long? What's it going to take to finish the interiors . . .

Even out of sight, Athena could tune into his thoughts,

invade his mind when she wanted to. He was in an early morning meeting with a contractor who was bidding to finish the million-dollar-plus condos on the top twenty floors of the Stargazer Tower. She could feel Kas's impatience growing.

Athena smiled at the two uniformed security guards in the lobby, drew out a smaller bag that held two of the six scones and passed it to the guard standing by the condo elevators. Sam was all she knew him by, a friendly, old man who'd grown accustomed to seeing her off for her morning walks and always said good morning. He thanked her and pressed the lower condo floor, number twenty-one. The first five floors were office suites, the next fifteen comprised the Stargazer Hotel, and the top twenty floors the luxury condos. Kas had assigned her to one of the smaller condos on the twenty-first floor since she insisted on having her own place. His larger condo reveled in bay views at the northeast corner of the twenty-second, his condo ownership in exchange for two years of his salary as Chief Operations Officer of Skoros Enterprises. The Skoros business office, located on the first floor of the tower, had become Kas's headquarters.

Where's Thena? Should be back by now with those scones . . . better not eat more than one . . . can't get fat and blubbery . . . that'd turn her off . . . God, I love that woman . . . should be back . . . ah, Thena, you're inside my mind . . . I'm starving, sweetheart.

Images followed that made her flush with heat as she rode up to the twenty-second floor. He was teasing her, purposely thinking about their last night's lovemaking as his mind wandered during his business meeting. The erotic images disappeared suddenly as the contractor presented him with a written bid. Athena shut off the channel. One thing she didn't want to do was spy into his business affairs.

His sexual fantasies were another story.

Her mind switched to gallery business. The painter, Ian Chen—a local hyper-realist, landscape stylist—was due at ten. He was meeting her in the gallery and bringing at least

eight of his cityscapes to display in a one-man show scheduled for that weekend.

Unlocking the door to her one-bedroom condo, Athena
scurried to make coffee and scrambled eggs to go with the
scones. When Kas still hadn't arrived, she texted him a quick
note, took a shower and changed into a gray pantsuit, sof-
tened with a pale chartreuse sweater. She'd just combed her
damp hair into her usual ponytail when she heard a familiar
knock. One, pause, two-three-four. She daubed her lips
lightly with red lipstick and fastened on gold hoop earrings.

It was nine-thirty.

She opened the door and there he was. Kas smiled at her
from his six-foot-two height. In a navy-blue business suit and
red tie, he looked every inch the smart, handsome and savvy
businessman his father had raised to take his place alongside
his brothers. Only she knew the real Kas Skoros. The man
she'd fallen in love four years ago and had pined over from
afar.

Looking a little fatigued from lack of sleep, he approached
her, favoring one leg by taking some weight off the other. After the car accident two years before that had killed his
brother and injured him, Kas had left the Placer County Sheriff's Office as a deputy and joined his two remaining older
brothers in the family firm. He still limped a bit, was still
haunted by memories of that night, holding his dying brother
in his arms.

The man whose mind she could read whenever she
wanted. His heart was also an open book.

He took her into his arms and held her, kissing her forehead, her hair, sliding his hand down her back, caressing
every inch. Murmuring sweet nothings with his soft mouth,
stroking her buttocks with firm palms. She turned into a plia-
ble noodle under his touch. His mouth moved to the V-neck
of her sweater, laved the smooth skin above her breasts. He

began breathing heavily, his breath coating her bosom with warm air.

"God, I can't get enough of you," he muttered, "you've bewitched me, you sorceress."

"You've never called me *that* before," she whispered. As his breathing grew more urgent and his hands more insistent, she slid one free hand down to his crotch. Oh yes, his body was telling her one thing. However, his mind lingered somewhere else. Back in that business meeting.

That bastard . . . trying to sucker me into paying double what he charged last time . . . sonuvabitch!

She sighed.

You never really knew a man if you couldn't read his mind.

CHAPTER THREE

She leaned back in his arms.
"Kas, why cover up your anger?"

For a second, Kas looked puzzled. But only for a moment, as realization dawned.

"Thena, I didn't want my meeting to ruin our . . . our cozy, little breakfast get-together. You know me, I have a hard time shaking off anger. It's just . . . just me."

Reluctantly, he let her go and walked over to the kitchen counter, from where aromas wafted over to him.

"The contractor that designed and built the first section of condos did such a great job, I wanted him back to do the rest but he bid double the price he charged last time, just a year ago, for chrissakes. One thousand bucks per square foot! I pointed out to him that market values of San Francisco real estate have increased only thirty percent in the past year, not one-hundred percent."

His agitation spilled over, his speech flowing rapidly, gaining momentum. He raked a hand through his thick, dark-brown hair, which he wore combed straight back. Taming a straying forelock that flapped over his forehead was always a struggle. This morning he gave it up and let it hang over his brow.

"So that's where we started out. Not where we ended up but wasted a lot of time getting there. He hung in tough, that persistent dude, but then he started to move when he saw how upset I was. I knew he wanted this contract. I talked him down to forty percent over last year's costs. Still, more than what we wanted to pay. Pop and my brothers . . ."

He shrugged off the concerns of the other Skoroses, with whom he shared a quarter ownership of Skoros Enterprises. The Stargazer Tower, to date, was their biggest development. A huge financial investment, it was an enormous potential risk as well as a potential long-term reward. If all went well, the Skoros patriarch and his three remaining sons could retire and live off the income generated by this city tower.

"So we're at an impasse. I did my best negotiating with the guy. George and Leon will say I caved, Pop will frown . . ." He shed his suit jacket and took a seat on one of the kitchen stools. "Sorry, enough shop talk."

George was CEO, Leon CFO and Pop-Philip the patriarch-was Chairman of the Board. Kas was officially now COO, having taken Alex's place.

She spooned some scrambled eggs into a salad-size dish, added a sugar-encrusted berry scone, adding a different viewpoint to the equation while he poured them both cups of black coffee.

"Look at it this way, Kas. By the time the condos are done and sold, the market price will have gone up another fifty percent. You said yourself that the condos on the top floors have doubled in price since a year ago." She shook her head. "This city is as bonkers as London, everything overpriced to the hilt. The townhome that was handed down to my father and Uncle Terrence almost ten years ago has increased in value, according to Father, two hundred percent. Real estate values are mad, aren't they?"

Kas smiled in assent. "Indeed." He was picking up some of her Brit-wit expressions. "It's all supply and demand, 'Thena. People want to live in big cities. Y'know, where the action is. The buyers of these condos are highly paid techies working in Silicon Valley, making big bucks. They've got buses and vans picking them up and taking them forty miles down to their jobs. Hell, why not live in the city? And there's no end in sight. 'Least, my mother hasn't seen one."

Lorena Skoros, a sweet, wise woman in her early seventies, was clairvoyant and precognitive, another Delphi descendant and Athena's distant Italian-Greek cousin. She had been the source of the Skoros fortune over the years, always advising her husband where and when to build his strip malls and apartment buildings.

"Least, Mom says the Big One won't hit for many years to come, long past our lifetimes, anyway," Kas added.

The Big One referred to a sizeable, life-changing earthquake like the one that hit the city in 1906.

Reflexively, Athena glanced out of her living room window. Blue sky and wispy clouds were visible beyond the elevated freeway on-ramp that marred her view. She tried to imagine what it would feel like to live in this skyscraper during a jolting earthquake. Would the tower sway and then crash into the bay?

She shook herself. "Please, don't even mention the Big One. You Californians are so fatalistic. It's like, you're worried but you refuse to think about it."

Kas laughed. "Maybe we're in deep denial."

Smiling, she sipped the dark, richly flavored Italian roast coffee she'd brewed. The redolent scent and flavor infused her senses as bracing caffeine surged through her body. "Hmm, delicious. These techies may not be painters of fine art, but the ones I've met in the gallery can sense a good design and that's why it's important that you hire the best to design their condos. No matter the price."

She joined Kas at the granite counter, swiveling into her bar stool. Kas elbowed her arm gently.

"Techies rule the Bay Area. It's also why gifted painters like you take jobs as art gallery managers. Doesn't seem fair, does it, but grateful I am for that."

He leaned over and kissed her cheek. "Last night was . . . amazing. Thena, I've never . . ." She faced him, noted the pinkish blush spreading over his face, could've helped him find the words but wanted to hear him verbalize those same feelings that had swamped her in the middle of the night. " . . . I've never felt that kind of intense bonding, connection. It wasn't just sex. It was . . . we . . . our bodies kinda melted together. But it was more, more than that. I felt our minds . . . meld together, fuse like one mind." He threw his hands up. "I can't explain it. It was just amazing. I'll remember it the rest of my life. Last night."

Athena knew exactly what he meant. She reached around his big shoulder and clutched at the hair at the nape of his neck.

"I felt it, too. I think for the first time, I not only read your mind, but you read mine." His eyes glazed over, he nodded, retrieving that moment of total fusion.

"You've never experienced that before, have you?" she asked him quietly.

His eyes swung over to hers, questioning, looking for answers. He smiled and shook his head.

She continued, "I experience that all the time, when I open the Flow channel. I read the thoughts, feel the emotions, almost see the world through that person's eyes."

His arm wrapped around her back, his big hand clasping her left shoulder. Dark brows furrowed but a side of his sculpted mouth slid upwards.

"This was different, Thena." He grinned helplessly while rubbing her shoulder, then fondling her neck with his chin. Goosebumps trilled up her spine to the base of her neck. "I can't explain it, it was so . . . so . . ."

"You don't have to. I felt it, felt you enter my mind but also felt you expand yours and take in what I was thinking and feeling."

He turned his body fully towards her in his stool, opening his legs to her knees as the same hand left her shoulder and landed on her thigh, running it from her knee to her thigh.

"Wanta try it again tonight?" He chortled. "Though I might not have the energy to do both physical and mental."

Another sip of coffee, avoiding his searching stare, and she was ready to pose an idea to him. A new idea for her, too.

"You're the son of a Delphi descendant. Maybe the sons of such clairvoyants and precogs, like your mother, have the ability, the gene, that allows you to be a little like us."

His frown deepening, he then chuckled and sat back.

"Huh! No, that can't be. With you and me, joined like we were, sharing that physical thing and the emotions—no, that was intimacy, not like what you can do. I can't read minds, don't want to. Ever. Maybe it was just a one-time, flukey, really crazy kind of bonding thing."

She could see his discomfort, so their conversation turned to more mundane topics. Still, his long, muscular legs continued to wedge in hers, applying pressure and suggesting another rendezvous that night. Her heart skipped, the heat in her cheeks intensified. His blue eyes traveled over the length of her body, challenging her to try a repeat performance. The visuals in his mind provoked her in a teasing, playful way. A part of his mind wondered whether she was up for a quick, mid-morning shag.

"I know what you're thinking, you cheeky devil. I have work in the gallery. In five minutes, to be exact."

Disappointment etched his countenance, like a little boy denied an extra piece of candy. She laughed at his exaggerated, self-mocking, childish frown. At five before ten, she slipped off her stool.

"My ten o'clock appointment, Kas. Gotta go."

He relented and smiled broadly, freeing her legs.

"The painter, Chen? Wish I could join you, but I have a

desk loaded with costs and invoices to slog through. Fun and games, huh. I'll be catching lunch on the run later, so . . . how 'bout dinner? Six? Something simple, like downstairs in the Grill?"

Agreeing, she grabbed her pantsuit jacket, flung it on and blew him a kiss as she pocketed her condo and gallery keys. A glance at the half-finished canvas on her standing easel in the living room made her cringe a little. The room served as a painting studio because the light was generous as it faced south. Not a great view, with the Bay Bridge entrance ramp and concrete pillars monopolizing part of the window, but oddly enough, there was more light as a result. But the mess she'd left after her last painting session would be called slovenly by her fastidious mother. She pointed to the mess and shook her head.

"Indeed, aren't you happy I didn't move into your condo? Your living room would look like this," she tossed back, laughing and exiting, not waiting for his reply.

After all, she already knew what he was thinking.

Ian Chen, the son of an Irish American mother and a Chinese American father, had studied Fine Arts at Cal State University, S.F., but he was mostly self-taught, she'd learned. After a decade of teaching high school art classes and trying to follow Degas and Monet in the Impressionistic style, he'd begun to follow his own heart and preferences. Which led him to his current hyper-realism style in which cityscapes of his home city were filled with recognizable landmarks, detailed minutiae and hundreds of people, details so tiny on the canvas that a brush with one or two hairs was necessary to capture each figure.

They shook hands and then watched as moving men, apparently Asian pals of his, carried his canvases out of a van at the curb and deposited them inside the Stargazer Tower's gallery. They managed very carefully to stack each canvas in a neat row against the east wall, then took off but not before shaking her hand as well. They all mumbled something to Ian in Chinese, a language she didn't understand or speak, as they left. Wishing their friend good luck, no doubt, as they left.

Chen was a petite man in his forties, shorter than her five-foot-eight. His receding hairline was barely visible amid a buzz cut. He had a full, round face, and was dressed in paint-smudged jeans, a black tee that managed to avoid any smear of paint, and a rumpled, burgundy-colored velvet sports jacket. A knitted black scarf, wrapped around his neck at least twice, covered his chin. Expressing his pleasure and excitement about his one-man show, launching that Friday evening, Chen sidled alongside her as they moved down the row of cityscapes propped up against the wall.

"I'm so happy about the exhibit! So is my family, all my friends, my girlfriend Cynthia."

"Me, too. I'm jolly excited. This is the gallery's first one-man show. I'll do my best to make this a total success."

They moved along the wall, gazing at the paintings. They were all the same size, twenty-two inches by thirty-four inches. Some were horizontal, some vertical in composition. One vertical painting featured Hyde Street, seen from the perspective of the top of the hill and looking down at the cable car turnstile, the bay waters and Alcatraz Island in the distance. Another one-of-a-kind oil painting was a horizontal one, seen from the vantage point of the bay, looking up at the city skyline, with Coit Tower the focal point, the two hundred and ten foot tower built in the early 1930's by the city's Italian workers. Another horizontal one of the southern end of the Golden Gate captured the true colors of the orangey bridge. Fisherman's Wharf was especially busy with fish stalls, people in colorful clothes shopping, walking, biking, driving. The bay waters just as crowded with boats of various sizes and types. A very colorful vertical captured the top of crooked Lombard Street, the yellow lights from the buildings lending warmth to the fog-shrouded streets on the hillside below.

Athena loved the style, hyper-realism at its best and most whimsical. Perhaps a carryover from the American primitives she'd seen and admired, but they also reminded her of early Dutch Masters and their realistic depictions of town folk in medieval Amsterdam. She told Chen so, smiling and exclaiming at each one in turn. Chen, a seemingly modern man in every way, could barely hold back the full extent of his gratitude. Evidently, every teacher he'd come across had advised him to paint either in the abstract or post-Impressionistic style. Instead, he'd found his own voice.

"Yes, and it shows," she told him. "Your style is authentic, yours alone. That's what I'm still trying to find in my own work. My own voice, my own vision."

Chen nodded. "Keep looking. Maybe you'll find yours before you get to be my age." He laughed, reached over his thick wooly scarf and scratched the scruff of black hair growing at his chin. "Y'know, the former manager of this gallery—I forget her name—wouldn't even look at my work."

Athena grinned. "Well, things have changed here. I keep an open mind and I do want to promote local artists. Will you encourage your family and friends to come to the Opening?"

That elicited a larger laugh. "You bet! I have eight siblings, twenty nieces and nephews, and many colleagues who keep asking when, where, what time."

She seized a stack of promotional flyers from the sales counter and gave them to Chen, encouraging him to pass them around. The flyer featured his photo, a proud man standing next to one of his realistic cityscapes.

"We'll serve champagne, hors d'oeuvres, give away prizes to the first five who buy a painting. Also, Mr. Chen-"

"Ian, please."

"Ian, I'd like to enter into an exclusive contract with you to produce giclee prints of your one-of-a-kind artwork. That will enable collectors who can't afford to pay ten to twenty thousand for a one-of-a-kind to buy a print-on-canvas for one or two-thousand dollars. We can make two hundred-fifty Studio Proof prints, maybe two hundred Artist Proof prints, all hand embellished and hand-signed by you. In time, they'll increase in value, too."

Chen's face shone with tears, her offer rendering him speechless. He managed to nod, and they shook hands again. They were discussing the framing of his sold artwork, a sideline she'd added to the gallery. In fact, she'd just hired a framer who also doubled as her assistant manager. She and Ian were discussing frame styles when her cell phone rang. Not recognizing the local number, she excused herself and stepped away.

"Hello, Miss Butler? Athena Butler?"

"Yes? This is she." The voice was unfamiliar to her, but her stomach flip-flopped suddenly. Whatever it was, it most certainly wasn't good news.

"This is SFPD Inspector Sergeant Mike Villalobos. I'm a cousin of Juan Pablo Ochoa, the Metro homicide detective you worked with in D.C. He told me you were moving to The City."

"The city?" Her stomach flipped over, her insides churning with fear.

"The City, with a capital C, is what locals in the Bay Area call San Francisco."

No! Why did she give permission for Ochoa to tell his cousin about her? She'd liked the D.C. detective a lot and, with her help, they were able to apprehend the disturbed serial killer who had eluded the Metro police for years. But helping Ochoa had almost cost her, her brother Chris and Kas their lives! She'd told Kas and her parents that she'd given up on helping the cops. Forever.

Silence droned on. But not for long.

"My cousin said you'd be reluctant to meet with me. The case in D.C. was god-awful, from what he told me. The murderer returned to D.C. dressed as a woman! After having cosmetic surgery and taking gender-replacement hormones! Jeez, what a nut case he was. The whole case a train-wreck! But you managed to point my cousin in the right direction when no one had a clue. The perp's in prison, I hear, recovering from his injuries."

She cleared her throat and summoned the courage.

"Yes, he is. His brother is still at large, however. Uh, Detective."

"Inspector. Inspector Villalobos, or you can call me Mike. Here in The City, we go by *Inspector*, a British carryover from the old Gold Rush days."

"Well, Inspector Villalobos, with all due respect, I don't do that, anymore. Police consulting, I mean. I promised people . . ."

"Oh, I see." Villalobos paused but went on as if she hadn't turned him down, "Well, it's a case that has us all stumped. A serial killer preying on the city's homeless, from all the evidence. He's got us in a stranglehold, many more will die, no doubt. My cousin said the Metro cops owed you big time. Whatever the case, I need you to consult with us. No strings attached. Just a lot of gratitude for the lives you'll save. Juan Pablo said you're the real deal. You're not a charlatan, not a fake psychic."

Her heart rate had shot up, pulsing blood in her ears like a thunderstorm. This chap knew how to pull all the heartstrings. Her right hand fisted and raised to her mouth in a gesture of fear and tension. She pounded her lips in fear.

Say no, Athena. That's all you have to say. No.

CHAPTER FOUR

"Sorry, Inspector, I can't. It's . . . it's too soon."

"All right, Miss Butler, but keep me in mind, please. You can find me at the Hall of Justice, Bryant Street, SOMA district."

"Soma?"

"South of Market. SFPD's southern station. I know that's where your gallery is. In the Stargazer Tower, in the SOMA district. I've been keeping tabs on you, courtesy of my cousin. Juan Pablo owes you, so he told me to look out for you."

That statement took her by surprise. Why would the police in San Francisco need to look out for her?

Hearing the side rear door from the hotel entrance open, she looked up to see Kas enter. He saw her, smiled and waved a greeting. Then he went over to Ian Chen and extended his hand. A conversation between the two men ensued, mostly out of her earshot. She spoke into her cell phone.

"Really, there's no need, Inspector. Lieutenant Ochoa owes me nothing. I was just helping him out."

"Yes, but you put yourself at risk by doing so. He told me all about it, how you went with him to that electrical business, saw or felt things no one else could. You told him the killer had returned but looked like a woman. Passing himself as a transgender. I gotta say, no one saw that coming, that ingenious ploy of his. Lots of serial killers are just that. Clever, cunning psychopaths."

Athena wanted to end this phone call, for just the mention of that disturbed man, now thankfully in prison, sent chills down her spine.

"But it was all so pointless. If the killer, the motorcycle dude ... chick ... whatever, if he hadn't made the first move." Athena huffed her impatience and sense of futility. "That deranged man would have continued killing. It was his mistake, not my insight, that stopped him. Anyway, all this is moot, Inspector. I don't want to be involved anymore."

She motioned to Kas and Chen that she'd be with them shortly. "I must go. The gallery's busy and I have customers."

"Yes, of course. Just keep me in mind, Miss Butler. Bryant Street, Hall of Justice. I'm located in the Homicide Division, fifth floor. Drop by any time and I'll clear my desk. We'll sit and have a chat. No pressure."

That wasn't true, Athena knew. By the time she rang off, both hands were shaking. She stood still a moment, willing them to stop, making herself calm down. No, she wouldn't do this again. Regardless of what her mother did consulting with the police in Milan, Athena would not jeopardize Kas's safety and her own. Helping to solve murders might be her mother's destiny but it wasn't hers!

Her heartbeat under control, she plastered on a broad smile and joined Kas and the painter.

"I see you've met. Jolly good." She went to Kas's side and slid her arm around his waist. Still dressed in his navy-blue suit, his red tie hanging loose and askew, he looked like a haggard businessman. He leaned down and bussed her cheek.

"Just a few minutes before I get back to the spreadsheets. I looked up and saw my bare walls, felt I needed some color, something colorful to look at. I thought of a painting I'd seen here in the gallery. By the way, Mr. Chen, I like your stuff."

The painter bowed his head quickly, a force of habit, it appeared to Athena. "Ian, please, Mr. Skoros."

Kas smiled. "I'll be here at the Opening, Ian. And Thena, give me some of those flyers. I'll put them in my office and in the lobby."

After she gave him a handful, including three table-size, transparent plastic stands, he turned to leave.

"See you at seven, the Grill?" She nodded.

Then Kas pointed to one of her cityscapes of Washington, D.C. that she'd brought with her when she left her former place of residence. Where she'd spent four years at the Art Academy while her father served as cultural attaché to the British Embassy, where her brother Chris had finished his high school studies and where her mother had continued translating books and consulting with the Baltimore PD. How many missing children had her mother located during that time?

Athena's eyes followed Kas's pointing finger. The twenty-four-inch by thirty-six-inch painting hung on the southern wall of the gallery, next to the inquiry counter. She had sold the other four in the D.C. city series to Martin Larsen's gallery in Georgetown. "That one?"

Kas nodded solemnly, looking at her fully.

The painting's subject. The street she and her roommate Mikaela had lived on, depicted in darkness and shimmers of rain, reflections of lamplight on street puddles. And a motorcycle and genderless rider parked at the curb. All in black, the face hidden a bulbous helmet.

"You know who that is, don't you?" Athena was referring to the serial killer who had appeared at her doorstep one night, had talked Chris into letting him in, and then had tried to kill them all. If Kas hadn't stopped him.

"You don't need to look at it every day, Thena. It's a good painting but I'd rather you didn't have to. It's a reminder of how close we came to—" Kas glanced over at Chen. "Make up one of those sales and title cards, whatever you call 'em, and I'll hang it up on my secretary's office wall. Lots of flow there. I'll have it sold in no time."

Why she'd insisted on hanging it in the gallery, she didn't know. Except that it was an exceptionally good painting and it did bring back memories of D.C. Not all those memories were bad, for she and Mikaela had shared many good times with quirky, artistic friends as well as their own personal and career triumphs and failures. Now Mikaela was launching her fashion design business and living in New York City with her fiancé of three months.

However, the image of the lone motorcyclist at the curb did evoke a stark lesson for both her and Kas. That Athena's extraordinary clairvoyance only went so far. She had sensed something disturbing about the motorcyclist from the very first time she'd laid eyes on what had appeared to be a young, mannish appearing woman. A few months later, the young woman was barking at them in a deep voice, the muzzle end of a pistol pointing at their heads.

Athena shook off the memory. The sooner that painting disappeared from her sight, the better.

"Yes, take it, Kas. You're right. I don't need to look at it every day." Her gaze turned away and swept down the wall of Chen's paintings. "This work is more cheerful. And free of negative associations."

"Let's hope so," Kas added cryptically, a shade of sarcasm in his tone. He was also remembering that horrible night in D.C.

In the minutes that followed, as Chen decided on the frame style for each of his paintings, Kas removed the D.C. street-scene painting from the gallery wall and collected the card imprinted with the artist's name, size of painting, brief description and sales price. While doing so, she read Kas's lingering thoughts. Even his countenance showed more than a tinge of worry. She drew him aside.

"How did you know I was talking to that police detective?" she asked him quietly. He hoisted the painting under his arm and turned to leave the gallery.

Kas lowered his voice in reply. "He called the lobby, they patched him through to me and I referred him to your cell phone." His eyes shuttered a moment as he took a deep breath. "Tell me, Thena, you turned him down. You're not going to get involved in that police crap anymore, are you?"

To console him, she reached up, clasped his shoulder and pecked him on the chin.

"No. I told him no."

He smiled ruefully. "I would've told him, Hell no."

When Kas was gone, Athena turned back to Chen and smiled. Yes, she was glad — even relieved that painting of hers was gone. It was a constant reminder of their close call, their brush with an early death. All three of them . . . Kas, Chris, herself. And for what? Because the coppers couldn't solve a case!

Time to paint happier things!

Like Chen's sunlit park scene of children at play before a background of windswept bay water and limpid blue sky.

Yes! Time to paint happy scenes.

And forget D.C.

CHAPTER FIVE

K as had changed into dark-washed jeans and a cobalt-blue sweater, long-sleeved and collared. Smart and casual, looking more like an off-duty Sheriff's deputy than COO of Skoros Enterprises. Athena still wore her light gray pantsuit, having just closed the gallery for the night. The newly hired gallery assistant, Dale Dargent, had arrived and was now busy framing Chen's paintings for the one-man exhibit on Friday evening, working frantically to meet the deadline. Dale had agreed to work part-time for the gallery, taking the evening shifts for after-work customers in exchange for exclusive framing jobs. A good arrangement, for Athena now had freed up her evenings to paint and spend time with Kas. When spring came and the daylight hours grew longer, she'd be able to explore the city more. Other than Mondays, when the gallery was closed.

Kas smiled and indicated the stool at his bistro table in the corner. She sat down after they kissed over his beer glass, guacamole and tortilla chips.

"What're you in the mood for?"

She inhaled deeply. "Long day, a bit tired. I'll have a Moscow Mule."

Kas eyes widened in mock shock. "Bad day, so vodka, huh?"

They chatted playfully and snacked on the guacamole until her drink arrived. She took a long swig of the cocktail, then heaved a sigh.

"Just glad you took that painting from the gallery. It was

making me shiver every time I glanced at it. Don't know why I held onto it. Guess I just wanted to sell it. That's the practical side of me, by Jove, as Father would say."

Kas clicked his beer glass with her copper mug. "Well, good news. Ryan Speck, the condo designer and his assistant came by, saw it and bought that painting for one of the condos they're decorating. The one-bedroom facing north that's for sale on the twenty-first floor."

Athena laughed. "Really? I'm sure that clause you put in that design contract, where decorative wall pieces must come from the gallery, played a definite role in getting that sold."

Kas shot her a lopsided grin. "Probably didn't hurt, but he wouldn't have paid the price he did if the picture hadn't been really good. I think it was one of your best cityscapes. He'd like to commission you to paint some cityscapes of San Francisco, to put in the new condos and to use with their other design projects."

She frowned as the street entrance door blew in a group of noisy, laughing diners, forcing her to lean over the table. Kas scooted his stool closer to hers, his leg meeting hers under the table. The accidental touch became an affectionate caress.

"That's wonderful but I wouldn't want to compete with Chen at this point even though my style is Impressionistic. Maybe later. But it's certainly an idea."

"You've been all over Europe. Why not a cityscape of London? Rome? Your grandmother lives in Lake Como. What about the small villages around Lake Como? What would you call them, village-scapes?"

She smiled and nodded, then sipped her drink and grew contemplative. The iconic Italian villages dotting the famous Alpine lake would make beautiful subjects. Ah, so many wonderful subjects in the world to paint, so little time.

"I'll certainly think about it. Anyway, thanks for promoting me and my work. Happy it sold. How much did he give you?"

Kas's boyish grin widened into full-out joy. The check he handed her said it all. She couldn't believe it!

"My full asking price! Ten thousand! Crikey, Speck Design Associates must be doing a bang-up business! I daresay, thanks to you and Skoros Enterprises!"

His modest shrug reeled her in. She wanted to hug and kiss him!

"Gotta get back some of that money we'll be paying their firm. The gallery benefits, the condos benefit, our sales numbers benefit. More importantly, Thena, you benefit. Besides, you deserve it, baby. That was a damned fine painting. Your reputation's growing, too. He said one of their clients owned a pastiche of yours, one of the Manets. So, how do you plan to spend it—after giving the gallery its twenty percent commission?"

The check in her hand quivered a little. Eight thousand after gallery commission was the most she'd ever made from one of her own paintings. Her pastiches or legal copies of Edouard Manet's paintings were different, didn't count. The D.C. cityscape was her first original, one-of-a-kind to sell for that much. She was thrilled. Thrilled, also, that the amount would pay for both her and Chris's roundtrip airfare to Milan. And a few very nice Christmas gifts as well.

She clicked drinks with Kas and laughed excitedly, her automatic British urge to suppress emotions not at all in check for the moment.

"Spend it? On plane tickets, for one. I don't know. Kas, I don't know how to thank you!"

He winked. "Oh, I can think of a few ways . . ."

She laughed. "Indeed. Always in a—what do you Americans say—horny-toad mood?"

"Just horny, sweetheart. Around you, an unqualified yeah." His penetrating look roamed over her face, neck and bosom. Salacious, X-rated images came through loudly and clearly in technicolor and three-D, causing heat to rise from her chest to her cheeks. A tingling sensation traveled from her breasts to her female center. She was both annoyed and excited.

"You do that on purpose, don't you? Just to rattle me, you cheeky wanker. Whatever, it can wait until after dinner. I'm starved. Skipped lunch today."

Kas looked immediately chastised, like a teenaged boy caught with a girlie magazine. "Sorry, jeez. No, really, I forgot you can see my thoughts."

Athena laughed. He hadn't forgotten and he wasn't the least bit sorry.

"Hmm, matey, lovely that you understand. Truly, it is. One of the things I love about you. Few men would take me on, knowing what I can do. They wouldn't want to lose their privacy. Men like you, my father, your father. Only the men of the Delphi women would tolerate us."

"Well, what choice do I have? It's part of you. It's who you are but you also have the sense not to invade at times. I like that, too, that you're considerate."

"I try to be, Kas. It takes self-control. My mother showed me how to turn it off. Furthermore, I don't want to know every little thing you're thinking."

Kas chuckled. "With all my business crap, you'd be mostly bored to death."

She smiled offhandedly. "It's more a matter of brain clutter, too much clutter. I need to simplify my life." She was surprised that he looked perplexed. His thoughts came through.

What does she mean by that? What is she trying to tell me?

She had to clear her throat, so she downed the rest of her drink. The liquid heat filled her insides and her head swam a little from the vodka. But the rest of her body felt electrified by him, by his heat and desire for her. By his very handsome, masculine presence. He'd always had that effect on her.

31

"I just mean," she said, "I want to be more normal. Like other women. I don't want to have to use my clairvoyance. Not all the time. Only when I want to. Or have to."

Kas appeared to understand. "Okay, I get it. Your ability to read minds complicates your life in ways you don't want. Yeah, I get it. Brain clutter. Now let's eat."

Menus appeared. A moment later, both barely suppressing smiles, they ordered.

Two hours later, hunger and sexual needs satisfied, they lay in Kas's bed. The brown silk sheets and blankets tangled around them, Athena stretched to her full length atop Kas's long, hard-muscled body, her bare legs flanking his as she rubbed her breasts, midriff and pelvis against his. His moans of pleasure mixed with her sighs of total relaxation.

Being naked together had always calmed them, as if their basic, primal selves had sloughed off alien skins. Gone were the stresses of doing business in a competitive, dynamic city. Gone were the follies of a human populace outside their cozy walls, two hundred-odd feet above the hustle and bustle of the streets. Gone were their individual concerns and questions about their future.

Their future together? Their future apart?

Her new dilemma.

The present was certainly more satisfying than she'd ever hoped for. Her being with Kas in the Stargazer Tower was becoming the most exciting adventure of her life.

"Kas, you asked me how I was going to spend some of that money?"

His hand caressed her shoulder blades, then roved over her vertebrae, traveling down her spine inch by inch until his long, strong fingers found her left buttock cheek. Five points of sensations, of gentle kneading followed.

"Yeah? Any ideas?" His voice was but a whisper.

"Next week, we'll be at your parents' house in the Sierra Nevada foothills, right? For Thanksgiving?" His reply was between a soft grunt and another moan. "Then Christmas. Would you be able to get away for a week or two and go to London to see my parents? They want to spend Christmas in London with Uncle Terrence. Last year we were in Milan and Lake Como with Mother's family. Could you get away and come with Chris and me?"

"Hmm, maybe not two weeks. One week, maybe."

She suddenly thought of Kas's family, his parents, two brothers, their wives and children. His brother Alex's little boy, now almost two years old, would miss his father-substitute if he weren't there for Christmas. It would be unfair to take Kas away from his family. Still, one week . . .

She raised her head and looked at him. His eyes were closed but his chest rose and fell to a reawakening need. His fingers felt more urgent as though tensing for another rush of desire. They couldn't get enough of each other, it seemed, and yet here they were, facing another compromise. Another test.

"Perhaps you should tend to your family," she said, "Chris and I will fly home and tend to ours."

His eyes blinked open. "Isn't this your home, 'Thena? You don't feel it, do you?"

She lowered her head to press her lips against his. His mouth was pliant, warm, pouting to meet hers.

"Home is where family is, isn't it? This is my second home." When his forehead furrowed in a slight frown, she added, "We made no promises, remember?"

"Right, no promises," he murmured, looking away. "Play it by ear, one day at a time." His whisper had an edge to it.

No, I can't lose her . . . I can't lose her . . .

"You can't lose me, Kas, I love you."

Sometimes love is not enough, babe. Life has taught me that.

His wisdom saddened her. But his sad, soulful eyes, now focused on her, troubled her and made her wish she could commit to him and his lifestyle. In earnest, she cupped his face in her hands and kissed him with all her heart.

She loved him and, god help her, she would make this work!

CHAPTER SIX

A t five o'clock exactly, Athena texted Kas and reminded him to wear a dark suit to Ian Chen's Opening Night affair, in keeping with the more formal event, as she intended. Such an occasion always took on a more glitzy and festive air. Already dressed in a cocktail sheath of mauvre satin, a rhinestone choker and earrings, black shear stockings and black silk pumps, her hair dressed up in a French twist, she was ready to greet the early guests into the gallery. Multi-colored lights hung like garlands along the walls, lending a Christmasy décor and highlighting Chen's paintings on the walls, their new frames correspondingly ornate or plain depending on the painting's subject matter.

Ian Chen stood by a podium near the entrance, nervously tugging on his black bowtie, straightening the hem of his jacket, shifting from foot to foot. At least twenty members of his immediate family milled about, sipping from champagne flutes offered by tuxedoed servers. They gazed doubtfully at the canapes presented on silver trays and picked at the cubes of cheese tooth picked with baby pickles. Athena admonished herself for not having the caterers make up Asian style hors d'oeuvres like Dim Sum. Oh well, too late now, she commiserated. Chen didn't seem to notice, and the younger members of his family appeared not to mind. In fact, they seemed to enjoy the Teriyaki chicken wings and various dips, so at least that was a good choice.

By six o'clock, twenty-five more Asians had shown up, followed in short order by more than a dozen or so Stargazer

Hotel guests and an equal number of condo owners who'd stopped by after work, curious to see the artwork. The noise level rose, the volume of English-speaking voices punctuated by several dialects of Chinese.

Then things started to happen as guests turned into customers who approached her sales counter to reserve their painting of choice and leave deposits. Meanwhile, Kas directed two photographers from the Daily Examiner and City Crier to the painter, capturing poses of the artist with various excited relatives and friends in front of his artwork.

Athena lost track of time as she took orders, ran credit cards and wrote down delivery addresses. Those who couldn't afford the one-of-a-kinds inquired about prints on canvas, which she assured would be available for delivery in one month. After writing down an order from one of the condo owners, a young software engineer, she looked up to see a man who appeared a little out of place.

An older Hispanic in his fifties, at her estimate, he was wearing a gray and black tweed sports jacket over gray flannel trousers and a black turtleneck sweater. His dark, thick hair flecked with gray, he was moving from painting to painting desultorily, as though he wasn't really interested in the artwork but had just come to munch on the canapes. Or conduct other business. There was something about him that shrieked, cop! A couple of Chen's friends noticed him, too, and moved to the other side of the large room. When he turned around, Athena spied the badge at his belt. Kas noticed the man, too, and approached Athena's business counter.

"Either he's a customer," he murmured, "or he's a man who doesn't give up. Which one do you think? Thena, do your vibes."

She smiled, pleased with the evening's success and not the least daunted by the prospect of refusing the man. Again.

When the Hispanic man approached the counter, grinning dourly at Athena, then Kas, she took the initiative.

"Inspector Villalobos, I'd like you to meet Kas Skoros, from Skoros Enterprises, owner of the Stargazer Tower."

Mike Villalobos stared at her, initially astonished but quickly recovered and shook Kas's hand. As he turned back to Athena, his handsome, lined face showed amusement. He ran a hand through his well-groomed, salt and pepper hair. His clean-shaven face was swarthy and handsome.

"Juan Pablo told me to never be surprised at what you're capable of. I forgot his advice." His voice was a mellifluent, deep bass. All in all, he gave her an impression of a solid character, a man who didn't give up easily. Certainly an important trait for a homicide investigator.

"Lucky guess," she replied, extending her hand. "Are you an art lover? Mr. Chen is a remarkable painter of cityscapes, don't you agree?"

His dark eyes swept around the gallery walls. "I don't know much about art but yeah, if I could afford one of his paintings, I'd probably buy one."

"Please, don't let the price tags discourage you, Inspector. We're having prints made. Giclees on canvas, they're called. It's a new process, well, not so new . . . at least forty years old. The process makes an accurate copy by transferring one color at a time. A tedious, slow process but the result is a perfect match to the one-of-a-kind oil or acrylic painting. And the price is like, one-tenth of the painting. Five-thousand instead of fifty. Two thousand instead of twenty."

Kas excused himself and moved to corral the two servers, pay them and dismiss them for the evening. Three-quarters of the guests had left and there were no more buyers in line to make their purchases.

The police detective glanced around and then leaned his elbows on the counter, lowering his voice to within only her earshot.

"Let's strike a deal, Miss Butler. I'll order a . . . what did you call it?"

"A giclee. French term. Which painting?"

He pointed to the one featuring the orange-red Golden Gate Bridge from the perspective of the northern end, the bay waters dark and churning below the vast span, the city outline on the distant shore shrouded in low-hanging mists.

"That one, the bridge. I've lived here all my life and no matter where I go in the world, the Golden Gate's like a magnet. A welcoming beacon. I get a sense of home whenever I see it. Do you know, it was built in the 1930's, a huge government works project, twenty-five lives lost in the construction. My great grandfather and great uncle worked on the bridge." The detective smiled broadly, showing a row of yellowed teeth. Athena knew he was a habitual smoker and coffee drinker. A dedicated public servant who put in long days and nights on his homicide cases.

His smile faded under Athena's intense stare. "Even now, people get chills when a cruise ship or cargo ship sails underneath. The Blue Angels fly under it on Fleet Day. Over a hundred people have committed suicide jumping off it." He raised up, let his arms fall to his side, and shot her an ironic grin. "There's good and bad in every human endeavor, I suppose."

She waited for the detective to say what he really came to the gallery to say. Even as she read his thoughts with a certain amount of uneasiness, she glanced over at Kas, who was chatting with Chen, his girlfriend and his lingering relatives. Her boyfriend and boss hoped to clear out the gallery soon so he could retire for the evening, and he wasn't about to let her close up alone. Ever mindful of security, he always helped her lock up at night whenever Dale Dargent was off duty. Tomorrow was Saturday and her assistant was due to take the morning shift so that she could sleep in.

"Back to our deal . . ."

"What deal, Inspector?" Playing dumb gave her extra time to think about it.

"Let's strike a deal. I buy a print of that painting, the Golden Gate one, and you come down to the Hall of Justice for a quick look at some jackets."

She sighed, pretending not to know the images indelibly etched in his mind now. A homicide detective might not appreciate her invading *his* mind.

"Jackets?"

"The jacket of a homeless man, a drug addict thirty-nine years old. Found this morning near Market and Ninth Street, stabbed to death as he slept in the doorway of an apartment building. And another jacket found nearby. Juan Pablo says you're good at psychometry. Feeling things, getting a sense of them, maybe getting images of who owned them, other information . . ."

"Yes, I do that. But not anymore, Inspector. I'm sorry."

The detective's dark brown eyes took on a sad, desperate look, shadowed by black, bushy eyebrows. His thin lips folded inwardly as he planned his next move.

"All you have to do, Miss Butler, is touch the two jackets, tell me what you see, feel. You'll be in no danger, I promise you."

She cast him a skeptical smile. "Your cousin made me the same promise."

The man nodded soberly. "I understand. I guess we cops can be ruthless in our own way, especially when there's a serial killer on the loose in the city. There've been several murders of homeless vagrants, all in the past two months."

"What makes you think it's the same person murdering these homeless people?" Her smile dissolved as an image came through. "Oh, I see. A note is always left behind. Same type of paper, generic spiral notebook paper. Creepy coincidence? I suspect not."

His countenance morphed from shock to surprise to finally understanding. He continued to frown. "You know cops don't believe in coincidence."

"A one-man vigilante?"

"So it is a man, seeking justice?"

"Most killers are men, and in their minds, anyway, they're seeking something. Their own perverted justice. Or revenge."

"So you agree our killer is a psychopath, a clever man who depersonalizes his victims. Playing God and handing out justice-his perceived justice, anyway. It's a type of thinking that angry kids display. But a smart, cruel man who's seeking revenge for some wrong in his past. That's what the FBI profilist has told us." The detective showed his growing impatience with a barely suppressed harrumph. For him, she knew, it had been a very long day. "Five minutes is all I ask, Miss Butler, in exchange for . . . how much for that giclee?" He pointed to the Golden Gate painting.

Athena took hold of a pen and her order form. "Two-thousand dollars. It could be ready by December twentieth at the latest."

Detective Villalobos scowled. "Just in time for Christmas, huh? Well, I'll pass it on to my captain, work related costs, research. Hang it up in the squad room. Or eat the damned cost and give it to my wife. How about Monday morning? Just touch two jackets and give me what you get. That's all."

Athena sighed deeply. Kas was ushering a couple of Chen's admirers out the door, smiling and shaking their hands, the painter gesturing his thanks, bowing to the oldest among them.

Kas wasn't going to approve.

"All right, Inspector. Just a few minutes handling the jackets. I can't guarantee I'll get anything useful but it won't hurt to try, I suppose."

A moment later, still scowling, Detective Villalobos gave her his credit card details and a professional card displaying the address of the Hall of Justice. However, by the time he shook Kas's hand and left, Athena detected a slight upturn of his thin mouth. He'd accomplished his mission. After Chen, his girlfriend and the last of his friends departed, Kas locked up, pressed the button that automatically lowered the window shades, and set the alarm.

Together, they locked and alarmed the side rear door leading to the lobby and approached the condo elevators. She knew he was struggling with the urge to complain about the detective showing up. Instead, he asked about the sales.

"Sold everything," she told him, "even twelve giclees from six of his paintings. The Golden Gate was especially popular."

"Awesome, Thena!"

"I think we should make prints of all his work. He's that good. If we do this, the gallery's profits will soar in the Christmas rush."

Kas's hand rested on her shoulder, then slid up to the nape of her neck. Her blond hair was coiled upward, so his fingers rested in the tendrils curling around her neck. Alone in the elevator, Kas pulled her to his side and hugged her to him.

"It's your call, babe. Tonight turned out great! Except for . . . y'know, the cop showing up. Hope you told him, Hell no!"

Athena steeled herself. "He bought a two-thousand-dollar giclee, so I owe him a few minutes of my time. Not a big deal, Kas."

Kas let her go, raised himself to his full, six-foot-two height as he stepped away from her. "Thena, I can't stop you, so I just hope like hell you know what you're doing."

"Just five minutes of my time. What harm can it do?"

To mollify him and his instinctive worries, she leaned into

him and wrapped her arms around his waist.

"Thank you for all your help tonight, luv. You were wonderful."

In response, he grunted softly, then settled a wry grin on her.

"You've come a long way since I first met you."

"You mean, the nineteen-year-old who wanted all men to be like her father? The teenage twit who fell hard for you?"

He smiled, gave in and hugged her to him.

"What can I say after that declaration? Have I disappointed you?"

"No." She kissed his mouth. "Not a't'all." She recalled something the detective said. "So what are the Blue Angels? And why do they fly under the Golden Gate Bridge on something called Fleet Day?"

By the time they arrived at his door on the twenty-second floor, Kas had explained, followed by her blank look and quizzical, "Navy planes?"

She shrugged. Would she ever understand Americans and their strange customs and traditions? One thing she could rely on was Kas and his customary behavior.

Melding her mouth to his, she unbuttoned his navy-blue jacket and ran her hands up the front of his shirt, then ruffled his hair. Instantly, she found herself pushed against the front door of his condo, his body's full length pressed along hers.

"Feel like spending the night?" he rasped.

"And sleep late tomorrow?"

"Maybe not sleep . . ."

"Sounds positively delightful."

CHAPTER SEVEN

Mondays, the gallery was closed and Kas's first meeting with the tower's new realtor's sales rep was not until eleven AM. And so, like the protector he intended to be, he drove Athena to the Hall of Justice's Southern station on Bryant Street. After parking his SUV in the All Day public parking lot across the street, the two walked across to the main entrance.

As they entered the stark modern, gray granite building that housed the criminal court, the DA's offices, a jail on the top two floors, and the Southern Station of the SFPD, Athena tried to quell the rising uneasiness churning inside her. She kept reminding herself that she'd done this before. She had met Detective Ochoa and his partner, Lieutenant Palomino inside their squad room at Metro PD in D.C., had advised them on their serial killer case. Mostly to no avail. Their captain had discouraged the use of psychics and had convinced Palomino to do likewise. Ochoa had listened to Athena and taken her seriously, had followed the leads she'd given them, and all ultimately to her peril. And to the peril of her brother and Kas. Nevertheless, Ochoa was the one to claim capture of the killer. According to his latest email to her, his promotion to lieutenant was the result of that arrest.

Entering the granite-floored lobby, they had to clear security with a metal detector, a wand and a pat-down. Next, a uniformed officer searched her shoulder-handled, satchel-styled purse after it emerged from the x-ray machine over the conveyor belt. When he pulled out a cartridge of pepper spray, she exclaimed in surprise.

"I'm so sorry. I forgot I'd put it there."

The officer placed the cartridge in a cardboard box and told her she could pick it up on her way out. Then he dutifully examined all the stuff that Kas pulled out of his sports coat pocket and trouser pockets. As an ex sheriff's deputy, he'd known better than to bring anything into the Hall of Justice that could be remotely construed as a weapon. Not even a nail clipper. His wallet was given back but his cell phone were placed in another box for safekeeping.

Finally, they were cleared to take an elevator to the fourth floor where they met another officer and had to repeat the entire process. Detective Inspector Lieutenant Mike Villalobos met them on the other side of a bullet-proof, glass door. They shook hands before following the inspector into the gritty bull pen of robbery and homicide detectives. At least thirty men and women worked diligently at desks, most with coffee cups steaming by their open laptops and old-school notebooks, cell phones raised to their ears. The lieutenant led them to his glass-walled office in the rear of the vast room. Athena noted the pale green exterior walls were lined with computers, printers, reams of paper, plastic evidence bins waiting to be processed, and other work tools. A large television flat screen hung in one corner. Most of the windows above these counters held various city views but the low-lying fog today obscured most of these views. It was like being inside an enormous whitish gray cocoon.

Another glass-walled, corner office was most likely the captain's bailiwick, Athena surmised. She couldn't help but wonder if Villalobos's boss was aware of her consulting session and if he approved. After all, this was California. Maybe protocols were different in this state. Or the police were more open-minded here.

No noises from the outside broke through. The noise

inside, however, was all clatter, bells, low-pitched voices, occasional muted laughter. Kas looked interested in the hustle-bustle of the squad room. She even detected a faint smile from him. The public's watchdogs at work must have reminded him of the Sheriff's Office in Placer County, where he'd worked for several years. He had turned down a detective's job to work for his family's company.

Villalobos's office was inviting. Family photos abounded, and one wall was covered with photos of snow-covered ski trails and mountains, skiers shushing down steep slopes. The Sierra Nevada Mountains were only a three hour drive away. Huh, so the detective was an avid skier, she noted. That tidbit of personal information hadn't come through her channel.

Villalobos invited them to sit down in the two captain chairs facing his desk. As if he sensed Athena's tension, he smiled warmly as he closed his office door.

"Although you've consulted with the police before, Miss Butler, I know how daunting this experience can be. I didn't mind approving Mr. Skoros's visit if he helps put you at ease."

Athena smiled. She was keeping her channel into the man's mind open, preferring to be further informed by his thoughts. She would close the channel at the right time.

"Yes, thank you for that. Kas." She glanced over at her boyfriend, who at the moment was gazing silently at the photos of skiers. "Kas does keep me calm. As your cousin, Detective Ochoa, told you, Kas was instrumental in capturing that serial killer in D.C. In fact, he and my younger brother were almost killed in the process. So, I dare say, he has earned the right to be here with me. Besides, I do my best work when I'm fairly calm."

"J.P." — referring to Juan Pablo Ochoa — "told me how this works, this psychometry gift of yours. You touch evidence collected from a crime scene, or from something touched or owned by a possible suspect. You get visions or you sense things."

"Yes, something like that." Athena wasn't about to enlighten the man with all the complexities of her gift when she sensed her visit today was mainly a test. Clearly, Mike Villalobos was not convinced she was *the real deal*, as Ochoa was wont to say.

The detective looked from her to Kas, back to her again, as if he were waiting for a parapsychology lesson.

"Detective," she began. Maybe an explanation wouldn't hurt.

"In the city, we're known as inspectors," Villalobos said.

"Oh, sorry. Inspector Villalobos" Athena used the correct Spanish pronunciation of his name, having learned Spanish in addition to perfecting French while her father was with the Foreign Office in Lyon, France. "Inspector, what I do is difficult to explain but here's a thumbnail sketch. While I touch something, I open a mental channel that connects to an all-knowing consciousness that exists in the universe. I'm not certain what it is. Maybe it's like the Buddhist belief, the Akashic Records of past, present and future human existence and knowledge. Or maybe it has to do with the Earth's electromagnetic fields. The ancient Greeks believed this insight came from the gods. Who knows?"

Athena saw Ochoa's eyes glaze over. With a quick glance over to Kas, who was straining to suppress a smile, like an I-told-you-so, she frowned and changed her tactic.

"At any rate, what comes through is often flashes of knowledge, words, names, sounds, feelings, images. I try to interpret these transmissions, but my interpretations aren't always complete or-or spot on. I'm still human and therefore limited."

At the end of her explanation, the detective looked confused. Another glance at Kas and his now open grin made her

recall how most people reacted to such an off-the-cuff explanation. Totally perplexed, scowls of disbelief, faces pinched
with confusion or anger. She might as well have said that the
Archangel Gabriel revealed the truth to her and then flew
back up to Heaven. After all, this was how the Prophet Mohammed explained his divine visitations to his followers. If it
worked for Mohammed, why wouldn't people believe her?

Who knew? If there was a divine being that guided her insights, she'd never seen it or him or her, not even in her mind.
Her own mother believed their insights came from some spir-
itual, omniscient realm. Athena's own convictions were
grounded in modern science and physics. One British physi-
cist at an English institute for psychic research had told her
that theories of multiple life dimensions abounded and had
been mathematically proven. Thus, the all-knowing consciousness which she could mysteriously dip into must be a
fountain of knowledge in some other dimension. For reasons
unknown to them, the descendants of the Delphi bloodline
had access to that other dimension.

Villalobos planted his hands on his desk and heaved himself up. From his closed expression, she surmised he'd already dismissed her explanation as pure bunk. "Right, well,
let's go into one of the interview rooms and we'll see whether
you can receive those so-called transmissions or not. Wherever they come from."

Kas shot her a knowing look. *You see, they never believe until
you prove it.* They followed the detective into a small, window-
less room. A two-way mirror lined one wall and a Formica-
topped table sat in the center. On top of the table was one
transparent, plastic storage bin, the kind someone might use
to store a large collection of sweaters in a closet. Villalobos
shoved aside a metal chair, wrote something on the Crime Evidence chart taped on the black plastic lid, and opened the bin.
Inside was a dirty, blood-stained, olive-green parka.

Athena couldn't help but grimace at the jacket and shrink away. The stench emanating from the jacket was overpowering. Reflexively, her hand covered her nose. Kas's eyes widened from the smells, but he stood fast and quietly along the distant wall. He stared alternatively at her, then the disgusting jacket, looking like he'd rather be walking on coals than standing there in the cop's interview room.

"Put these gloves on, Miss Butler." The detective held up blue latex gloves he'd taken from a box on the table. She did so and then tentatively touched the top of the bunched up pile with both hands.

Then closed her eyes and let the channel open wider.

A vision rapidly flowed into her mind. Then another and another. Almost in disbelief, she scrunched up her face at what came across. Seconds later, a sense of rage flooded her mind, assailing her in colors of red and orange. Then a wave of black hit her, followed by a white sheet of paper. A large number in black felt ink had been smeared on the paper, like someone had prepared it beforehand with an abundance of anger. Someone let go of the paper and it drifted down to an elongated lump of dark, smelly rags. The dark, smelly rags were a human being whose soul had just departed his debilitated body. A homeless person who had once been sleeping in a drug-induced stupor was now dead. But not before he'd struggled against the slamming effects of the chemical that had been injected into him. Another vision flashed before she frowned and tossed down the parka.

Athena opened her eyes and swiftly peeled off the gloves. Involuntarily, she stepped back from the table, her mind still in the grip of the visions. Kas reached her side.

"You okay, Thena?"

"Miss Butler?" Villalobos asked as he replaced the jacket in the bin and put the lid back on. "Would you like to write down what you saw or give it to me orally? If orally, would you mind if I record it?"

With the heaviness of someone half asleep, Athena stepped back further and touched the wall behind her with her fingertips. It felt solid and secure even as her insides quivered and quaked. Kas helped her into the chair that the detective had pushed aside. He stood behind her, his hands resting lightly on her shoulders. Reassuring her.

"Yes, that's fine. Orally and you can record me."

Villalobos took the chair opposite her at the table, slid the plastic bin over to the floor on his side to mute the acrid smells. He put his cell phone on the table and pressed the recording button.

"All right, Miss Butler, go ahead. It's November eighteenth, ten-thirty-five in the morning. Miss Athena Butler, a clairvoyant, is giving her impressions of the jacket found on top of the victim at the latest crime scene, reported into the South Station on November sixteenth. Homicide case twelve-forty-two. This is Inspector Mike Villalobos."

He looked up at her, waiting for her to begin. Athena stared at the table, recalling the visions of just moments ago.

"First I saw the jacket from the point of view of the man who handled it. It was used but clean before he did something strange. He emptied all the pockets, dropped it in the mud, stomped on it. I couldn't see his face or body, just his hands and what he was doing."

"You couldn't see his face? So it was a man? A young man, an older man, maybe middle-aged?"

The detective's sudden interruption startled her.

"No, I couldn't tell. His hands were big, though, so I think he's a large man but not fat." She sighed deeply. "Please, let me describe what I saw before you stop me to ask questions. Okay?"

Villalobos nodded, apparently taken aback by her insistence. She wanted to report her visions in her own way.

She continued. "The blood is animal blood. Could be cow blood, no, maybe deer blood. Strange, but you already knew that. Hmm, maybe he's a hunter . . . or lives in the country near animals. Maybe your coastal hills. Anyway, then I saw him . . . uh, urinate on the jacket. So it smells badly. He wears it at night so he blends in, in look and smell. Blends in among the homeless. He finds a homeless person on the street . . . no, crouched in a doorway. This time, anyway. He walks among the homeless until he chooses one to kill. I see a needle in the man's hand. He stabs the homeless person in the chest, presses the plunger. He knows something about the human body, and he kills in that way. He's filled with rage and hate. Horrible, so much hate. It goes back to his childhood, fills him up, almost blinds him but only at certain times. Otherwise, he passes as quite normal. He's very self-controlled, self-disciplined."

Athena paused and exchanged looks with Villalobos. "I guess you would call him a clever sociopath. Very intelligent but filled with hatred towards the homeless, especially towards drug addicts."

She sighed before going on.

"When he knows the person is dead, he drops on the body a piece of paper. The paper I saw is white, y'know, just regular eight-and-a-half by eleven binder paper. Blue lines. Black ink. It shows the number thirteen. I have no idea what that means, Inspector. Maybe he's keeping track, and this is his thirteenth victim. If this is true, oh my god!" She paused for a moment, realizing what she'd said was true.

Looking at the lieutenant, she shook her head at the terrible truth. "But he plans many more, Inspector."

Villalobos nodded, frowning and rubbing his chin, so she continued.

"He hears someone yelling. He takes off the jacket in a hurry, throws it on the homeless person he has just killed and runs away. Like I said, he wore this jacket to blend in."

Athena looks at the detective, whose jaw has dropped open and whose droopy, dark eyes appear wide and awestruck.

"That's all I saw, Inspector." She touched Kas's forearm and he helps her rise shakily to her feet. "I'm sorry I couldn't see his face. I'll be going now, sir, if you don't mind."

The detective barely moved his head up and down as he stared after her. Automatically, he turned off the recorder.

"Y-yes, thank you, Miss Butler."

She stopped in the open doorway of the interview room, Kas behind her, holding onto her waist for support.

"Oh, one more thing. The last thing I saw was a police badge. Or it could've been a firefighter's badge. A silver badge of some kind. I don't know what that means. Sorry."

They left Villalobos hunched over the interview room table, staring down at his cell phone.

Down in the lobby, Athena retrieved her pepper spray cartridge and put it back in her satchel bag. Kas retrieved his cell phone and immediately checked for messages. He appeared relieved.

On the sidewalk, she and Kas looked around. The fog had lifted in the hour they'd spent inside the Hall of Justice.

Kas took her hand. "Well, thank god that's over. I don't know about you, babe, but I'm hungry. My lunch meeting with the realtors was postponed 'til two. Wanta grab an early lunch before I meet with them?"

Athena blinked repeatedly, trying to shake off the aftereffects of those disturbing visions. Her stomach was in no condition to welcome food but to placate Kas, she was willing to go along.

"You're kidding, of course. I'll join you but won't eat. Hot tea will do me just fine."

"You did well, Thena. You kept your cool."

"Kas, do you think he believed me?"

"He'd be a fool if he didn't. What was that about a cop's badge?"

She slid her arm around his waist, as he did hers while they walked across the street to Kas's car. On the way, they saw two homeless women pushing their grocery carts filled with their possessions. A dirty sleeping bag hung out of one of the carts.

She turned her gaze away from the two women, over-whelmed suddenly with a mixture of emotions. Sorrow, disgust, guilt.

"I have no idea. It was just a flash of a badge. I think it was important, but I pretended it wasn't."

Kas made a soft grunt, then leaned over and kissed her hair at the side of her head. His tenderness and support made the last of her creepy quivers vanish.

"You did well, Thena."

She smiled. "You're such a luv."

CHAPTER EIGHT

The door to the interview room opened. Two detectives walked in, both wearing sports jackets over slacks and button-down shirts and ties. Len Wycott, a mocha-complexioned, clean-shaven African American male in his late twenties, a Cal Berkeley graduate, was the first to approach the table. He wore eyeglasses with gold frames, always bore the serious look of a scholar. Frank Vecchio, a Caucasian in his mid-forties, was second. His Van Dyke beard and sideburns were dark brown but peppered lightly with gray. His head hair was thick, dark and bore a prominent widow's peak. He always wore a sardonic half-smile but in that moment, both men's countenances were pinched with sober reflection.

His serial killer task force team.

Inspector Villalobos, their team leader, motioned them to close the door, unwilling to let their voices drift out into the squad room. Vecchio closed the door behind him and took a position standing beside it. Wycott pulled out the second chair, the one that Athena had just occupied, and sat down.

"You saw her, heard her. Want me to play it back?"

Wycott took a little notebook out of his jacket breast pocket. "Sure, wouldn't hurt. I'll take notes."

Vecchio nodded in assent, so the lieutenant played the recording on his police-issued cell phone. Athena's voice came across at first tentative and a little hoarse, then strengthened with resolve and confidence as she continued. With each revelation, both Wycott and Vecchio showed little reaction. Both took notes and when the recording finished, their gazes settled on Villalobos. Wycott was the first to speak.

"Well, she certainly got it right. The clean jacket soiled on purpose by the perp. The animal blood, not the victim's or perp's. Unfortunately, the bodily fluid DNA was so degraded, it was useless. The underlying rage focused on the target victim, another homeless person. The injected chemical — according to the ME, a fentanyl overdose into a thoracic artery going into the heart. The MO, the deadly injection, that wasn't in the papers. What else? Oh yeah, the note and number thirteen, the thirteenth victim in two months. It's been all over the papers, TV. Everyday notebook paper used, felt pen, black ink. Those details were never issued to the press, either. The second jacket left at the crime scene, another detail the press didn't have."

Vecchio interjected, "There were two jackets in the bin, Lieu. She could've assumed the perp wore the jacket so he'd pass as one of them, so the homeless in the area wouldn't become alarmed. A given. He's someone with a massive grudge against the homeless. Another given. So far, she could be making lucky guesses, trying to impress the cops, get her name out there."

Both detectives, Wycott and Vecchio, were outranked by Villalobos's lieutenant status and customarily deferred to his higher seniority in the SFPD.

"Yeah, that's right." Wycott's black brows furrowed with concentrated thought. "However, all things considered, I'm impressed. She could've known about the thirteenth victim but not about the sheet of paper with the number on it. That's a detail we never disclosed to the press. Nor the lethal injection?"

Vecchio piped up, "We gave that out to hospital supervisors. Hoping someone from the medical community might suspect someone. Maybe she heard some gossip from a customer at that art gallery."

Villalobos scraped his chair back and grunted loudly. An avowed conservative, who despised the City Hall establishment politicians, he never felt shy about expressing his disdain over the city's failure to warehouse the increasing homeless population.

"I still believe the perp espouses an ideology that resents all the government money our mayor and city council spend on the homeless population in this city. But he'd have to be a fanatical ideologue to carry his resentment that far."

"Or he has personal reasons, like the Bureau profiler told us," said Wycott. "As far as we know, nothing is ever stolen. 'Course, it'd be hard to tell with the mess of stuff they carry around in those carts. This girl — what's her name, lieu?"

"Athena Butler. Referred to me by my cousin in the Metro D.C.P.D. Like I told you guys, she works at the art gallery in the new Stargazer Tower on Main and Folsom. Looks to me like the girlfriend of one of the developers. Skoros Enterprises. The guy with her is Keriakos Skoros, the company's COO. Family's rich developers. She's a U.K. citizen, here on a work visa."

"So this girl, what is she?" Vecchio asked.

Villalobos gave them a small shrug. "Some kind of psychic. Or so she claims and so my cousin claims. Maybe she is, she was accurate about so much. Incomplete but accurate. We haven't notified the press or anyone outside the ME's office or the Department about some of those details of the crime scene she got right. She led us up to and included the crime as it was happening. Amazing, how she gets into the mind of the perp."

Wycott chuckled. "But can't identify him. Or she's the perp and she's trying to throw us off-track by describing a man's hands."

Vecchio shot him a mirthless smile and chimed in. "She was off about one thing. She mentioned the big hands, but the crime lab found no fingerprints or identifying trace evidence from that jacket. Diluting the DNA sample with water, dirt, other organics. Like the perp deliberately wanted to test our acumen. He knew what he was doing, probably wearing gloves. Smart fellow."

The three detectives frowned for a moment, then Wycott spoke up.

"That's right. The man's big hands. She didn't say that he wore gloves—"

"Right," said Vecchio excitedly, "she must be a fraud. That's a vital detail she should've seen in her woo-woo visions. Don't you think?"

Wycott nodded, and so did Villalobos. While smirks were exchanged among the two sergeants, Villalobos stood up and pocketed his cell phone.

"Well, worth a shot, anyway. I think we must conclude she's a good guesser. Maybe picked up on something that was reported in that news article. Or some leaked gossip told to her from someone at the Tower. I think my cousin exaggerated what she can do."

Wycott pointed at his notebook. "She didn't mention when or where the crime took place, did you notice that?"

Vecchio nodded. "Yeah. Not the fact it happened in the middle of the night. Not the fact that the vic was sleeping in the doorway of a restaurant on Ninth just north of Market. The heart of the Tenderloin. Nor the screams of another homeless guy that brought the patrol cop to the scene." He paused, frowning. "She did mention a badge but didn't know what kind."

The lieutenant's cell phone buzzed. When he saw who was texting him, he recalled giving her his business card. Silently, he read the text, a wry grin slowly curving up one side of his wide mouth as he read. He looked up at his team and shook his head in wonder.

"That was from Athena Butler, Girl Psychic herself. She said she forgot to tell me that the killer wore black leather gloves before and after he pissed on the jacket. During the crime, which happened a little after midnight, he wore them. Old, worn leather gloves, like he'd had them a long time. Also, she doesn't know the city, doesn't know many streets or neighborhoods outside of the Embarcadero and the Financial District. So couldn't verify where the crime took place."

"Sonuvabitch," Wycott exhaled.

"No shit," Vecchio muttered. "So what about that badge she saw?"

Wycott added, "Maybe the badge on the beat cop that showed up about five minutes after the other homeless guy started yelling?"

The three detectives nodded in unison.

"So what now, lieu?" asked Vecchio.

Villalobos pocketed his phone. "We look again at the possible profile on the perp. Put all night-shift uniforms on alert, South and Central Stations. When they do their rounds, watch out for any talk about a stranger in those homeless encampments. Maybe some big guy dressed like a poor, homeless bastard but alone. Not quite fitting in among the known homeless camps all over the city and in the Tenderloin. Notify the North Station to do the same. Wait for the next one."

"Maybe call her again?" said Wycott. He looked pointedly at his superior. Vecchio turned to face the lieutenant.

Villalobos opened the door. "Yep, couldn't hurt. First, let's explore the fentanyl angle. Pharmacies, hospitals, street dealers, wherever that damned drug can be found."

The three men shuffled out, nodding and looking grim.

Chapter Nine

"Lovely, you'll be here Friday all day, and Saturday and Sunday, too. We're always closed on Mondays. I'll open on Tuesday as usual." Athena looked over her notes, reminding herself of all the business concerns at the Stargazer Gallery. "Oh yes, pick up the keys from the lobby's day manager, Mr. Andrews. Drop them off after you lock up." She tapped the ballpoint pen on the notebook, admonishing herself to be efficient and thorough. "Well, I reckon that's it, Dale."

Dale Dargent, a part-time art history instructor at the San Francisco Art Institute, had agreed to be the gallery's assistant manager. Inundated with work in the gallery and her own creative work, Athena welcomed his help wholeheartedly. He appeared more than competent and as an added plus, Dale was a skilled framer.

She finished her call with a cheery, "Happy Thanksgiving, Dale." Feeling chipper, she added the French pronunciation of his last name, which meant *silver* or *money* in French. When she looked up, Kas was standing there, smiling broadly.

"Dale pronounces his last name like sergeant, not the French way."

"Even though his name is French?"

"Well, that's Americans for you. We always Anglicize every name. Although we leave your name, Butler, alone."

"Thank heavens for that," she joked. "What would you do with my paternal grandmother's name, de Vesey?"

"We'd pronounce it D.V.C." He laughed shortly when she shook her head in mock horror. Looking downright spiffy in a charcoal-gray suit, white button-down shirt and a hunter green tie, he pinned her gaze expectantly, his expression turning serious.

"Thena, sweetie, our reservation's at seven. It's six-thirty. The cab's out front."

"Oh, bugger!" Athena jumped up from her metal-backed stool at the gallery's counter. She'd lost track of time while discussing the various tasks she assigned Dale during her upcoming, brief hiatus from San Francisco. The following day, Kas would be driving them both up to the Loomis Hills, about thirty miles east of Sacramento, for Thanksgiving dinner with his parents and the rest of the family.

"Bloody hell! I'm so sorry. Sorting out the things I want Dale to do while I'm gone—it took so much longer than I thought it would."

Kas shrugged good-naturedly but something in his eyes told her that he was disappointed. He'd obviously gone to extra lengths to dress up for the occasion, the fourth anniversary of their meeting. Her rather sloppy red tunic over black leggings, lack of makeup and haphazard ponytail didn't measure up to his shiny, urbane appearance. He'd even had his hair cut and scented.

Kas pointed to the gallery's wide, picture window. Dusk had descended rapidly upon the tall, glass and steel canyons in their neighborhood near the Embarcadero.

"Cab's out there, Thena, waiting for us."

Determined to make up for her thoughtlessness, she grabbed her purse and ran for the gallery's side rear door, which led directly into a hallway off the lobby.

"Kas, lock up for me. Just ten minutes, I promise. Ten max."

A rush up to her twenty-first-floor condo, almost tearing off her clothes as she went, followed by a slap-dash sponge bath, a spray of scent, a magical transformation of sloppy ponytail into a more sophisticated, side-twisted shoulder cascade. Next, she maneuvered a silk, royal blue sheath over her head, shoulders and hips, smoothed it down over her slim figure, and ending with a hop into matching blue-leather wedge heels. Currently, this was her best and dressiest outfit. She grabbed her ankle-length wool coat and stuffed her leather wallet and tube of pure-red lipstick into a pocket. With no time to change her gold hoop earrings, Athena returned to the hallway to find Kas motioning to her.

"Fifteen minutes, not bad. In fact, I'm totally amazed. The cab's out here in front." He grinned and steered her through the huge, marble-floored lobby and out of the glass entrance doors. "I told the cabbie to drive around to the front. By the way, you look great. Quite a transformation in fifteen minutes."

"Thank you, kind sir. You look smart, yourself, like a model from Savile Row."

Kas bent down and gave her a peck on the cheek. "Hmmm, I won't ask what that is. You're wearing a nice fragrance. What is it?"

"Chanel Number Five, my favorite."

"It's now mine."

Thirty minutes later, they were ensconced in a soft leather banquette, receiving cocktails from a waiter carrying a silver tray full of drinks. A vodka martini for her and a Jack Daniels on the rocks for him. The flamboyant, tuxedoed waiter moved on to the next table with a flourish of white serviette and whisked tray.

She looked around the restaurant, situated at the end of a pier in the heart of Fisherman's Wharf, an older building that appeared to have been renovated in an attempt to appear posh. The place was noisy, crowded with diners in various states of inebriation and bonhomie, all dressed in evening finery. The décor was minimal with white tablecloths and walls filled with old, framed photos of celebrities.

"Scoma's is my favorite on the Wharf," Kas said. "The fish is fresh, and it's been here since the nineteen-twenties. Joe Di-Maggio, the baseball player who was married to Marilyn Monroe, some old crooners like Frank Sinatra, Tony Bennett-all those famous Italians used to come here. You can see the photos of all these bigwigs all over the walls. They had to re-build after the big earthquake."

"The nineteen-oh-six earthquake?"

Kas laughed. "No, the nineteen-eighty-nine one. The city sustained a lot of damage. The Bay Bridge, the freeways. Some downtown areas experienced liquefaction. Collapsed like Lego toys."

"How do you know this? You were born in nineteen-ninety."

He shot her a wry smile at her teasing remark. "I do read, y'know, and I've seen photos. Older folks still talk about it. My parents remember it. The water in their pool splashed up and out, and the epicenter was a hundred-and-fifty miles away. One of the reasons I tried to talk my family out of build-ing here. We're smack in the heart of earthquake country. But also smack in the heart of big bucks."

Athena smiled and raised her delicate martini glass. With a feigned air of horror, as if the Big One might hit at any mo-ment, she clicked glasses.

"Cheers. Let's hope for a calm terra firma."

"According to my precog mother, good luck for some time to come. So here's to many more years, Thena, this time to-gether instead of apart. What a novelty that would be." His sudden seriousness surprised her.

She repeated his theme, "Many more. Together, not apart." Adding a smile to her words incited a warm smile from Kas.

After their first year of knowing each other and falling in love, their separation and estrangement over the next three years had been painful. Too painful to dwell on tonight. A strange toast, perhaps, but she knew it was Kas's way of expressing his relief that they had finally reunited. That they'd made it this far, considering everything they'd been through.

They had spent little time together, with her in D.C. and him in the Sacramento and San Francisco Bay Area. He'd married and divorced during their bitter separation, had buried his brother Alex and taken his place in the family real estate development business, Skoros Enterprises. He was even helping to raise his brother's child, a little boy named Alexander, who was now two-and—a half years old.

Athena had passed the time in a relationship with a fellow painter until it came crashing down. For months during this past year, Kas had pursued her, won her back—nearly getting killed in the process. And now here they were.

Kas put down his glass and covered her hand with his own. "I'm relieved you're here with me."

Athena felt just as relieved. "I know how you feel. There were times when I thought our relationship was impossible."

The past two months in San Francisco had been eventful, busy, fulfilling in many ways-the gallery was experiencing a wave of success. Gratifying to Athena, for this pleased Kas from a business standpoint. Gratifying, for Athena was developing a reputation in the city as an artist with a knack for finding other good artists. Ian Chen's one-man show had drawn good reviews in the two local newspapers and had fostered interest among the artists' community in the city. She had scheduled two more exhibitions of outstanding, innovative painters and one of a bronze sculptor's unique work.

Gratifying, also, for she was spending every day doing what she loved. And spending every night, or almost every night, with a man she was mad about.

Her gaze scanned the restaurant and its views of skyscrapers on nearby hills. Then her gaze returned to Kas. She caught him staring at her in a contemplative way.

"Shall I hold your hand and read your thoughts? Kas, you look so . . . so pensive."

His diffident smile was disarming. "I'm just thinking about tomorrow, the next couple of days. With my family. You're refined, reserved, Thena. Worldly. I love all that about you, don't get me wrong."

Determined to keep things light, she asked, "Do I hear a but somewhere in there?"

He took a slow sip of whiskey-on-the-rocks before setting the glass tumbler back down on the table.

"You know my family. They're nosy, want to know everything you're doing. Rambunctious, sometimes irritating, sometimes hilarious as hell. They're a maddening mixture of Greeks, Italians, over-the-top Americans, energetic kids. So don't let them get to you, okay?"

She leaned over, touched his hand and read his thoughts. "I think I can handle rambunctious adults and energetic kids. There's something else you're anxious about. My meeting little Alex?"

His gaze morphed from surprise to concern.

"Xander, the little scoundrel. You'll see, he's a little devil and charmer. Y'know, I don't call him Alex even though Alexander is his name. I can't."

"I know," she murmured softly. "It's okay. I understand. He's your brother's son . . . and you miss Alex . . . and yet he's your son, too, in a way. Rather, he thinks of you as his father."

"Well, I helped raise him as a baby. I'm the only father he's ever known, poor kid. Now, I'm just a part-time father. Most weekends, he's with my parents. Weekdays, his mother. Nikki loved my brother, I believe that, but she's moved on, has a new boyfriend. I've grown attached to the little guy, wish I could spend more time with him but the Stargazer Tower is not a place for a toddler. Besides, we . . . we both have too much on our plates to raise a child. I can only be his weekend father substitute. Eventually, Nikki will remarry and her new husband'll become the boy's father. I won't even see him on the weekends."

Astonished, Athena sat back and sipped from her martini, delaying her reply. So that was it. Kas would love to see the little boy more often, maybe even here in the city, but he was conflicted. *He's afraid I would resent the time he'd spend with the child. He's afraid he'd lose me. And he's afraid he'll lose the boy. His foster son.*

A waiter interrupted them and took their orders. Good timing, for she'd been caught off-guard by Kas's worries. She'd been too preoccupied with the gallery and her own creative attempts to think much about his family. Or the little boy, his dead brother Alex's little boy, whose framed photo rested on Kas's bedside table. It was apparent that he loved the child. Loved him more than that of an uncle.

She hadn't thought about Kas's torn emotions and what this predicament might mean to their own relationship. How would Kas's love for his little nephew influence their own tenuous situation? Was he hoping that she would volunteer to be a sort of part-time stepmother for the child?

Good grief! She was only twenty-three. Wouldn't be twenty-four until May of the following year. Was she prepared to accept the little boy into her busy life? Hardly.

For the remainder of their dinner, Athena adroitly avoided the topic of his nephew. She assumed she would meet little Xander, or little Alex, the following day and would be delighted by the child. According to Kas, the boy looked like a small version of his brother, Alex. And had his biological father's charismatic personality.

Over their bowls of cioppino, San Francisco sourdough bread and shared bottle of Riesling, they caught each other up on their respective families. Leon's wife, the mother of two girls, had gone back to law school since the twin girls were in middle school. The oldest of George's three boys was now six-teen and would be a high school sophomore. The patriarch of the Skoros family, Philip, now aged eighty-seven, had retired but was still Chairman of the Board. Lorena, Kas's precogni-tive mother and a descendant of the Delphi bloodline, was now giving private readings to people on a referral-only ba-sis. Staying under the radar and using the cover of a *life coach*, she was helping direct people who felt lost.

Having just received the change of plans that day, Athena told Kas that her younger brother, Chris, a freshman at Stan-ford had been invited by his roommate to come down to SoCal so he could enjoy Thanksgiving break with the room-mate's family. A trip to Disneyland was in the offing, an ex-citing lure that Chris couldn't pass up.

"I'm sorry on Chris's behalf, and mine, that it's such short notice, that he can't join us," she said while, at Kas's urging, they began soaking the delicious bread in the cioppino sauce.

In his usual easygoing manner, Kas shrugged off her apol-ogy.

"No problem. One less will make no difference at the din-ner table. Mom's cook makes enough for a regiment. But they'll be sorry not to see him."

"Chris says he'll join us all for Christmas. He promises."

Kas's dark eyebrows raised a notch.

"What about you? What's your plan for Christmas?"

Athena smiled sheepishly and watched his reaction. She might genuinely surprise him with her news.

"I've made up my mind. If I can get Dale to take over for two or three weeks, I'd like to visit my parents in London for Christmas. Maybe you'll be able to join me."

He clasped her hand, more than pleased. He was so joyful, his countenance lit up like a lamp.

"Yeah, I think I can swing a trip. A short one, maybe one week. I've never met your father."

His words, delivered low key, belied his countenance, so Athena let her clairvoyance channel open to his thoughts.

Wow, a weeklong honeymoon in England . . .

Suddenly, like a steel door crashing down, all she could see was a stone wall. He'd realized his mistake, their hands touching and that she was reading him. And he clearly didn't want her, she knew, to be scared off by his secret thoughts. Marriage was certainly off the table for her, he knew. At least, for the time being. She'd already told him that when he proposed a month ago.

"Damn, I was too late, wasn't I?" he asked her, his dark brows arched in dismay. She'd invaded his privacy and caught him with a thought he didn't want to share with her.

"No worries, I had my channel closed," she lied. She gave him an encouraging grin.

His slit-eyed frown told her he didn't quite believe her.

"Hope so," he muttered. He looked uneasy and displeased with himself and his gaffe, like a man who burps in front of a woman he's trying hard to impress. Like most men, he didn't like showing his vulnerability.

"Truly," she added, "I wasn't tuning in."

She smiled at him and sipped more wine.

Chapter Ten

In the cab on the way back to the Stargazer Tower, she leaned against his sturdy shoulder. From day one, she'd felt safe with this man. Felt a close bond with him. Probably because his own mother was of the bloodline and he seemed to understand the pitfalls and drawbacks of such a gift.

Regardless, she and Kas had always strived to be honest with each other. Guilt for lying to him chilled her blood but she forgave herself. After all, she'd wanted to spare his feelings. To distract herself, she sat up and gazed outside the cab window.

"We could have walked back, couldn't we? And enjoyed the fresh night air?"

Indeed, the night was unseasonably balmy and the streets buzzed with sightseeing tourists strolling around, small groups of them pointing at various city sights, consulting their guidebooks.

Chuckling, Kas ran his hand down one of her bare legs. "Huh, three miles in those heels? I don't think so. And I'm too tired to carry you." As they passed a darkened park near the Transamerica Building, Jackson Square, he pointed out to her. "Look at all the homeless camping out there, the guys begging for food, money. The prostitutes hustling the male tourists, giving them — the less discriminating, anyway — blow jobs behind the trees. You want to walk by that?"

"Not really, no." Her reply was truthful. "Where are the police?"

"They've given up trying to control these homeless camps.

If they round them up, the jails are full for the night, resources are wasted, nothing changes. The courts let them out the next morning, so all they've accomplished is giving some poor bastard a free meal and bed for the night. The cops concentrate their time on chasing violent offenders. So they say."

Shocked, she remained silent. She remembered Inspector Villalobos and the murders of the city's homeless. A difficult case, to be sure. Would it ever be solved? Would the police ever stop the murderer? Strange, but thankfully so, Athena hadn't thought about the case since that Monday when she'd consulted with the homicide detective.

"I take cabs, Thena, wherever I go in the city. Especially at night. When I'm not walking with you during the daylight hours along the Embarcadero, that is. Days aren't so bad but nights-well, some areas can be downright disgusting, especially when you see them defecating and vomiting on the sidewalks, shooting up in the grass, wherever. Mumbling to themselves, yelling at the air. Sure, many of them are mentally ill, drug addicts. But don't kid yourself, Thena. Some are dangerous."

"Also, the rats in the city have multiplied," he added grimly, "San Francisco is the fifth, most rat infested city in the U.S. Disease is rampant in these camps." He chuckled softly. "On a lighter note, there's a local poop app for our cell phones. It tells you where all the shit locations are so you can avoid them. Ingenious, isn't it? Some entrepreneurial techie's going to make a bundle from this poop app."

"You're joking," Athena said.

"No, I'm not joking. God, I wish I were."

They were quiet for awhile as she gazed out the cab's window. The passing scenes reminded her of another city.

"There were homeless camps in D.C., too. I usually stayed in Georgetown to avoid them . . . or stayed in at night." Her voice trailed off, but something nagged at her mind. "So why do people pay top dollar for real estate in this city, like your condos in the Stargazer Tower?"

Kas took her hand, his voice deepening and turning raspy. "What can I say? This is a city of dichotomies, of extremes. The very rich and the very poor. Lots of well-paid tech workers. Did you know, there's a billionaire for every eleven thousand people in this city. Also, lots of paupers who can't work, too drugged out, too crazy. Or don't want to work, too lazy. The city puts them on welfare, disability, whatever. What can I say? Our company builds housing for the industrious and the rich."

Absently, she nodded. Fatigue crept through her bones. Speaking of the industrious, she'd been working nonstop for two months. Tomorrow morning, they'd be leaving the city and three hours later, they'd find themselves in a very different environment. The semi-rural hills of Loomis, where the affluent enjoyed space and nature on expensive acreage. Like the grand manor houses in Herefordshire back in England. Her parents often wished aloud that they could afford to retire to a country estate in Yorkshire. That's where her father's family originated. Her mother often spoke wistfully of retiring in Lake Como, where Nonna and her uncle Giancarlo still lived.

Kas's deep, sonorous voice snapped her back to the present.

"Your place or mine, tonight?" Kas asked gently, his hand squeezing hers for a moment. His head canted downward and briefly she felt his lips on her forehead. Grateful for the change of mood, she lifted her face to his and returned his kiss, her mouth finding his. Her tongue tangled deliciously with his and she tasted the coffee he'd had at the end of their meal.

"Yours," she whispered, "Your bed is bigger."

"Ah, good choice."

CHAPTER ELEVEN

Athena and Kas were walking home in the twilight, their shadows on the wide sidewalk of the Embarcadero lengthening with each step. With each step, they seemed to be floating until all of a sudden, they were leaning on the railing by the Ferry Building. The bay water beyond beckoned them, like a mystic, fog-shrouded lake. Was there a Loch Ness monster, some prehistoric creature, out there calling them? Or Homer's sirens whistling them home? Then Kas went down on one knee and asked her to marry him. This time, to his delight, she said yes. Only she screamed it in an ecstasy of joy, like finally giving in to something already predestined. With abandon, they climbed over the railing and jumped into the bay water. Strange, but the water was warm, not the chilled water of winter. Like the water off Portofino that one summer . . .

She must have jerked. Something awoke her from the dream. A loud buzz on Kas's nightstand. Her bloody cell phone.

Half asleep she raised up, glancing over at Kas's still sleeping, supine figure, his mouth slightly open, his broad chest rising and falling with each breath.

Annoyed at the intrusion, she pressed the red stop button. His warm, nude body and musky scent lured her to his side. She snuggled up against him wrapping one bare leg over his lower torso. Contact with his loins caused hope for physical reaction as her thigh continued to rub against his erection until she provoked a deep moan.

"What time . . ."

"I don't know."

"Who called?" Kas opened his eyes, then closed them. However, not in sleep. His left arm circled around underneath her while the other reached under her smooth thigh until he found the spot hidden by her folds. It was now his turn to provoke her to moans of pleasure. She happily obliged.

A second round of buzzing interrupted them.

"For pete's sake, who's calling?"

A thought startled her. Her parents six time zones away? Was there an emergency? A crisis with her father's health?

Athena extricated herself from one of Kas's frisky hands and turned over.

"Um, uh, hello."

"Miss Butler, Inspector Villalobos here. Sorry to call but I thought you should know this."

A chill ran down her spine, prompting her to punch the speaker button. If it was a police emergency, Kas should hear the message.

"Yes, Inspector?"

She felt Kas tense up beside her. He raised himself on one elbow and stared into the darkness of the bedroom.

"I felt that I owed it to you to keep you abreast of our investigation. The homeless murders, as our homicide team is calling them. Well, there was another one last night . . . in the Noe Valley. Dolores Park, a large encampment there by the streetcar rails. Number fourteen on the binder paper left on the body. This time, a woman aged forty-seven. We have her name, stats. No Jane Doe, this woman had a life once upon a time." He paused and waited for a response.

"I'm . . . I'm sorry, Inspector."

Villalobos continued, in his voice the weariness of a man who'd spent a sleepless night. "Yes, we all are. After she lost her husband and son five years ago in a car crash, it appears she just fell apart. Turned to drugs, lost her job, her home, everything. So there she was, camping out with the others in her sleeping bag and makeshift tent. It was a nice, starry night. Almost spring-like."

Sorrow filled her throat and her eyes smarted at the rush of emotion. Ah, the tragic vagaries of life. Athena opened her clairvoyant channel, hoping some image would come through. Anything that might help the police.

She saw a shadowy figure all in black, wearing a long, dirty black coat and hood. He moved with caution as he left his car parked along the road. In his pocket was a long-barreled pistol, not a hypodermic needle this time. His face obscured by the hood, he moved with deliberation. He crossed the street, chose his victim at random and fired his weapon twice into the sleeping woman. Then dropped the sheet of paper as he wriggled out of the coat. Threw the ragged coat on top of her, then ran back to his car.

The car, a dark sedan. She couldn't see the front or rear license plate. Couldn't see the man's face. A tall man. That was all she got.

"Inspector . . ."

Kas was sitting up now, the blanket and sheet having fallen to his waist.

"Chrissakes," he muttered softly.

Athena had also sat up, her legs dangling over the edge of the bed. Her stomach was a bundle of knots, making her feel sick. She tugged on the blanket in a hopeless attempt to cover her nude body, as if the inspector could see her through her cell phone.

Despite her wave of nausea, she told Inspector Villalobos the images she'd seen, ending with an apology.

"Sorry, I never saw his face. Or the license on his car."

There was a long silence, punctuated by heavy breathing. Then the man's voice, hoarse from lack of sleep, came back.

"Long barreled pistol? Did it make a sound?"

She thought for a second. "No sound but he fired twice. He left the coat he was wearing. He drove a sedan, a dark color, maybe foreign made. I hope this helps a little."

"My god, all of it fits. Miss Butler, have you ever been to Dolores Park? Noe Valley?"

Kas quietly left the bed and walked into the adjoining bathroom. She heard shower noises soon afterward.

"No, I don't know where they are."

"Southwest of us. Southwest of Market by five miles at least, if that's a help. Is there anything else you saw? Any detail, however insignificant it might seem to you?"

Athena swallowed down the bile rising in her throat. Kas was upset, and so was she. So much for their cozy, cuddly morning under the sheets. Bloody hell, another murder! Poor woman! Mustn't be so selfish, should help if I can.

"No, not that I can think of at the moment."

"All right, will you call me if something else occurs to you?"

She hesitated. Did she want to get involved? Was it already too late?

"Yes, Inspector, if I think of something else that might help. Oh, just a moment." She closed her eyes for a second, conjuring up that brief vision and the certitude that came with it. "One thing that's important. It's a different man."

"Different? What do you mean?"

"This murderer is a different man from the one who used the hypodermic needle to kill that other homeless person. The one you asked me to come to the station about."

She heard a sound that sounded like swearing over her phone but was abruptly cut off.

"Okay, Miss Butler, thank you."

He rang off. Hunched over, the heels of her palms digging into her eyes, she sat there as still as a cemetery statue.

Dear God, what have I gotten myself into?

73

CHAPTER TWELVE

They crossed the Bay Bridge, then the Benicia bridge crossing the north eastern edge of San Francisco Bay. The hills whizzing by along Inter State eighty were still dark gold from the summer's drought. The winter rains hadn't yet begun in full force although it was already late November. For Athena, a Brit raised on English weather and wet autumns, California's dry climate was something new and alien. Like being on a different planet.

The silence between them had grown with each passing hour, causing each to withdraw into his and her own thoughts and feelings. Athena knew that Kas was upset with her growing involvement with the homicide detective's case. And she was angry that he couldn't understand her compulsion to help law enforcement whenever she could. She tried to explain that consulting with the police was part of her destiny, like the compulsion her mother felt, too. Why else would she have been given these gifts? Was that part of their destiny? Her mother believed so. That Kas's own mother didn't feel the same was Lorena Skoros's personal choice.

He made one comment to mull over. "Destiny is something we choose, Thena. Not forced on us."

"I don't agree." And she left it at that.

Nearly three hours later, as he drove up the half-mile long driveway of the Skoroses' Loomis estate, that was all that was spoken the last hour of their journey.

Everything was the same as it had been when Athena was there last. The dry, pale gold hills, the estate's manicured grounds, the mature trees, the large, Tuscan-styled mansion. Two luxury cars and an old foreign sedan were parked in line along the circular driveway. Two German shepherds bounded over to greet them as they pulled up in front of the four car garage at the side of the mansion.

Athena smiled. "Spartacus has a friend?"

Kas opened his car door. "Didn't I tell you? We got a mate for him. Leon's daughter, Cassie, named her Cassandra, after herself."

Spartacus expressed his joy at seeing Kas by making a couple of leaps in the air, then barking up a storm. His mate joined him in their noisy greeting until Kas kneed down, hugged each one and ruffled their fur coats.

"Okay, okay, I know you're thrilled to see me, aren't you? I'm happy to see you both, I am. Big guy, Spartacus. Pretty girl, Cassandra. Yes, you are."

Athena, relieved to see Kas happy again, joined them and bent down to give her own welcome of joy. Spartacus recognized her from before and gave a shrill cry as she hugged him. Cassandra barked until Athena hugged her, too.

By the time she and Kas entered the mansion with their luggage, their mood had lifted. George and Leon, their wives and children were all there in the living room. More hugs and loud greetings ensued, the three boys of George hanging back a little and shyly welcoming Athena with handshakes. Leon's eight-year-old twin girls, Cassie and Cathy, red-haired like their mother, Michele, hugged her after embracing and kissing their Uncle Kas, then stepped back to admire Athena's choice of outfit. A rose-colored sweater tunic, rhinestone studded and V-necked, belted and worn over rose leggings. They admired her wedge heels, also.

George and Leon took their bags and disappeared while Kas led Athena into the dining room. A long table with seating for fourteen sparkled with a gold embroidered tablecloth, a plethora of crystal glassware and silver rimmed china. The multi-faceted chandelier above the table glimmered like a hundred lit candles.

"Oh, beautiful," exclaimed Athena, realizing that the children would be sitting at the table with the adults.

Kas took her hand, pleased by her obvious delight at seeing everyone.

"Yeah, very nice. Mom always goes all out for Thanksgiving. Let's go into the kitchen."

"Sure it's okay?" she asked. British kitchens were forbidden to enter without an explicit invitation.

With just a nod and a broad smile, he led her through the large butler's pantry into the kitchen. There, supervising the preparations stood Lorena Skoros, dressed for the occasion. Wearing an off-white wool dress, scoop-necked, long-sleeved and cuffed with brown mink trim. Her dark, curly hair was cut short and styled. Diamond earrings shone in harmony with the lone diamond choker she wore.

The white haired patriarch, Philip Skoros, was seated on a high-backed stool at the kitchen counter. Bent over and taking turns between sipping from a wine glass and urging a little, tousled, dark-haired boy in his lap into drinking from a glass of milk.

While Kas went over to his father and little Alex, Lorena Skoros turned around and yelped a little cry of joy. The woman embraced her warmly, reminding Athena of their common ancestry, the Delphi bloodline, that bonded them. And another kind of bond, their shared love for Kas.

"Athena, it's so good to see you again! We'll have to catch up in private, tomorrow morning perhaps. Until then, the family madness won't allow us to sit down and have a heart-to-heart chat. We have much to chat about."

With that enigmatic declaration, she introduced her cook, Betty, an older woman Athena had never met before. Two younger women, kitchen helpers for the day, were introduced by name before Athena could turn her attention to the ruckus going on at the end of the long, granite counter.

Kas was holding a jubilant little boy who looked like a pint-sized Alex, letting him climb onto his shoulders and clutch Kas's wavy hair. Then, little Xander, as Kas introduced his nephew to Athena, looked fully at her and stopped his antics long enough to wave a shy *hello* to her.

Athena reached up to take his hand and said, "Hello, Xander. What would you like to be called? Xander? Alex? Alexander?"

The little boy looked serious for a moment and shrugged. "I don't know. Popu calls me Alex, and so does Imma. Uncle Daddy calls me Xander."

"Do you mind if I call you Alex? Because you look just like him."

When she said that, the little boy nodded and smiled. She knew by touching him, that the boy had overheard the family talk, had heard from his mother that his real father was a handsome, dark-haired man called Alex, who was now in heaven and that his Uncle Kas had taken his father's place. But it was still okay with the family if he called Uncle Kas, Uncle Daddy.

Kas blinked away sudden tears, she noticed, but nodded his approval to her. His grief over his dead brother, Alex, was a barrier, she knew, that somehow he had to overcome. Maybe she could help him cope with it. Maybe she already was.

"Alright, little man, Alexander the Great, let's go galloping and show your cousins how well you ride the big giant. Okay?"

Kas swung the little boy over his back and settled him on his ample shoulders. Little Alex whooped in excitement and away the two went. Philip Skoros swiveled heavy lidded eyes her way, his deeply lined, liver spotted face wearing a thoughtful expression. He raised his arms for an embrace, the Greek way of greeting even the most casual of visitors. Overcoming her own English reserve, Athena hugged the old man, surprised by the still brawny shoulders and arms for a man in his late eighties.

"How are you, sir?" She detected the resemblance between him and Kas. Indeed, between him and his other two sons. Alex, the third in line among his four sons, had looked the most like Lorena with her dark, feminine features. Kas, the youngest, and the eldest two brothers carried more rugged, masculine features. Athena suspected the father and three remaining sons were as soft as marshmallows inside. Tough but fair businessmen on the outside, though. Pragmatists and not above compromising when necessary.

"Fine, just fine. For an old man getting ready to kick the bucket." Philip Skoros laughed heartily as Lorena spun around and called out something in Greek. That made the old man laugh even harder. "She said it's bad luck to talk like that. I say, it's laughing in the face of fate, giving it the old finger, saying *I dare you*. Know what I mean?"

Athena laughed. "Yes, I do, indeed. My father talks like this all the time. Defying our mortality, is what he calls it. What else can we humans do?"

Philip smiled, showing a row of white-capped teeth, making Athena reflect again on the amount of money that Americans spent on their dental work. Brits, glad to have survived two world wars, tended to accept their yellowed teeth and gaps in their smiles with nonchalance. Americans wanted to put their best foot forward, so to speak, and that translated to their smiles.

"Oozo, my dear? I'm having some," Kas's father said, indicating the glass he held.

Lorena interjected, holding up a tray of *dolmas*. "No, Phil, it's too strong. She isn't used to it. Later tonight, after dinner." Her husband shrugged in a wily way, reminding her of Kas's playful nature.

Athena followed Lorena as she carried the tray to the dining table.

"May I help, Lorena?"

The woman patted her arm before pulling her into the living room. She took a glass of dry sherry from a tray that Leon's wife, Michelle, held, and encouraged Athena to take the other wine glass. Even the children, including the teenagers present, had little glasses of sherry. To everyone assembled, and to Philip who had joined them, Lorena made a toast.

"I'm sorry your brother Chris couldn't join us, so we'll look forward to seeing him at Christmas. Here's to our good friend and one of my distant cousins, Athena Butler. Thank you for joining us today for our traditional, family Thanksgiving dinner."

Murmurs of agreement followed, and everyone sipped from their glasses. Tears welled behind her eyes as Athena responded in kind.

"Thank you all for your warm welcome. I love being here with all of you. It takes the sting out of missing my parents and brother at this time. Thank you all."

Everyone sipped again. George's eldest son, a sixteen-year-old, gave an exaggerated cough and said, "I'd rather have a brewski, Dad." Little Alex insisted on a little sip from Kas's glass, and then screwed up his face in disgust. "Yucky!"

Everyone laughed as Kas put him down and came over to Athena. He put his arm around her shoulders and hugged her to him.

"Another tradition, which we'll do now or at the table. Each one says what they are thankful for. The children, too. So, now or at the table?"

A chorus of *Now* rose up.

"Okay, I'll start," said Kas. He glanced down at Athena and grinned. "I'm thankful that you are back in my life, Athena Butler, sharing life in the city with me. Doing a great job at the Stargazer Gallery, showing me that life goes on and we must make the best of it."

Amid appreciative murmurs from the assembled family, Athena embraced him and kissed his cheek. She knew that Kas had implicitly referred to the family's loss of Alex nearly three years before. Gone but not forgotten. Emotion filled her and threatened to spill over. So much for her stiff upper lip, she groused to herself. Maybe the sherry helped lower her natural inhibitions. Whatever it was, she'd just morphed into a mushy mood.

Oohs and *Aahs* followed her kiss to Kas, teasing remarks by his brothers, exchanged looks between Lorena and Philip, Athena observed. Realizing everyone was staring at her, waiting for her to tell them what she was thankful for, she took a second to gather her thoughts.

What to say? She didn't want to sound weepy or maudlin, or desperately grateful. Or half of the various emotions that threatened to engulf her. Now was the time to be gracious in a reserved, sophisticated way. The way Kas liked her.

"I'm thankful for all of you, your kindness and generosity. And most of all, I'm thankful for the love and friendship of your youngest son, Lorena and Philip. Keriakos Alexander Skoros is the man I've been waiting for all my life."

And as eyes around the room widened in surprised stares, as hushed murmurs and half-hidden smiles rippled around the group, Athena's tears began to spill over.

Oh my god, what did I just say?

CHAPTER THIRTEEN

After a long evening of food, drink, and more food and drink, the patriarch, his three sons and George's two eldest teenage boys settled in the family room in front of the large-screen television, cheering on their favorite football teams. Lorena put little Alex to bed while Athena and Kas kissed him goodnight. Then after Kas disappeared into the family room and Lorena went to play checkers with George's youngest boy in the upstairs rumpus room, Athena went outside.

She found herself warming up around a portable fire pit on the huge terrace behind the mansion. Joining her were the two wives, Helen and Michelle, and Michelle's twin girls, Cassie and Cathy. They cooked marshmallows on long handled grill forks. Made s'mores for everyone, some of which were shared with the men and children inside. To say that the wives' curiosity had grown over Athena's impulsive statement during the toasting would be an understatement. The women were bursting with it.

And Athena knew their questions before they began asking them. As soon as she sat down in the wicker rocking chair, the small fire blazing yellow and orange, warming the little circle of women, she prepared herself. Although everyone in the family knew that as a bloodline descendant, Athena had clairvoyant abilities like Lorena Skoros, they'd never asked her about it. Athena had assumed their reticence was a matter of respect but now she knew the real reason.

Pretty, raven-haired Helen was the first to probe although

she tried to sound nonchalant while holding her long-handled grill fork over the open flames.

"Athena, I hope I'm not overstepping boundaries but have you and Kas been discussing marriage?"

"No, not really." No one in the Skoros family apparently knew that Kas had already proposed and that Athena had declined. Lorena knew, of course. She knew everything that was happening in her family. How disconcerting that was, Athena thought, the mother of her boyfriend knew everything about their relationship. No doubt, even before Athena became aware of the situation, herself.

How strange it was, being on the clueless end for a change, like ninety-nine percent of the people she encountered.

"I'm not even twenty-four . . ." Athena continued, feeling the need to explain to these women who were firmly ensconced within the Skoros family. But even that excuse sounded lame to her now that she uttered it. "I don't know if I would want to spend the rest of my life here in Northern California. It's beautiful, truly, but I've spent most of my life in England and Europe. Kas's life is here and I know he would never leave. I have family in Italy, a grandmother and uncle. An uncle and cousins in England, even a few cousins in Switzerland. My uncle Giancarlo's grown sons and their families. My brother Chris is here at Stanford but that's just temporary. So you see, moving here permanently would be a terribly big decision."

That reply seemed to mollify Helen and she busied herself with assembling s'mores for Cassie and Cathy. A plate on the ceramic lip of the fire pit held chocolate squares and graham crackers. The two twins held up their napkins so the cooked s'mores wouldn't spill over.

"Here, Cassie, keep it on the napkin. Go and see if the men want any more."

Eight-year-old Cassie, red-haired and blue-eyed like her

mother Michelle, shook her head. Her two front baby teeth had fallen out and had been replaced by two big, permanent teeth, lending her a bit of a chipmunk aspect.

"No, they don't, Aunt Helen."

"How do you know? Go and ask, sweetie."

Cassie frowned. "I just do. Tony wants another one. He's in the upstairs rumpus room, Mom, so I need a plate."

Athena stared at the girl for a moment and smiled. The girl stared back and returned the smile. A telepathic message sprang between them. Just then, Cathy, an exact replica of her twin sister except for the front baby teeth she still showed, returned to the fire pit.

"Mom, Papa and the uncles don't want any more. They said they've had enough sweet stuff. They're drinking beer. Tony wants two more s'mores."

Cassie smiled, showing her buck-toothed look.

"See, Auntie, I told you so."

Tempted to tell both Helen and Michelle that the two girls were both psychically gifted, Athena nevertheless decided not to. It was up to Lorena and the twins' mother to discuss the pros and cons of the girls' incipient psychic gifts. Amazing, that the Delphi bloodline was so strong that even Lorena's son, Leon, could be a carrier and hand down the gift of clairvoyance. Athena and her mother had always presumed that only the female line could carry on the genetic gifts. Was Kas a carrier, too?

Athena knew that Michelle, the girls' mother and a high school science teacher, was averse to such a controversial concept. The woman didn't believe such a thing was possible. If it couldn't be objectively tested and proven, then it wasn't possible. And Athena didn't feel inclined to enlighten the two women what the research showed. Positive clinical test results from various institutes of psychic research spoke for themselves. Let Michelle learn, herself, that instead of brilliant mathematical minds, the artistic gifts of a Michelangelo or the musical genius of a Mozart, her daughters had been born with another mental gift. As strange as the vapors and mists of Delphi.

If one day, geneticists could isolate and identify the chromosomes that comprised their special mental gifts, the science world would be enlightened. It was all in the DNA. Of that, Athena was certain. Although her grandmother-her Nonna-her mother and Lorena might disagree with her. Some day scientists would prove it.

"Okay, Cassie," her mother said, "take these up to Tony. See if Grandma wants one, too."

The little girl started to say something but then stopped, nodded to her mother and carefully placed the latest completed s'mores on the plate her mother had handed her and left the terrace. She glanced back and winked at Athena.

Cathy, a red-haired and blue-eyed duplicate of her twin sister, patted her chest.

"Grandma's having heartburn. She doesn't want any, either. And she's very tired."

Michelle, the twin's mother, looked confused.

"How do you know, Cathy? Did you ask her?" her mother asked.

The little girl looked uncertain. "No, but . . ."

"Go ask her, Cathy. Ask if she wants one."

The mother frowned, staring at the flames as if trying to find verification in the burning logs. *She knows,* Athena thought. *But she doesn't want to accept the truth.*

Helen looked up at Athena. "Anyway, as I was saying, it sounded like you and Kas have grown a lot closer in the past two months. Since you've moved here from D.C., I mean."

"Indeed, we have," Athena replied. She turned over her barbecue fork to cook the other side of the marshmallow. One more s'more should do it. Meanwhile, Helen and Michelle took sips from their glasses of wine. Helen's thoughts swirled around a variety of topics, so many that Athena closed that channel. Michelle, the twins' mother, worried about her daughters and her growing realization of their mental powers. Athena knew the woman was working up to a serious, frank conversation with her mother-in-law. For the time being, however, she was in denial.

The night air was cold but the seating area around the fire pit glowed with warmth. Still, Athena sat huddled with her coat over her shoulders. She had gorged herself with enough food and wine to last a month. It was almost time to call it a night but she didn't want to seem unfriendly.

Michelle exchanged glances with her sister-in-law, then plunged in. Athena already knew the woman had been rehearsing her remarks internally for the past few minutes.

Reading minds without having to touch a person had become a recent reality for Athena as long as she opened her mental channel to The Flow. Tonight, her channel was wide open, especially to Michelle.

"You and Kas have been in love with each other for almost four years, haven't you?"

"Yes, about that long. Since we first met."

"Leon and I got engaged after three months of dating. We knew right away that we were meant for each other. Why are you and Kas hesitating? Is it simply the location problem?" She smiled and added, "If you don't mind my asking?"

Athena was ready with, she hoped, a tactful answer.

"Well, not only that. The very strange situation. Kas's marriage to little Alex's mother, all that's happened since then has, you might say, hampered our feelings of trust. He's been hurt, I've been hurt. Indeed, it's been difficult all around. For the present, we're enjoying just being together without any complications. Or long-term commitments."

That reply appeared to satisfy both Michelle and Helen.

Eight-year-old Cathy looked up at Athena across the flames. Her expression evinced a mixture of curiosity and worry.

"Athena, I think it's cool that you have police friends. And you help them put bad people in jail."

Both women stared at the little girl a moment before turning back to give Athena a quizzical look. Kas had never told his brothers or their wives that Athena sometimes consulted with homicide detectives. Obviously, Lorena hadn't revealed it, either. But the child, along with her twin, had *the Third Eye* and Athena suddenly realized how prodigious their psychic abilities were.

"Yes, I do. I consult with homicide detectives. I'm clairvoyant, like you and Cassie. This is my way of helping people, helping the police find the bad guys. Putting them away so good people don't have to be afraid."

Before anything more could be said, Kas appeared at Athena's side. He leaned over and kissed her forehead.

"Take a walk with me?"

"Of course."

Athena was happy to leave the little group around the fire pit, before the women could pelt her with additional questions. She stood up, shrugged her arms through her coat's sleeves, while Kas helped her. He was already wearing his brown leather sport coat.

"Excuse us, ladies," he said in mock gallantry.

"Watch out for the gazebo," Helen called out, a moment before both women dissolved into giggles.

CHAPTER FOURTEEN

He took Athena's hand as they walked down the terrace steps onto the graveled walk path around the patio and lawn bordering the pool's fenced off area. Out of the darkness by the garage on the east side of the property, the two German shepherds appeared suddenly, barking happily in greeting as they trotted over to join them.

"What was that all about?" he asked, "Michelle looked like she had stabbed herself with one of those barbecue forks."

"Glad you came when you did," she murmured against his sleeve, "Cathy just revealed that she knew of my police consulting."

"What? You mean . . ."

"Oh yes, both she and Cassie. Michelle doesn't believe they're gifted. Your mother will have to take on that task of convincing the mother and advising the girls. I say to that, stay calm and carry on."

"Hmm, that'll be interesting. Leon knows about the bloodline and Mom's precognition, of course. But he's never considered the possibility of passing on the gift. We always thought it was passed down from female to female. Are we wrong?"

"I'm not sure. In this case, Leon seems to be a carrier."

Kas soldiered on. "The female line of the bloodline is supposedly very strong. I mean, look at you and your mother. And your Italian grandmother with a Greek lineage, the one you call Nonna. So why wouldn't Leon's girls inherit the same genes? Oh well, that's their problem . . ." He looked down at Athena and grinned sheepishly. "Or their cause for celebration. Maybe the male line can be a carrier, too. If it's a strong enough male line." He let go of her hand and slid his arm around her waist. "Know what that means?"

"No, what, pray tell?" Athena smiled ironically. She knew what was coming.

The way Kas squeezed her waist told Athena something wise-ass was coming. The twinkle in his blue eyes and the smirk on his mouth reinforced that expectation.

"If I'm a carrier, too, what will our kids be like? Super humans? Mental giants? Omniscient gods? Will they get rich in the stock Market by the time they're five?"

She chuckled and squeezed him back. "Let's name the boy Superman and the girl Wonder Woman, shall we?" She shot him a wry look. "Down, luv. Let's not get ahead of ourselves."

"Ah well . . . one can speculate." Kas's hand slid up to her shoulder. "Thena, I wanted to talk to you out of earshot of the others."

"What? You left your football games to talk to *me*? I should feel honored." Her words were teasing even as her arm snaked under his jacket and stroked his back, felt the rippling muscles under her palm, his warmth and strength.

The two dogs trotted behind them for a minute, then darted in front of them for the remainder of their walk. Like two stalwart bodyguards, their ears perked up for any strange sounds. The balmy November night was alive with the clicking of crickets. An owl hooted in a tree nearby. Birds chirped in a nearby Blue Oak, a tree so voluminous that it appeared to be over a hundred years old.

The footpath narrowed a bit as they approached the diverging path to the boat house. Carriage lamps on brick posts, every twenty feet or so along the wrought iron fence line, lit their way as they veered away from the boat house path. The Skoros compound was entirely enclosed with a six-foot-tall wrought iron fence, the upright, sharp-as-swords railing spikes assuring the owners that no mountain lions or deer would try jumping over. And possibly no two-legged creatures as well.

He harrumphed to her teasing remark.

"George and Leon invited me to join them tomorrow morning for some fishing. There's a mountain lake we like going to, lots of trout. Popu's going to join us. Do you mind? I'll be back by noon. Tomorrow night, I want to take you and little Xander . . . I mean, little Alex . . . to Grass Valley. The Cornish Christmas Fair is going on. Y'know, Cornish and Welsh miners came over during the Gold Rush. Most of them stayed on and worked in the silver mines. A lot of their descendants have settled in the Sierra foothills."

"I didn't know that."

"Yeah, so they have an outdoor fair between Thanksgiving and Christmas with hot Cornish Pasties, California wine, Christmas carols, games for kids."

"Sounds like fun."

He's thinking about what I said at the toasting. And he's confused. Uncertain. Insecure. Hopeful.

"Good. It'll be fun." A few moments passed in silence as they arrived at a large, backyard gazebo, the hanging lights draping like garlands around the exterior perimeter, sparkling like Christmas tree ornaments, throwing the interior into deep shadows. She could detect the outlines of a lounge chair, a small patio table surrounded by four small chairs, all shrouded in tarpaulin covers. The gazebo was at least a hundred yards from the mansion, downslope enough to be unseen even from the terrace.

"Ah, the infamous gazebo," she remarked pointedly. He pulled her up the three shallow steps and took her into his arms.

"Yes, the scene of who-knows-how-many nighttime seductions by the Skoros men. Helen and Michelle can testify to that."

She evaded his kiss but gave in to another one. "It doesn't look too clean."

He chortled with amusement. "At least, let me plead my case."

"All right, plead."

"The guys and their families are going home tonight to their homes in Granite Bay. I've been assigned my man-cave over the garage and you've been given one of the guest rooms next to little Alex's room. You know my father, he's old school, Greek Orthodox. We can't throw it in his face."

"Throw what in his face?" She knew what he meant but she enjoyed teasing it out of him.

"You know, that we're sleeping together." His tone of voice was edgy and not completely appreciative of her tease.

"Of course, that's fine."

He sighed, then pulled her closer as he supported them both against one of the posts, and nuzzled her neck. "Not fine, not to me."

She made clucking sounds to counter his own gravelly whine. "Well, I daresay we'll survive a few nights of physical deprivation."

"Speak for yourself, sweetheart." He pulled her close against him so that their groins mashed together.

She could discern in the dark gazebo mounds of plastic-wrapped pillows on the covered lounge chair, an accumulation of swimming pool paraphernalia scattered about the perimeter.

"Don't even think about doing it in this place. I reckon there're spiders all over those tarps."

That comment made him growl against her hair. "Well, darn, wouldn't you know, I have a fussy girlfriend."

"You bet, ol' chap."

Her hands snaked up his back while his roamed under her

coat. They kissed long and hard, their mouths open and searching, tongues touching. She stroked the back of his head, loving the silky feel of his thick, wavy hair. When their heads parted, they were both breathing heavily.

"Can't you sneak out? I'll keep my door unlocked."

"That wouldn't be respectful, would it? Remember the last time we tried that? The alarm?"

"Ah, well, I had to try."

"You brought me here on purpose, you sly dog."

He smirked and they kissed again. Impatient to hear what she knew was on his mind, she nearly broached the topic herself. Finally, he screwed up the nerve to bring it up.

"Thena, what you said at the toasting. I know you were caught up in the moment. You didn't really mean what you said."

Said with a questioning tone at the end.

She had to admit the truth. "I was caught up, wasn't I? The sherry, the family scene?"

"I'll say. You had tears in your eyes. You're my dry-eyed, stoic Brit. I've never seen you get so emotional so fast."

She smiled at the way he described her character of reserve. The old stiff upper lip, so British, so like her father.

"The sherry was fairly potent, you know," she said.

He pressed on. "So you're saying, the wine, the emotional toasts. It all got to you, didn't it? You didn't really mean what you said, did you? About me, you and me. That you've been waiting your whole life for me."

Kas was dying to know how she truly felt, and he wasn't going to let her off without a blunt, honest answer. And for that persistence, she was going to give him the courtesy of the bald faced truth.

Before she had a chance to answer, he continued. "None of my family knows that I've already proposed to you. Well, except Mom. She knows everything though she's never mentioned it. The rest of 'em, they don't know that you turned me down. I don't want them to know, either, if what you said isn't what you really meant to say. They weren't the only ones blown away by what you said. I couldn't stop thinking about it."

Athena rose up and pressed the full length of her body against him, her plump breasts, her soft midriff, her hard thighs. His body was long, muscular and powerful. She felt safe in his embrace, always had, probably always would. An embrace so achingly familiar, it seemed to recall a time long past.

She leaned her head down between his strong shoulder and the curve of his neck.

The truth.

"I didn't mean to say what I did, Kas, not in front of your family, in front of everyone, the kids even." His chest rose as she felt him inhale deeply. "But I meant every word I said. I've been waiting for you my whole life. Maybe for several lifetimes." She heard him expel the breath he'd been holding. He was deeply relieved, she knew. She could feel it in his muscles, his abrupt, relaxed posture. The unabashed joy flowing through his body.

Would she tell him the rest? The ancient truth that was revealed to her in one of her most recent Flow dreams? How familiar his embrace was, across the span of ages. No, now was not the time.

"I won't trouble you with another marriage proposal, Thena. I understand it's too soon, you're not ready. But if and when you are ready, will you let me know?"

"I will. I promise."

And despite the possibility of spiders and other critters, they found a way, a spot on the lounge chair, disposing of the plastic-covered pillows and pool toys, to express their passion for each other.

The two German shepherds sat below the steps, like sentinels keeping vigilant watch over the gazebo and the humans within. The peculiar human sounds they heard reassured the dogs. The occasional chuckle and sigh let them know that all was well.

CHAPTER FIFTEEN

They'd gotten a later start than planned and the fish-the damned, smart trout-weren't biting. The patriarch and three brothers sat in a shallow hulled fishing boat, its aluminum sides glinting in the sunlight. Eagle Lake, a stocked mountain lake north of the mountain town of Truckee, shone and glimmered in the soft, November sunlight.

Kas smirked to himself. Four executive types playing fishermen in the great outdoors. His grouchy father and impatient, older brothers kept complaining at their lack of progress. Rich men expecting the fish to jump into their laps, as fast as their eager-to-please employees. The morning was almost gone and they'd caught nothing but a few insect bites.

Still, Kas felt the world was his oyster. Withdrawing into himself, he'd obsessed over last night's revelations. After hearing Athena declare her love for him, that she'd been waiting for him all her life-well, nothing could puncture his balloon of exultation that day.

Not even the stubborn trout.

Leon, who'd taken over as the company's CFO, was doing a good job of keeping track of expense details, the bottom line of the company's real estate investments, was born to be a numbers cruncher. Now, he gingerly moved from his seat next to his father and hunkered down next to Kas. He leaned over, elbowed Kas and whispered conspiratorially.

"Heard you christened the gazebo last night?"

"What're you talking about?"

"Ha, you and Athena disappeared on a walk last night?

Think you're the first one to get gazebo love?"

"Damn, are there no secrets in this family? How did you guess?"

"Hey, Keri, you think you're the only one to bypass Papu's strict rules? Been there, done that, bro. Wanta share any details?"

Kas shook his head and clammed up. Not the first time his older brothers ribbed him about his love life. He smiled in spite of himself.

"Huh, didn't think so," said Leon.

"Perv," Kas muttered and looked out at the lake.

Leon chuckled and returned to his seat next to his father.

Vicarious voyeurism, Kas groused, almost as bad as a Peeping Tom. Did marriage, years of perfunctory sex, and the responsibility of children cause that? He hoped not.

Maybe staying unmarried kept sex fresh, exciting? Maybe changing partners kept sex fresh? No, he couldn't see himself making love to any other woman. Ever again.

Hell! It used to be exciting to go through the whole seduction-and-conquer scene, test his manhood with a variety of women, a variety of bodies and female minds. Always wondering what they really thought about him, what games they were playing, what needs they had that were wanting to be fulfilled. Then, letting them down easy and moving on. The whole merry-go-round of changing partners.

His train of thought turned back again to Athena. How did she capture his heart? He'd not thought about another woman for over three years, even when he was in that sham marriage with Nikki. Why was he so fixated on one woman? How did this happen? Would it-the excitement, the mystery-be ruined if they got married? But he wanted to father her children. His mother had told him that Athena would someday have his children. Could his mother, the precog, be wrong about such an important revelation?

How was Athena doing with his mother? Their big heart-to-heart chat that morning? Would his mother advise her to quit consulting with the cops? The risks weren't worth it, not if she planned to marry and have children someday.

Would Athena marry him? Would their children be gifted in that psychic way? Would she give up England, her other possible homes in Europe to stay with him in California? Was he asking too much of her?

At least, he hoped that's what his mother would say to Athena, that her future was more secure if she married Kas. Only his mother, a sister of the Delphi bloodline, could also persuade Athena that using her clairvoyance to try and catch killers and rapists wasn't worth the risk. He remembered all too well the last bad guy in D.C., and the three of them-him, Athena, Chris-staring at the business end of the freaky ass-hole's gun muzzle. They'd been lucky that Kas had gotten hold of Athena's borrowed revolver in time. That the bastard had run instead of fired.

Next time-well, he hoped there wouldn't be a next time.
C'mon, Mom, talk her out of it. You can do it.

Athena and Lorena each carried a mug of coffee into the study that also doubled as Philip's office, now that he no longer made the trek downtown to the Skoros Enterprises office in the multi-storied Wells Fargo Building in downtown Sacramento.

Both dressed in casual pants and sweaters, the two women settled on the leather sofa and faced each other.

"I'm so happy you came for Thanksgiving, Athena. We've enjoyed your company, the children, too. How're your parents doing in Milan?"

"Father's having neuropathy issues, cardiac problems. He may have to have a bypass, too. Mother says that some of the arteries around his heart are clogged with plaque. He's more concerned that the Foreign Office will yank him back to London and retire him early on disability. He's only fifty-four and now he's paying Chris's way at Stanford. Which is not cheap, of course. Father was hoping to make it to sixty before returning to London."

Lorena looked away into the distance. Athena knew the woman was seeing her father's future and she didn't want to know. She closed her channel into Lorena's mind.

"Please don't tell me," she said, "I couldn't bear it if it's bad news."

Lorena's gaze turned back to her and she smiled tentatively.

"And your mother? Is she still helping the-what do you call them, the Italian police?"

"The carabiniere. Yes, she is. She's also working with the Polizia di Stato on counter-terrorism cases. As you've heard, with the increase of migrants from Muslim majority countries into Europe, all the growing unrest and threats of terrorist attacks, those kinds of problems are increasing."

Lorena pursed her lips thoughtfully. "Your mother's very strong and brave. She'll be fine." She took a sip of the caramel flavored coffee she'd prepared for them both. "What do you know about Greek history and how your mother and I are related?"

"Not much about Greek history. Only that you and Mother share a common great-great-grandmother from Italy who had a Greek heritage. Her mother, my Nonna, was born in Greece but raised in northern Italy. Emigrated to Italy sometime in the nineteen-thirties. Before World War Two."

"Would you like to know more? About our heritage from ancient Greece?" Lorena asked her. Athena nodded.

"Did you know the ancient Greeks believed they were the people of the serpent? The serpent, they believed, was a creature of knowledge and enlightenment-not the symbol of Satan that the early Roman Christian church would have people believe. Western civilization demonized the serpent but not the Greeks."

Athena sat back and waited, wondering what this bit of ancient history might have to do with her.

Lorena continued. "The Goddess Athena is always shown with a serpent wound around the bottom of her spear. She symbolized enlightenment and was always portrayed as ready to defend the importance of knowledge and enlightenment. That's how the spear and serpent became the symbol of medicine and healing. The ancient enlightened ones, the Greeks believed, were the temple priests and priestesses. They were ancient psychics but they were also healers. These temple priests and priestesses believed they got their powers from the Goddess Athena."

"Blimey." Intrigued, Athena didn't move.

"We're descended from one of those temple priestesses, perhaps one of the most gifted of her era. She spent time at the Temple of Apollo on Mount Olympus, and at the Temple of Aesculapius in Athens."

Athena sat up straight, nearly spilling her cup of coffee. She set it down on a nearby table.

"You mean, she was one of the Oracles of Delphi?"

Lorena steadied her gaze on Athena. "Yes, her name was Porphyra. The Oracles rotated in and out of Mount Olympus near Delphi but she stayed the longest, as did her mother. She was the most gifted of the soothsayers. When she returned to Athens to the Temple of Aesculapius, she had a Macedonian guard assigned to her. His name was Kyriakos and he became her private guard and protector. And her lover, husband, and father of her children. Scrolls from the Temple have been found, scrolls that told their story."

Athena consciously closed her mouth, then smiled in a puzzled way.

"How do you know all this, Lorena? The details, their names? The guard, Kyriakos? Porphyra? Where Porphyra lived and the temples she served at? It's incredible."

Lorena shrugged. "The various temples of ancient Greece had scribes that kept detailed records of their priests and priestesses. When I was much younger, I went to Italy and met your mother. She and I traveled to Athens and read the records, with the help of a Greek scholar. Those records explained a lot and helped us to understand our strange ancestry. And our strange gifts. I named my youngest son after Porphyra's guard and lover because I sensed something about my son. Keri-or Kas, as he calls himself-is special. Has a special spirit."

Athena considered her words. Yes, Kas was special. She sensed it, too, had sensed it all along. Yet, she remained confused.

"Why is it my mother has never told me this? She just said that we had a Greek and Italian heritage, that our psychic gifts came from our ancient Greek ancestor. A woman who was a soothsayer and healer."

"Yes, the priestess Porphyra." Lorena drained her cup and set it down. "Would you like more coffee, Athena?"

Breathlessly, she shook her head. "No, thank you. My heart's pounding as it is, just hearing all of this."

A moment passed as Lorena sat back and sighed. She closed her eyes for a couple of seconds before opening them again. Again, she had that thousand-yard stare, this time pinning a point on the wall.

"There's more. Do you believe in genetic memory, dear?"

"Yes, I realize if the lowly salmon can have it, why can't we? Is this what determines the existence of our bloodline?"

"Yes, but there's more."

CHAPTER SIXTEEN

"Why are exceptional music gifts, or the ability to understand high-concept mathematics or theoretical physics, or world-class athletic abilities, passed down from generation to generation in some families?"

Athena smiled brightly. "Genetics. My grandfather Butler was an artist, a painter of some repute, I'm told. He died when I was ten. I'm sure I inherited his artistic ability."

"Yes, exactly," Lorena said. "Which is why enlightenment, or psychic abilities, are also passed down in families."

The common sense of it struck Athena, confirming what she already knew was true. But the exception to this theory simultaneously made her frown.

"So why just the women? Why not the men in our bloodline? Why not Kas or his brothers?"

Lorena's hands rose, her palms lifted upward. "That, I don't know. They have other gifts. Smart, analytical minds like their father. Sensitivity to others' feelings. A need to protect. Or maybe they're carriers, like the carriers of recessive genes that cause blue and green eyes. Do you know, only seven percent of the global human population have green-hazel eyes? Only one to two percent have red hair? It could be a mutated gene that began with the ancient Greeks."

Athena's head swam. The memory of her recent Flow dream made her dizzy.

"Oh, Lorena, my dream. The dream I had several nights ago. I must tell you my dream."

Lorena patted her hand before clasping it tightly. "Tell me

telepathically. I'll close my eyes to concentrate."

Athena did the same. The visuals and audio memories flooded back, all of which she strove to convey to the mind of this extraordinary woman, whose bond with her ran much more deeply than she ever expected or thought possible.

The tentmaker looked up and shielded his eyes from the relentless sun. His dark eyes were sun-weary but wizened. There was an intensity of spirit and purpose about him. Even when he bent over the handmade grommets, an iron awl punching the holes that he would then encircle with tough, thin strips of hide. Just then, though, he steadied his intense look upon her.

Porphyra wondered if he recognized her as the servant girl from Philippi. This man had claimed he'd driven out, with help from the Holy Spirit, the demon that possessed her.

"I see your protector is a Macedonian," Saul said kindly as she stood before him quietly. The hand holding the iron awl pointed behind her to the young, muscled guard, who wore a Macedonian arm band made of bronze. "I shall go there next spring, to Macedonia, and spread the Good Word."

"Teacher Saul, oh, forgive me, my fellow Greeks call you Paul now." Porphyra smiled meekly before this great man. All the Greeks in Corinth were speaking about him.

"Yes, I remember you. After I exorcised the demon spirit from your body, you followed me to Thessalonika, then Athens. Now you find me in Corinth. What do you wish of me, child?"

He spoke fluently in Greek but he was a Jew who spoke Greek and Latin as well as Hebrew. She heard the impatience in his voice, she seemed to make him restive, uncomfortable. Of course, a Greek priestess walking in the Jewish Quarter of Corinth was somewhat unorthodox.

"My mother was in Delphi at the Great Temple of Apollo. She foretold my capture and enslavement in Berea but also foretold I would meet a great teacher and would be freed soon thereafter."

Saul shifted on his short stool. "Who is this soothsayer, child?"

"Persephone, now the High Priestess at the Temple of Aesclepius. I am a priestess, too, and it is now my turn to serve at the Great Temple of Apollo." She bowed her head slightly. "I thank you again for my freedom, Teacher Paul, and I wish you success in your travels."

She turned to leave, glanced over at her dark haired Macedonian protector, Keriakos, who stood silently, a sheathed sword at his side and a bronze shield on his arm. He gave her an encouraging nod, implying that she should deliver her message before they left.

Saul of Tarsus, or the Jesus disciple Paul, peered at her beneath his thick turban.

"You, a priestess at the temple? What do they call you, child?"

"Porphyra," she said, radiating pride. "At the temple, I shall heal and foretell, just as I did for my Macedonian masters in Philippi. I shall also interpret dreams and give advice. The light and wisdom of Athena is my beacon in this dark world. You see, Teacher Paul, the Sacred Goddess has given me a gift. Just as she has blessed my mother and her mother before her."

Saul frowned deeply and looked away. She sighed deeply, deciding to be completely truthful.

"I thank you for making my master believe a demon was inside me and that you released me from its power. I pretended I had lost my prophetic abilities and so my captor let me go. What could he do? Certainly not blame me. He even gave me money for the journey home and ..." She glanced over at Keriakos. "One of his guards whom you entranced. Keriakos is now my protector and bodyguard. The Goddess Athena sent you to me, Teacher Paul, so I could come home. Forgive me if I seized upon the opportunity to win my freedom."

Saul snorted loudly and surprised Porphyra by erupting into laughter. She withdrew a few steps into the sunlit cobbled street. Her head and shoulders were covered, but it was not proper for her to be seen in the Jewish quarter.

"I thought you were following me because you were a convert to the Jesus discipleship."

"You have many devotees, Teacher Paul, but I am not one. We

Greeks are by tradition an openminded and tolerant people, are we not? Can we not accept your philosophy as well as our own?"

"You misunderstand, Porphyra. The teachings of the Lord Jesus are not a philosophy. They are a faith, a belief, a way of life."

She smiled. "You are a great orator. I listened to you in the agora in Athens and on the bema here in Corinth. You have enraptured Keriakos by your eloquence. Still, he tells me he prefers Apollo and Athena to your Lord Jesus."

Porphyra looked over at her Macedonian bodyguard. His duty was to guard and protect her from all harm. Each of the temple's priestesses had a Guardian. The young, dark haired man was lean, muscular, and had a handsome facial profile, framed by a short, dark brown beard. He was as handsome as Apollo and as strong as Zeus. She loved him with all her heart and soul.

Saul waved her away. "Go, child, you tarry too long and I must work."

"First, I must tell you that I have had a vision about you. Athena has shown me a great temple of stone in a faraway place, which is now a Roman camp called Londinium. This temple will be named in your honor and your words will be read by nations on the far side of the world."

The Jesus disciple stared at her, awestruck. Aquila and Priscilla, his companions and fellow tentmakers, clamored for a translation from Greek to Hebrew but Saul ignored them.

"What you say, child, is nonsense. I do not seek riches or temples in my name. I simply seek to spread the Good Word of our Lord Jesus. Surely, you mean well but it is clear that a demon has possessed you again."

Porphyra ducked her head in embarrassment. This teacher had just gently rebuked her. Nevertheless, she had come to see him with a purpose in mind and she would not leave without warning him with the message that Athena in her divine wisdom had imparted to her.

"I have come to implore you, Teacher Paul, do not go to Rome. It is dangerous for you there. Nero . . ." She whispered now, bending over so that no passersby could hear her, " . . . Nero is an evil man

and will destroy you. Athena wanted me to warn you."

Saul chuckled mirthlessly. "Dear maiden, I do not fear the Ro-mans. I am a citizen of Rome."

Porphyra's heart squeezed with disappointment.

"You should fear them, Teacher, for they will learn to fear you."

She withdrew to Keriakos's side on the cobblestone walkway, which led back to the Greek section of Corinth. Raising her right hand, she said, "May the light and wisdom of Athena keep you safe, Teacher Paul."

Her last glance back at the Jewish tentmaker revealed his troubled countenance. He gruffly nodded to her before turning and speaking to his friends.

Keriakos strode beside her, his brilliant cobalt-blue eyes warming her. She felt safe and secure, just walking beside him.

"You warned him, Porphyra. Your duty is done."

She smiled up at him. "Yes, it is done."

Athena opened her eyes and looked over at Lorena. The older woman was open-eyed as well, staring at the wall and smiling.

"I've had the same dream. Our ancestor wanted to tell us where and whom we came from."

The image of Keriakos's face, Porphyra's bodyguard, still swam before her eyes.

"Lorena, Keriakos is Kas. He looks just like him."

Kas's mother continued to smile. "I know. And now, Athena, he is your protector. If you will have him."

CHAPTER SEVENTEEN

"This reminds me of fairs at home, the Christmas street fairs of North Kensington in greater London. The Portobello Road fairs."

Kas smiled. "Maybe I'll see them for myself."

Happy that Kas was actually planning the Christmas trip to London with her and Chris, Athena scanned the downtown area of the mountain town of Grass Valley, deep in the Sierra Nevada foothills. Once the home for hundreds of Cornish and Welsh miners hoping to cash in on the California Gold Rush, now a thousand or so locals and tourists strolled the downtown streets, lighted with carriage lamps and overhanging, varicolored and lit ornaments. Crowds wrapped in heavy clothing meandered about the coronas of light. Some carried glasses of wine and beer. Exhalations of breath misted and clouded in front of faces flushed by the cold and boozey, festive cheer.

The night air was chilly but there was no wind. Still, aromas of all kinds from outdoor food booths wafted through the cold air, warming and tantalizing everyone who came near. Booths outfitted with barbecue grills sizzled and popped with English-style sausages. Deep-fried fish fillets were hawked as well. Signs of "Chips" advertised cardboard bowls heaping with fries, bottles of malt vinegar available to drench them with. Athena exclaimed at the familiar food and proposed to Kas and little Alex, who rode atop his shoulders, that they take home a bag of fish and chips.

"And Cornish pasties," reminded Kas as he pointed to the

pastie shop further down the street.

Holiday music drifted from the open doors of saloons and shops, background streams of notes to the Christmas melodies sung by a roving quartet of Victorian costumed singers.

Kas carried the toddler on his broad shoulders so the boy could view everything above the crowd. Athena, bundled in her coat and muffler, kept replacing the little boy's knit cap every time he flung it off his head.

"Don't like it, Thena. Scratchy."

"Your ears'll get cold, Alex," Kas warned mildly.

"Don't care, Daddy. Don't like it."

Athena shot him a wry grin. Where did little Alex get his stubborn, willful nature? Ha! With a biological father like Kas's brother, Alex, who probably never saw an obstacle he didn't want to challenge, and an uncle like Kas, ex Sheriff's deputy, the boy was never going to be a milquetoast kind of kid.

She relented. "I'll carry it, it's okay, Alex. I'm not wearing a hat, either, am I, luv?"

The little boy looked down at her and laughed his high, little-girl laugh, sounding a little like one of the singing chipmunks. He looked up at the night sky, a halfmoon shining but not blotting out the millions of bright stars dotting the black velvet sky. Athena couldn't help but notice the difference between the city night skies of San Francisco and those of the Sierra foothills.

"Look, Alex, the moon and the stars!"

"Ooh," the toddler gushed.

Kas grinned. "We look at the stars together when I'm in town. Every weekend, don't we, little buddy?"

The toddler pointed suddenly at a man carrying and eating a pastie as he walked.

"What's that, Daddy?"

"It's a Cornish pastie. A meat-filled turnover. Want one?"

"Yeth." The boy clapped his tiny hands together, a silent clap from his mitten covered hands.

Kas found it nearly impossible to deny the child anything, Athena knew. When they arrived at the pastie shop, he pointed to a bench with an empty seat in front of a store, whose sign bore the bold-lettered words in red *Cornish Pasties*. Another sign of a red dragon breathing fire in front of a field of white and green drew Alex's attention.

"Look, Thena, a dragon."

"Yes, a dragon. That's the flag of Wales, where many of these locals came from. Or rather, their great grandfathers. They came here to mine for gold and silver," she said, feeling foolish after Kas looked at her and shook his head in disbelief. As if to say, do you really think a two-year-old understands what you just said?

Oh well, she was out of her element, unaccustomed to conversing with small children. Kas put Alex on the bench, where he promptly clambered off. She caught the back of the boy's jacket and held him fast before he could run off.

"Alex, you must stay here with me."

"Watch him, Thena. If he runs off, we'll be looking for him all night."

She nodded. "I'd love a pastie, too. A beef one. Alex, a chicken one?"

"Yep, easier to chew. I'll give half a dozen," Kas agreed, who promptly disappeared into the store. A line had formed inside, she saw, as the door stayed open for a moment.

She sat down on the bench, continuing to hold onto the toddler. Helping Kas watch over little Alex was exhausting, she'd discovered, confirming her suspicion that she was too young to have children of her own. How Lorena could have dealt with four little boys was beyond her! It must've been like the American Civil War all over again. She may've had some help, a nanny perhaps like many well-to-do families, but crikey! Chasing one little boy was like chasing down a dozen cats.

A few minutes passed. Little Alex had settled down a bit, was staring at several children who had just walked by. She noticed he seemed bewildered but excited by all the people in this small downtown area, especially drawn to the children close to his age. He watched them walk by, occasionally smiling at some, bashfully glancing down at others.

Athena knew he would benefit from attending a pre-K school, even for a few days a week. He needed the companionship and energy level of little kids his age. The Skoros grandparents meant well but they couldn't keep up with the little tyke. A weekend father like Kas wasn't enough. Athena could only hope that his mother, Nikki Skoros, would see the wisdom in finding him a part time pre-K day care. So far, according to Kas, she hadn't.

Just then, her mobile phone buzzed. She looked down and saw the area code for Italy. Her mother or father? They'd just rung her Thursday evening, to convey their best wishes to the Skoroses for a happy Thanksgiving.

She answered, holding on to an increasingly squirrelly little Alex. A little girl had diffidently approached him. A woman's voice came on, drawing her into her phone.

"Mum?"

Pleasantries were exchanged, and then the real purpose of the call ensued.

"I wanted you to know straight away that your father is in hospital today, undergoing a procedure. A plaque removal via microsurgery."

Athena's attention wavered from little Alex to her mother's message. What! Her father in surgery and she's just now hearing of it? Her mind launched itself to Milano, where her parents now lived. She visualized the city for a second, the streets by La Scala and the cathedral, her parents' spacious townhouse next door to the British Consulate. Her heart was pounding so loudly, she felt the pulse in her ears, in her neck.

"He's in hospital now?"

"Yes, dear, a sudden thing. He saw his cardiologist today, and without a moment's hesitation, the man insisted that Trevor see the surgeon immediately. The blockage has worsened, ninety-five percent in the arteries around his heart. He's breathless all the time, can barely walk up a step or two. It has to be done now."

"Oh, Mum, I can't believe this."

Distracted, Athena just now noticed she'd let go of the boy's jacket. Little Alex had wandered off with the little girl — no, an older girl around Cassie's and Cathy's age. The girl was holding Alex's hand, talking to him, handing him something, pulling him away.

"Mum, is this surgery happening in Milan?"

"No, figlia mia, we're going home to London for the procedure. His physician here advised this."

"Mum, so London . . ." Athena lurched to her feet, raking her gaze through the crowd, desperate to keep sight of little Alex and the girl.

A man on the fringe of the crowd milling around the side of the pastie store, a scraggly dark, graying beard and mustache concealing most of his face, was watching the girl, calling to her, bending down to speak to little Alex, taking his hand —

"Mum, I must call you back!"

Athena pocketed her phone and took off in the direction of the man. Thirty feet away, now forty feet away, the man was now running, carrying Alex under one arm.

Her heart leaped into her throat, rending her voiceless with panic, her voice screaming in her head. Stop him! Stop him! Kidnapper!

She pushed through the crowd, flung one woman out of

her way, didn't stop to apologize, no time!

"Stop him! Stop him!" she screamed at anyone who would listen. The crowd parted and stared at her. The man with the scraggly beard was taking a handkerchief out of his pocket with his left hand.

"Stop! Let him go!" She screamed at the bearded man as loudly as she could, but he wouldn't stop. His pace picked up but so did hers.

"Stop him!" Her screams did no good and just hampered her breathing. In full panic, tears burning her eyes, pumping her legs as fast as she could, she ran after the man an entire town block. Alex began to scream as well, a high-pitched scream that wrenched her heart. The crowds had thinned at this end of town.

The man had reached the perimeter of a small, outdoor parking lot filled with cars, vans, pickup trucks.

Then suddenly, she remembered the personal alarm she carried at all times on her cross-body purse. It dangled from a carabiner lock attached to the purse's strap. She snapped downward on the chain that connected to the bright pink, plastic alarm device.

The device emitted an ear-piercing, high-pitched shriek, steady like a fire alarm. People strolling nearby turned around to stare and point.

She was running out of breath but knew she couldn't stop!
Dear God, help me!

CHAPTER EIGHTEEN

The shrill, screeching alarm drew the attention of people nearby, walking in the opposite direction.

Athena could only point and holler, "Help me!"

One man from the crowd began walking her way, his gaze following hers and shouting, "Hey you!"

The bearded man approached a row of tall shrubs that bordered the parking lot. Caught in his viselike arm, little Alex kicked and screamed. Athena's heart stopped! She couldn't let him get beyond the shrubs and out of sight.

Running after them, closing the distance, she reached down and picked up a rock the size of her palm. She pitched it towards the man as hard as she could. It hit him in the back of the head.

The thin, bearded man stumbled to a halt, dropped the child, sending the toddler to his hands and knees on the asphalt. Swooping up the girl at his side, he began to run at full speed to the parking lot, now just yards away. They disappeared behind the hedgerow of shrubs.

Athena reached Alex and picked him up, held him to her as he cried in shock and fear. *Oh god, oh god —*

She choked back sobs but managed to whisper, "It's okay, sweetheart, I've got you. The bad man's gone."

Kas sprang past the man who'd shouted and came running up, lunged for the two of them, flung himself down on his knees and encircled them in his arms. He held them tightly, breathing hard.

"What the hell happened? I heard your alarm."

111

Athena just pointed in the direction of the parking lot before catching her breath.

"Skinny man with a bushy dark beard and a girl about Cassie's age, grabbed Alex, ran to his car."

"Hold him, don't let him go! Where is he?" Kas yelled as
he let them go. Athena pointed to the parking lot behind the
shrubs. Kas arose, dropping the white bag that held their pasties, and ran past the shrubs.

She held tightly onto Alex, soothing him while he wept,
simultaneously following Kas at a walking pace. She knew he
had a CCW permit. Conceal and Carry Weapon permit. As an
ex-deputy, not difficult to get in California, she'd been told.
He carried a pistol with him most of the time, even in the city.

Now, as clear in her vision as the lamppost she walked
past, Athena knew what the bearded man was, what he was
trying to do.

The horror of it chilled her to the bone.

Such a close call!

And now worry for Kas's safety set in. The moment she
moved around the waist-high shrubs bordering the parking
lot, still carrying little Alex, she saw they were too late. The
man was pulling out, his tires squealing on the asphalt, the
girl in the passenger seat of the dark-colored pickup truck
looking back at them, her eyes bulging with fear.

Her head and heart filled with clamorous alarms, she
watched Kas jog after the truck, then skid to a halt.

"Kas! License plate!"

He turned around and bent over, breathing hard, trying to
catch enough wind to speak. Finally, he nodded.

"Got it. Gotta write it down."

She rushed up to him and handed him a pen from her
purse after first shutting off the shrieking purse alarm. Kas
wrote a line of letters and numbers on his forearm.

"Didn't catch the last two, covered with mud or dirt."

He heaved a couple of breaths, took the little boy from her arms and held him tightly against him. As little Alex quieted, Kas stared at her, waiting for an explanation.

"I'm so sorry. I was distracted for a couple of seconds, call from my mother, Father needs surgery, heart arteries all clogged up, returning to London."

Kas alternated between kissing the toddler's head and cheek, shaking his head at Athena, holding back his own tears, and glancing around the crowd. Strangers had returned to their own business, murmuring to each other. A Sheriff's deputy, on overtime duty at the Cornish Christmas Fair, hastened up to them.

In a gray and tan uniform, the young deputy, in his late twenties at the most, recognized Kas and greeted him.

"Kas Skoros? That you, sir?"

Kas gulped back his anxiety, refrained from shaking the young deputy's outstretched hand, showed him why.

"Tom, Tom Buckley," he said in greeting. "Deputy, I need your help. Write down this number." Kas showed the young deputy the letters and numbers on the palm of his hand. "I managed to get five of the seven. This guy, he tried to kidnap my nephew, Alex." He turned to acknowledge Athena. "This is Athena Butler. She was watching—"

Tears streaming by now, as the shock was wearing off, but the horrible reality continued to settle in.

She tried to explain. "I was talking on my mobile, distracted by bad news, horrified actually. A little girl, dirty blond hair, in a jumpsuit, a kind of coveralls that farmers wear. Dirty coveralls. She took Alex to that man, a skinny man in his forties, I think. Wearing jeans, jeans jacket, big bushy dark beard, dark eyes, a scar along one cheek." She raised her hand to indicate her left cheek. "His left cheek. He's a child trafficker, steals children, sells them. The girl was the lure, the bait."

"Wait, how do you know all this, miss?" The young deputy asked, his gaze dancing from Kas to little Alex, to the numbers written on his notepad, back to Athena.

She looked at Kas, uncertain how to proceed. "I-I just . . ."

Kas stepped between the deputy and Athena, his height and broad shoulders blocking Athena's view of the shorter deputy. Athena got the implied message, after which Kas moved aside to finish introductions.

"She's just guessing, Tom. Athena, this is Deputy Tom Buckley. I trained him before I left the Sheriff's office." Kas stepped aside, cast a glance at Athena, then at a sniffling Alex.

The deputy tipped his cap, took in the whole situation in silence.

Kas stepped closer to the younger man.

"Do me a personal favor, Tom, and look up those numbers on the CLETS database. Keep it quiet and, for chrissake, don't reveal where the complaint came from. If you need to, go to the NCIC, check on out-of-state warrants. BOLOs, even. That kind of asshole usually moves around, takes his victims with him, keeps them close, tied up, locked up until he can unload them."

Deputy Buckley nodded, then gazed back at Athena.

"Are you certain about this, Miss Butler, that he was trying to kidnap the boy?"

"Yes, absolutely. What else would a total stranger want with the child?"

"Tom, the child's my nephew, Alex's son. And yes, Athena wouldn't make such an allegation unless she knew it was true."

"You should make a formal complaint, Kas. Come to the Sheriff's office tomorrow."

Kas patted the boy's back, soothing him, Alex's head lolling on Kas's shoulder from exhaustion.

"No, I don't want my parents' name involved. They're too

old to deal with the fallout. We know what he's going to do, this asshole. Deny, say the girl told him the little boy was lost, get rid of any evidence of wrongdoing or kidnapping tools. Get rid of any kids he's got somewhere in some hellhole."

Athena interjected, "It looked like he might've had a chloroformed rag. He was taking it out of his pocket when I hit him with a rock. He stumbled, almost fell. Then he dropped Alex."

Kas's dark blue eyes grew big. He hadn't known this detail of her chase.

"Tom, you know the drill. Just quietly look for him. Navy blue pickup, five to six years old, maybe older."

Kas followed with a more detailed description of make and model in addition to the partial plates. Deputy Tom Buckley dutifully wrote everything down.

Athena opened her channel and read Kas's thoughts, which explained a lot.

The California Law Enforcement Telecommunications System and the National Crime Information Center would be two of the databases to start with. If there were no outstanding warrants from the California DMV or these law enforcement databases, they would have to proceed in a different way.

Surveillance. A search warrant, perhaps? Kas knew he was prepared to do whatever it took to put this predator behind bars. She shivered as she read Kas. Or six feet under.

Kas and Deputy Buckley exchanged a few more comments in low voices before the deputy touched his cap and left them.

Meanwhile, Athena had retrieved the bag of pasties, hoping their evening could return to normal, but knowing that it couldn't.

"I'm so sorry, Kas. I let down my guard. Just a few seconds . . ."

Her tears dried as she dropped her head onto little Alex's drooping back, kissed his curly head. The little boy's eyes had closed, overcome with fatigue and the sudden letdown of adrenalin and emotion. With his free hand, Kas hugged her to him, his own face wet now with belatedly shed tears.

"This happens when you least expect it. The element of surprise is always in their favor." He started to say something else but stopped. "Let's go home."

Their happy evening over, she hugged him and little Alex to her.

For dear life and limb.

CHAPTER NINETEEN

It was after nine o'clock by the time Kas drove his SUV into the far-right bay of his parents' five car garage. He carried a thoroughly exhausted, sleeping little Alex up to his so-called man-cave above the garage, a spacious studio apartment. The apartment next to his was not used, not since the boy's father, Alex, had died in a terrible car crash. The empty apartment was always a reminder of the brother he'd lost.

Athena followed them up the exterior wooden stairs, still holding the bag of uneaten pasties. While Kas gently took the boy's jacket, jeans and shirt off, Athena put the bag into the small fridge in the apartment's kitchenette. Their appetites gone after their harrowing ordeal, she heated up the single cup coffee machine's water tank. After all, why not settle one's stomach with some hot tea? Hers was still roiling from the abduction attempt.

When she suggested as much, Kas shook his head morosely.

"I need something stronger. Join me in some bourbon on the rocks? Then you'd better get to bed. We're leaving early tomorrow morning. When we get back, I have to prepare for a meeting first thing Monday morning."

He hadn't looked at her since he'd begun the twenty-minute drive from Grass Valley back to the Loomis Hills. She knew through her Flow channel that he was torn between blaming her for her carelessness with such a precious child and regarding her as just a normal caretaker who was human and had let down her guard. But she also knew Kas was not the kind of man to welcome or excuse human weakness, not when the welfare of a child was involved. A child who was like a son to him.

"Yes, I'll take that drink." Sighing, she turned off the coffee machine.

She watched him gingerly place the little boy on one side of his own king size bed. He removed the boy's jacket and shoes, then covered the still sleeping child, staring at him for a long moment. The wretched expression on Kas's face said it all. Letting something horrible happen to little Alex would be like spitting on his dead brother's grave.

With heavy, slow steps, Kas moved away from the bed and absently took a bottle of bourbon out of the makeshift bar next to the fridge. Silently, he half-filled two hi-ball glasses with bourbon, handed one to her, and then sat down at the foot of the bed. Athena took a seat on an armchair covered with a red and black Buffalo plaid blanket, the chair situated halfway between the bedroom area and the kitchenette. Kas's entire demeanor said *don't approach*.

A wide screen TV hung on the wall opposite the bed. Apparently, Kas's favorite TV viewing spot. It stayed off.

The memory of their first passionate moment in heated foreplay came readily to her mind. She'd known Kas just a few days, had crushed on him immediately and when he swept her off her feet with a passionate kiss, she knew then and there that he would be her first lover.

They were undressing each other when he'd received a call. His father had collapsed with a heart attack and his mother needed him. After that, after his father had recovered, Kas had flown to D.C. to be with her. He'd made her no promises and she'd wanted none. The nascent lovemaking was enough . . .then.

But what about now?

And what about her own father half a world away and his

health issues? Surgery on his arteries, back to London . . .

Her attention snapped to the present. She realized she'd already swallowed the whole drink.

Kas's gaze swept over her. "Take it easy, Thena. Tell me about the call you got. Your father?"

She got up and poured herself another three fingers of bourbon. His first glass was only half empty. His steady, accusatory gaze on her made her want to weep. Did he hate her? She knew he couldn't decide for certain what he felt.

"Mum called from the hospital in Milano. Tests showed the impacted arteries around Father's heart. They're flying home to London for emergency surgery tomorrow. Nothing to do but wait for the outcome. I'll ring her back tomorrow morning. It'll be seven or eight in the evening there. Things should be sorted out by then. Right now, I can only pray that he'll survive the procedure."

"Tell me about your father's health history."

As she settled back down in the armchair, she felt the pain of losing Kas's respect, the pain lessening a bit with each sip of the bourbon. The alcohol gave her a buzz, a numbness that calmed her a little. For a few minutes, she sketched for him her father's various physical problems since leaving the Royal Air Force in his late twenties, a helicopter pilot. The broken bones, punctured ear drum. Then, as he rose up the ranks of the Foreign Service, a bout with bladder cancer.

By the time she'd finished her second bourbon-on-the-rocks, she was weeping again. Unable to swallow down each rolling sob, she gave up and buried her face in her hands. Kas came over to her, sank to his knees before her and held her, lifting her up to her feet as he stood, tightening his embrace.

Then, he was kissing her, and she was kissing him back. Each kiss grew briefer and less passionate until he drew back and dropped his arms. He stepped back and sat down again.

"Do you forgive me? Kas, can you forgive me for being

such an idiot tonight?"

In a frosty voice, he muttered, "We all make mistakes."

"But I should've held onto him."

Despite her buzzed state, a glimmer of Kas's mind came through. *Yes, you should've. Too young. Too young for marriage, too young for children. What was I thinking?*

Her heart broke in two. Would he ever forgive her? Probably not.

She started towards the door. Swiping her face a couple of times with her hands, Athena then dug into her jacket pocket and withdrew the house key that Lorena had given her.

"I better go back to the main house. Go to bed."

Kas did not approach. His face had crumpled with pity, empathy but suddenly closed off to any love that normally would've flowed from him to her. Both his look and mind were shuttered.

"Yes, go to bed."

Guilt swamped her as she visualized the horrors that had awaited the child if the abductor had succeeded.

"Alex needs you. He may have bad dreams tonight."

Kas nodded slowly and looked away. "Yes."

Athena said her goodnight, took another look at the little, sleeping child on Kas's big bed, and left.

The question was not only if Kas would ever forgive her, she realized. Would she ever forgive herself?

She trudged along the lit, pavered walkway to the mansion, let herself in with the exterior key that led directly into the kitchen. The small light over the stove enabled her to make her way to the back stairway, where a hallway sconce took over. Inside her assigned guest room, she disrobed, shook off her sneakers, and fell back onto the coverlet over her queen size bed.

Consciously, unable to help herself, she opened the Flow channel to Kas's mind. What was he thinking? Feeling?

Would he ever again respect her or love her like he used to?

A red brick wall came through. He was purposely blocking her out. He was in effect telling her, Bugger off!

Acquiescing, she closed the channel to his mind.

Oh god! Would she lose him over this? This terrible night?

With effort, she gathered her wits about her. She didn't trust the occasional telepathic visits she had with her mother. The emotion-laden, white noise might obliterate the factual information that Athena needed.

She punched in numbers on her mobile phone and heard it ring on the other end. A half-minute passed before her mother's voice could be heard, sounding as clear as if she were in the adjacent bedroom. Even though Athena could hear the intense worry in her mother's voice, she didn't hesitate with pleasantries.

"Mum, how's Father?"

"Oh, Athena, there's nothing to report. We're en route to Saint Paul's Hospital in London." What followed was an Italian expression of exasperation. "The surgeon said the time needed to repair all four arteries might be eight hours or more. He's there already in preparation."

"Alright, Mum, I shall pray."

"How are you, *figlia*? And Kas and the little boy, Alex's son? I know you had a close call over there."

Of course, her mother had *seen* the abduction attempt at the fair in Grass Valley. Not surprised, for this telepathy had occurred before, Athena filled in with her mother what had happened afterward.

"Kas is having a Sheriff's deputy look into this, try and identify the man, where he lives, whether he has a police record. Kas is determined to find this man."

"Believe in yourself, Athena. You will help the police find this man. He's evil and must be stopped."

"I shall try, Mum." Athena choked to a silent sob,

reminded of Kas's disappointment in her. Would he ever forgive her or trust her again?

"Athena, don't be afraid. Use the gifts you were given. The bloodline never balks at the chance to right a wrong. Do you hear me?"

"Yes." Athena squeezed out the sound although her heart was pounding inside her chest. "Yes, Mum, I shall do what I have to do."

Yes, right a wrong. Whatever the cost.

CHAPTER TWENTY

Athena and her assistant manager, Dale Dargent, handled the new Chen painting carefully as they hung it on the two wire cables dangling from the ceiling. This technique of hanging artwork on cables instead of walls lent an openness to the gallery floor, creating a flow of air and light which enhanced the artwork and made it more accessible amid the others displayed in a like manner. Gone were the traditional, claustrophobic walls of old-fashioned galleries. Those walls enclosed and hid rather than exposed the artwork.

"Oh, lovely. Ian's doing so well with his cityscapes of San Francisco. I think this one'll sell quickly. We need to make giclees of this one, price them at least one to two thousand each."

Dale agreed. "I'll send it to the printer as soon as some orders come in. What do you want the one-of-a-kind priced at?"

It was the Tuesday following Thanksgiving, and they were catching up after the busy weekend that Athena had missed. Since the gallery was closed on Monday, she and her assistant manager were both dressed casually in jeans and working tops, hers was a sage green, knit tunic, his was a dark blue, button-down shirt. She'd already reviewed the account books with him, had expressed her surprise at the big sales figure from the Thanksgiving weekend. Evidently, the residents of Stargazer Tower and neighboring towers had done some early Christmas shopping in the gallery, its reputation having gained prestige in the past few months. She hoped the total sales figure would please Kas.

Apparently, Kas was still displeased with her.

Her boyfriend had removed himself from her company as soon as they had returned to the city and she hadn't seen him yet that morning. Nor had he called or texted her. Understanding why he was doing this but nevertheless feeling the pain of it, she didn't pursue his company, either.

Apparently, in his view, her one careless, distracted moment was defining her life. Deep inside, she felt Kas's judgment of her was unfair. Didn't ten-second lapses of attention happen to most parents all over the globe? Such lapses could end in tragedy, she conceded, and such was the awesome burden and responsibility of parenthood.

She certainly wasn't ready to take on parenthood or even step-parenthood. Was she even ready to take on marriage? Bloody hell, no.

Although still swamped with guilt and self-reproach, Athena knew she had to redeem herself in some way. Catching the evil, creepy kidnapper would be one way of earning his forgiveness.

At the very least, she could try.

But how could she unmask the creepy child trafficker if she was stuck in the city? And what about the poor, little girl who was forced to do his bidding, be the lure that pulled children away from their caretakers? Didn't she deserve to be rescued, too?

"Athena? The asking price for this one-of-a-kind Chen?"

Dale was tall, built like a basketball player, which he was at one time, he'd told her. Now he hovered over her, looking down at her with a worried look. She flashed to the present task at hand and turned her gaze upward to the painting, assessing this work of art. This was a realistic view of the bay waters with Coit Tower off to the right. Like an apparition above the fog, the Bay Bridge was visible in the distance behind a gray curtain of mist, only the top of the gates visible.

She compared this painting to Chen's treatment of Hyde Street with Alcatraz Island in the distance.

"It'll sell as well as his Hyde Street painting. People loved the downward, all-encompassing view from the top of the hill. He's doing the same thing here, giving an expansive landscape that takes in the city landmarks and the iconic bridge. You can see the influence of so many Realism masters."

"The one-of-a-kind for Hyde Street sold for twenty-five," Dale reminded her, meaning the five-figure number. "Don't you think this one's capturing the light better as it glimmers off the fog?"

"Yes, good eye, Dale," Athena murmured. "What do you think? Thirty-five? Forty?" She knew that Chen spent six months on the painting, slaving over it with twelve-hour days. "Let's try forty-thousand for the one-of-a-kind and two-thousand each for the giclees."

Dale nodded vigorously. "Yes, yes, I agree! Let's go for it. This is his best cityscape so far."

There was a firm knock at the exterior street door. The shade was down and obscured the identity of the man, no, two men outside. She went over, drew open the shade and recognized Inspector Villalobos. Another man was standing next to him, a younger, mocha-skinned black man. Another cop?

Athena sighed. Now what? Another homeless victim?

She unlocked the deadbolt, opened the door and beckoned the men in.

"Good morning but we haven't yet opened."

Both men stepped inside before Inspector Villalobos introduced Sergeant Len Wycott to her. She smiled politely and introduced Dale Dargent, who looked perplexed. Athena hadn't revealed her clairvoyance to anyone else in the city, including her assistant manager.

The lieutenant took the lead and asked to speak with her in private. She glanced at her watch, it was ten o'clock, maybe time for a coffee or tea break. She mentioned the idea to Dale, who took the hint.

"I'll go over to the coffee shop on the corner for, how long, Athena?"

She shot the lieutenant a questioning look. His reply was curt, to the point.

"Fifteen minutes max."

After Dale left, she invited them to take the two stools at the sales counter while she sat on the other side in full view.

"Where's the other detective, Inspector Villalobos?" she asked pleasantly. She'd envisioned a third shadow as they stood on the other side of the counter, had drawn her own conclusions.

Villalobos reacted with surprise. "How do you know there's another detective on my team, Miss Butler?"

She explained briefly what she'd seen.

Villalobos gave her a rueful grin. "Sergeant Vecchio's with forensics this morning." He sighed deeply. "If you know that, then I suppose you already know about the fifteenth homeless victim? Thanksgiving evening, around midnight? Lafayette Park, between Clay and Sacramento Streets. We were called away from our homes to the crime scene."

The African American detective shook his head with disgust. "Yep, I had just taken my first bite of turkey. This time, a young man, a Desert Storm vet, knifed to death, his throat cut. We think the perp came up from behind. Blended in with the other homeless, as before, attacked when everyone was asleep. Again, no witnesses."

Athena lowered her gaze to her hands, folded together on the counter's lower desk surface. Silent for a moment, her vision blurred before she saw something she hadn't seen the last time she opened her channel to this case.

Shocked, she said nothing.

The lieutenant pulled something out of a paper bag that Sergeant Wycott was holding. Inside a glassine evidence bag, the size of a quart size freezer bag, there was a plain, black baseball cap, folded upon itself. Villalobos slipped on latex gloves and with a thumb and forefinger, extricated the cap from the bag. He unfolded the dome part of the cap.

"Will you try your psychometry on this cap, Miss Butler? We're so desperate, we came to you this time."

Wycott held up a pair of blue latex gloves and waited for her affirmative.

What choice did she have? She already knew too much. Her involvement in this case was turning dangerous, she knew. With misgivings, she nodded and took the gloves.

It took a moment to fit them on while she considered how much to reveal. Quietly, she handled the baseball cap as the two detectives watched. The cap was dirty but otherwise gave no outward appearance of being worn by a killer. She turned it over and looked at its underside. Suddenly, in her mind's eye she saw something.

When she lifted her eyes again to take in Lieutenant Villalobos's troubled countenance, she felt the moisture of unshed tears. She wondered why she hadn't seen it the first time the homicide detective had consulted her.

No explanation.

"We're stymied, Miss Butler," Villalobos said, his voice hard-bitten with frustration. "Two months and we have no leads, no hard evidence. We've followed what few leads we've had. Nothing. We're still waiting on the ME, sorry, the Medical Examiner, hoping beyond hope for a fingerprint, a trace of DNA, a witness, any piece of evidence to show up. Now we have this cap. We think it might've been worn by the perp, the killer. We interviewed the others at the encampment at Lafayette Park, but the vic . . . this young vet was suffering from a major case of PTSD, had taken to booze, drugs. This kid was off by himself, drinking, doing drugs. Coke, meth, you name it. Had it bad. The city-paid food truck came around, fed most of them. Then everyone fell asleep in their tents and sleeping bags, their cardboard boxes. No one saw anything, heard anything." The inspector snorted loudly. "The DA's office doesn't regard drugged out or mentally ill homeless reliable witnesses, anyway."

Sergeant Wycott interjected at this point. "The DA doesn't regard psychics as reliable witnesses, either, Lieutenant."

Wycott apparently was no believer in clairvoyance, Athena surmised. Villalobos fired off a fulminating glance in the sergeant's direction.

"True, but any hint or clue that might lead us to other physical evidence would be helpful."

Her sympathies evoked, she could only shake her head in sorrow, hoping that what she saw would help them pull the dragnet in about the killers. Physical evidence was what they needed.

"Tell the Medical Examiner to look closely at the victim's hair. This killer was careless. He approached from behind, grabbed the victim's head and as he sliced his throat, one of his hairs broke off and fell onto the poor man's head. Despite the cap he wore, or maybe because of it. The killer and the victim both had dark blond hair so the ME might not have noticed."

Villalobos looked stunned. "A hair the same color? On the vic's head?"

Sergeant Wycott gave a slow, astonished nod. "Correct, sir. Dark blond hair on the vic."

"One more thing, Inspector Villalobos." She took a deep breath. Would they believe her next revelation?

"Miss Butler, did you see the perp's face? Can you give us a sketch?"

"No, I'm sorry. I didn't see his face. I'm usually inside the killer, inside his head. This one is just as enraged as the others."

"What do you mean, others?" Villalobos asked. Both men were hunched over the high counter now, their bodies tense with expectation.

"This last killing, the man's neck was slashed. I see the knife in the killer's left hand, so he must be left-handed. He slashed from right to left." She demonstrated with her left hand upon her own neck.

Silent, both detectives, looking dumbfounded, were noncommittal.

"There's something else," she said.

Villalobos and Wycott exchanged glances, their foreheads furrowed with disbelief.

"There are three of them. Three killers. Not one."

CHAPTER TWENTY-ONE

"Three killers? Are you sure?" Villalobos looked at her as though she'd lost her sanity.

Athena took a deep breath. *Right, well here goes.*

"There are three killers. They know each other or at least how to contact each other. Each one uses his preferred weapon, one the hypodermic needle, as you said, Inspector. Another one a gun with a sound suppressor, and the third a knife. A slightly curved knife, like a hunting knife. Maybe that's what they have in common. They're hunters at heart. Out for revenge. Or maybe just from pure hatred. I think each one has a different motive."

The vision of a cop's badge flashed before her, the one she'd seen before. She held back on that piece of information, hearing Kas's warning in her head about seeing the badge.

Hold back information that might endanger you, Athena. You don't know what the badge really means.

The two detectives were silent, awestruck, but simultaneously skeptical. Their clouded expressions showed it. Athena had no choice but to go on. It was too late to back pedal now.

"They choose their victims at random because they see themselves as avengers, a sort of vigilante team. Rid the city of the losers, the crazies, that sort of thing. But also personal. All three. And they communicate via code messages."

"Personal?" asked Sergeant Wycott. "Y'mean, the killers might've been attacked by a homeless person?"

She nodded. "I don't know. I'm sorry."

"On the internet?" Villalobos asked, his curiosity clearly

piqued. "You mentioned code messages, via the internet? Like an encrypted chat room?"

She shook her head, deep in thought.

"No, I don't think so. Maybe in a more old-school way, like the way World War II spies communicated with each other. What do you call those? When the two spies go to a prearranged place and leave notes for each other? Or other things?"

"Dead drops?" Wycott chimed in.

"Yes, I think that's it. They go to a place, a bar." She stopped herself and closed her eyes, forced the Flow that had turned foggy to clear and let her see. "Yes, I see it. It's a bar inside a hotel and there are posters of movie characters on the walls, framed posters. Superhero comic book and movie characters."

"I know that place!" Wycott's loud exclamation surprised her and Villalobos. "I've been there. Pete's Place in the Park Hotel. Financial district."

"It's a hangout for law enforcement," added the lieutenant, frowning, "security guards, firefighters, EMT techs, other First Responders." He looked steadily at Athena. "Are you certain, Miss Butler? Have you ever been there?"

"No, never. We, my boyfriend and I, we don't go to bars. Just restaurants with bars." Her thoughts flew to Kas, the pain of his silence enveloping her again. "Anyway, have the ME look for that strand of dark blond hair. It's not the victim's, it's the killer's hair. And the bullets you retrieved from the woman's body. They come from a stolen gun, the same pistol that was used on the other homeless victims that were shot."

She felt the Flow channel close, so she handed the baseball cap back to the detective and peeled off the latex gloves. She'd done all that she could. Maybe revealed more than she should have. Her stomach was revolting with nausea. She felt the rising urge to vomit.

Villalobos put the cap back into the glassine evidence bag

and wadded up the gloves into his sports jacket pocket.

His thick, dark eyebrows were spiked downward, his forehead lined with contemplation.

"You're certain about everything you've said, Miss Butler?"

Dale Dargent appeared at the front entrance, two cardboard cups of coffee in his hands.

"Yes, I am. As certain as I can be under the circumstances," she said, moving to let her assistant manager inside. "Are we finished here?" she added, holding the door open. She was hoping they'd take the hint, for she didn't want Dale to know about her clairvoyance.

Villalobos didn't look happy, but that she couldn't help. She'd given him and his partner all she could, all that she had accessed.

Or nearly all.

The rest of it, she'd keep to herself.

Out of self-preservation.

The two men thanked her for her time and left.

Dale handed her the coffee he'd bought for her. The smell of it made her reel with a wave of sickness.

"Two SFPD detectives? What did you do, Athena? You a prime suspect for murder?"

His joke made her grimace. For she knew who should be.

One they'd never believe.

"It's a long story, Dale."

His back to her, Dale hadn't seen her sudden pale, rueful countenance.

"Don't tell me, you're a spy on the run, wanted by Interpol."

He turned around and saw her face. His tone of voice immediately changed. "Or maybe I watch too many James Bond movies."

She held up a hand to her mouth and rushed to the small

bathroom in back. When she returned, feeling better and her face cooled with water, she sat on her stool behind the counter.

"Hope you haven't caught the flu," he said, commiserating, adroitly changing the subject.

"No, not the flu, something I ate for breakfast. No, they thought I might've witnessed something. An attack on the Embarcadero." She gave him a flaccid smile. "I didn't."

Lame. Who throws up after a visit from the cops? Unless they're guilty of something. Or knows who is.

CHAPTER TWENTY-TWO

The tall, broad-shouldered man opened the side door to Pete's Place, the one he usually took from a shortcut through the hotel lobby. That way he could slip in and out without attracting too much attention. A couple of men recognized him and nodded. Although he sometimes acknowledged those he knew, tonight he was in a dark mood. This time he hurried by the bistro tables. Men hunkered over their mugs of beer, their mixed drinks, hi-balls of whiskey on the rocks littering the tabletops, faces weary, angry, intent on venting, forgetting. A few women hunched over their drinks, joining their male counterparts in these moments of release from the traumas of their jobs, their intense, often dangerous workplaces.

Finding his usual place on the far-right side of the glossy walnut wood-covered bar, he grabbed a coaster with the featured lager beer logo on the top. There was a stack of coasters which the bartender kept along the wall. He casually looked at them before selecting one.

"Hit me the usual draft," he told the bartender, a man he didn't recognize, as soon as he got the man's attention. This was his second and last visit to Pete's Place. Yeah, Wycott had spilled the beans, all the incredible revelations from that crazy broad. Fucking nonsense. The dark blond hair hidden in the vic's thatch of head hair. Lucky guess.

Every hotel in the city had a bar, but the super-hero posters on the wall—that was another lucky guess. On the opposite wall, a garish caricature of Captain America glared at him, his

134

round shield glancing off bullets from left and right. The man averted his gaze and glanced down at the coaster, where the bartender had just placed a filled beer glass. The amber liquid glinted under a layer of white foam, mocking him, warning him.

Teetotaler Villalobos found her credible.

Now, thanks to that crazy chick, this watering hole was off-limits.

They'd have to find another dead-drop place for December. Or maybe kill the campaign for a while.

Fuck.

Big crowd tonight for a Tuesday night, he thought as he looked around the bar. A classic rock tune played in the background, barely audible above the dull roar of voices as a touchdown by the Forty-Niners lit up the TV screens hanging over the bar.

As he sipped his draft beer, he stewed silently. While in the ME's autopsy room, he'd eavesdropped as a call had come in from the lieutenant. Check the vic's head of hair. So the female MD did.

The doc had combed the scumbag's hair as if she were a world-class barber, carefully, almost studiously. A partial hair had separated from the rest, a curly strand unlike the straight, dark blond hair of the vic on the stainless-steel autopsy table. She examined it visually while handling it with tweezers.

He watched her look at the hair under a microscope and then place it in an evidence bag. She dated and signed the outside of the bag and put it into a cardboard box along with the bags holding the scumbag's filthy clothes.

What that meant, a DNA analysis test would follow. Also, the doc verified the victim's right-to-left deep cut on his neck, indicating the killer was left-handed or possibly ambidextrous. Definitely not right-handed.

A fucking, unforgiveable mess up. He could physically feel the dragnet tighten up. Time to change venue.

They'd been so careful not to leave trace evidence behind, the cops had gotten no clues for two months and then this chit of a girl launches a barrel of leads at them. Unless, of course, she knew the third killer, the knifer.

That must be it. She knew No. Three, and he'd spilled his guts. That lunatic. He'd not only jeopardized the mission, he'd endangered his partners.

Enraged, cursing under his breath as he hunched over the bar, he sent out a signal to anyone who might be tempted to approach him. Leave me the fuck alone. After a moment, he calmed down, put his analytical mind to work.

That damned girl. Did Number Three brag about their foolproof mission while trying to pick her up in some bar? Or was she the real fucking deal, a real psychic, as Villalobos believed? Whatever she was, whatever happened between Number Three and the damn broad, it was no big fucking deal. He could handle her. Number Two or him, they'd handle it. Take care of their two little problems when the time came.

Hey, besides, no DA would take seriously the word of a so-called psychic, or any one of Villalobos's crazy notions. Legally, whatever she said was inadmissible evidence, fruit from the forbidden tree.

Meanwhile, he had to warn No. Two.

He casually lifted his glass of beer and turned over the coaster. The number sign, *Three,* then a hyphen and a small number *One* could be seen, hastily inked by Number Three. Meaning, I did my deed. Now, it's your turn, Number One.

Their code to each other, saying "My job is done this week. Your turn, good luck, do it for the cause."

No way in hell, not now. Too risky. He would tamp down his rage, forego his deep satisfaction and pleasure at doing his part to rid the city of the filthy, crazy-ass scum that the fucking cowards at City Hall were too afraid to deal with.

For him, it was a personal vendetta as well as a cause.

Personal, because his druggie mother had taken off with her dealer boyfriend, leaving him at age ten and his six-year-old sister alone with their abusive father. Finally, after neighbors reported the constant abuse and neglect, the CPS took them away and placed them in separate foster homes. Now he rarely saw his sister, who had left the state and had grown up god-knew-where. All that misery and loss, thanks to his fucking, selfish, miserable bitch of a mother.

Getting his thoughts and heartbeat under control, he willed himself to calm down. The cause at hand was too important to fuck up.

He took a ballpoint pen out of his pocket and drew a short, horizontal line next to the number *One*. Over the line he drew a cartoonish, setting sun. The code to stop.

Time to call a halt to the operation.

Maybe temporary. Maybe not.

Wait and see what would happen with that damned strand of hair. He drew a, five-pointed star, ornate with multiple fleur-de-lis circling the center, the star of medieval crusader knights. Their crusade was still important but would have to be suspended.

Should he warn Number Three that he'd screwed up and left evidence behind? A strand of his curly, dark blond hair. If that fucking asshole was somehow identified, he and Number Two would have to clean up the mess. Their righteous crusade would be in jeopardy.

He turned the coaster over and finished his beer. Glancing at his watch, he decided it was time to leave Pete's Place. Number Two was due in about thirty minutes. They had to make extra sure they would never be seen in the same place at the same time.

No physical contact. That was the plan.

Number Two had just been warned that the mission was now on hold. The man drew a rough Number Three, circled it, then drew a diagonal line through the circle. He replaced the coaster, back into the stack along the wall, paid the bartender and left.

Number Three's fucked up. Abort.

CHAPTER TWENTY-THREE

Athena closed her digital account books, logging off. She was pleased with the day's progress, having taken the orders for four giclees or prints of Ian Chen's one-of-a-kind paintings. While Dale spent the day framing, she also sold an Avant-Garde brass sculpture made by a local sculptor and the giclee of one of her D.C. city scenes. It was time to celebrate.

The following day, Thursday, she'd take off and paint all day, a well-earned luxury. Dale would take over and when he could, he'd matt and frame the sold giclees.

Her mobile phone sat on top of her clutch purse. She hadn't received a call or text from Kas. No word from him since Sunday night. Three days of silence. He was freezing her out.

He despised her, he'd never forgive her, and they were over. The man who'd asked her to marry him just two months ago now hated her.

Could she blame him? No.

Tears of despair collected behind her eyes, her sinuses and nasal passages filled up. She snatched a tissue as the first stream wetted her cheeks. Every time she had tried to open her Flow channel into Kas's mind, he'd sensed it and had thrust up his brick-wall image.

Ohh, the man was infuriating. Why, oh why did she ever fall in love with that stubborn, unforgiving wanker?

She should leave and go to Milano, where she might find a nice Italian boy. No, an Englishman like her father. Steadfast, reserved, undemanding . . .

Grabbing her mobile, she punched several numbers and

waited. When her mother finally came on the line, her voice clear and calm, Athena began to relax.

"Pronto."

"Mum, how are you? How's Father?" He'd come through a successful surgery, repairing the four clogged arteries near his heart but was still recovering in the London hospital.

"Oh, *figlia mia,* how happy I am to hear your voice. Don't cry, *cara mia.*"

"I'm not." There was no point in trying to fool her mother. She saw and knew everything. "It's nothing, just a misunderstanding with Kas. Do tell me, how's Father doing today?"

They had been in touch with each other, telepathically and via phone calls, every day since Saturday night, when her mother's call had distracted her, resulting in little Alex's near horrible abduction.

Her father was recovering slowly but steadily after his arterial scrubbing procedure. If he continued to improve, he would leave the hospital by that weekend or the following week. Her mother suggested that she ring her father up in his hospital room later that night, which would be the following morning, London time, when he was at his best. It was a relief to hear her mother's voice and her encouraging, optimistic words.

They spoke for a few minutes, half in English, half in Italian, before ringing off.

"*Te amo, figlia mia.* Come home for Christmas, see your father. He would love to see you and Chris."

"Te amo, Mum. Ciao."

Athena had called her brother at Stanford at least twice during the past week, wanting to hear about his Thanksgiving visit to Southern California with one of his dorm mates. They'd played phone tag for days, leaving messages for each other a couple of times each day, each relaying updates on their father. She and Kas had planned to drive down to Palo

Alto to visit Chris on Sunday.

Now, she wasn't certain that Kas wanted to do anything with her or Chris ever again.

The Stargazer Tower Grill was only half filled with patrons. She carried her clutch purse, knowing that anything she bought at the bar or for dinner, she'd have to pay for, herself. She kept a credit card handy for that purpose, of course. Even though she disliked dining by herself, she had no choice for the present. She half hoped that she'd stumble across Kas in the Grill, forcing him to confront her and communicate to her his anger or whatever emotions he was experiencing. If Kas wanted to break up with her, he should have the courage to tell her to her face. Didn't he think she could handle it? Or did he consider her a weak ninny who'd fall apart? Or was he simply reluctant to lose his gallery manager?

She'd no sooner sat down and ordered a glass of red wine and the chef's specialty for the evening, French pot roast, than who should enter the Grill but the man, himself. And next to him, a pretty brunette in a short skirted, cream-colored suit with matching jacket, tightly fitted black sweater, black suede high heels and matching shoulder bag. She was gazing admiringly at Kas's face while he spoke to her.

With one bejeweled hand, the woman flipped one long brunette lock over her shoulder and scanned the Grill as if she were looking for someone. Kas followed her gaze until his dark blue eyes settled upon Athena.

Their gazes locked. His was unreadable but his mental brick wall that had blocked her clairvoyance for days instantly crumbled.

So that's where Kas's attention had been for several days. With the pretty brunette at his side. Of course, she should have known. Her handsome, rich and single boyfriend was a great catch for any woman looking for a mate. Or a fling.

When the waiter delivered her wine, Athena looked away and closed her Flow channel. She didn't want to know how he felt about the brunette. It would be too painful.

Angry at herself, she'd sworn years ago to never let Kas Skoros break her heart again. Now she was going for heart-break number two! Was she ever going to learn?

Bloody hell, he was walking towards her.

CHAPTER TWENTY-FOUR

W hen Athena looked up a moment later, Kas stood before her, his expression somber, expectant. The pretty brunette was strolling to a table at which sat an urbane man in a dark suit. As Athena watched, the brunette bent over and kissed the man's cheek, then sat down next to him.

Slowly, the truth dawned on her.

"May I join you, Thena?" Kas asked, his expression uncertain and somber.

She remained silent but shrugged and indicated the chair opposite hers at the high, bistro table.

Admittedly, Kas looked especially handsome in a dark gray suit, white button-down shirt and blue, gray and white paisley tie. His dark brown hair had been cut, styled in a casual way, parted on the side. She could smell his usual cologne, a mixed scent of musk and citrus. By contrast, she felt rather shabby in her black, work pantsuit and matching black tank, her Goddess Athena medallion and gold hoop earrings her only shiny adornments.

His eyes, however, held a haunted, pained look as if he'd lost sleep or felt ill. Dark smudges encircled his deep-set blue eyes. He was working hard, probably late into the night, trying to finish the remaining floors of condos. Despite her anger at him, she felt sympathy for him. The pressures on Kas were monumental. She knew he felt the weight of the world on him, a modern-day Atlas, bent in two by his family's high expectations.

"That was the wife of the design team that's doing the

luxury condos on the upper floors. Speck Design Associates. I've been in meetings with her and her husband all day. They wanted me to join them for dinner and I was going to—" Kas glanced over at them and smiled as the husband and wife team gave him a little wave. "I told them I had to speak with my gallery manager."

Archly, she spoke. "You should join them, Mr. Skoros, if that was your plan."

"No, I'd rather eat with you. And talk. We need to talk."

She stood her defensive ground. "If I hadn't been here, would you have reached out to me? Rung me up or texted me, at the very least?"

"Tomorrow morning. I was planning to come and see you. I know you like to take Thursdays off to paint."

"No need to see me. I'm doing my job and making you and the gallery a lot of money."

"Thena, c'mon. Sweetheart, that's not what I'm talking about."

"Then explain why you haven't spoken to me for the past three days. Not even to say hello."

His eyes dropped to his hands as he appeared to marshal together his thoughts.

"What happened in Grass Valley scared the shit out of me. I can't let anything happen to that child. I owe it to my brother, Alex. I owe it to my family, to everyone."

"I know, and you blame me for what happened."

He looked at her then. "I did, yes. Then today I was talking to Mrs. Speck, talking about her family, her kids, how old they were, all that. I asked her, how do you keep kids safe. She told me about her worst nightmare, every mother's worst nightmare, every father's worst nightmare. And she told me a story."

Athena sipped her wine, waited for the story to continue while a waiter took Kas's food and drink orders. Bourbon-

and-seven, a glass of iced water, a hamburger with a side or-der of salad for him. The French stew was on its way, alt-hough she doubted she could eat even half of it. She contin-ued to nurse her glass of cabernet.

"One day Mrs. Speck was shopping with her three-year-old son in a large department store. She was distracted for a moment, the boy disappeared. She called for him, looked all over the store for him, became frantic, got the security people at the store involved in looking for him. Had the PA system announce his name, became even more frantic, reduced to tears, imagining the very worst that could happen to him. Y'know, the whole, god awful nightmare."

Athena nodded, understanding the woman's ordeal. Transfixed, she encouraged Kas to continue after he took a long draw from his drink.

"Finally, one of the sales ladies looked in the center of one of those round carousels. There he was. He'd gone into the middle of the it to hide, as a prank, then fell asleep."

Kas spread his hands before him in a helpless gesture and shrugged his broad shoulders.

"A child's mind is so different from ours," he added.

Athena smiled. What a bloody understatement.

Kas swigged down more bourbon, like a parched man in a desert cantina, and, with a gesture of his hand to their waiter ordered a second one.

"I learned this type of thing is very common, more com-mon that you'd think. It's a miracle that most end well for the child and the parents. I learned that even devoted mothers can become distracted and lose track of their children."

"Yes," Athena concurred softly.

"And I learned that I blamed you unfairly. I left you with a squirrely child, a child you're not accustomed to. In a big crowd, a strange town." He ended by shaking his head mo-rosely.

At long last, proud Kas Skoros was apologizing to her. The satisfaction she thought she would feel was replaced by a surge of affection and respect for this man sitting across the table from her. And another wave of guilt and self-reproach at her own shortcomings.

Not ready for marriage or parenthood.

The self-awareness sat heavy upon her heart.

His dark blue eyes glittered and shimmered with emotion as they steadied on her face. His right hand rested on the table, halfway between them both.

"I love you, Athena Butler, and I don't want to lose you."

Her throat clogged up with gratitude. She cleared it and slipped her hand over his. Was this a temporary truce, or something more?

"Thank you for saying that." She cleared her throat again, determined to acknowledge her fault in the incident. "But it was still my fault for getting distracted. When my mother rang, all other thoughts fled. I was there in Milano with my mother and father. This hyper focus, I suppose you could call it, is both a blessing and a curse. Blessing, when I paint. When I access the Flow channel. A curse, when I'm with people and they need me."

Kas's gaze on her face remained steady. He nodded in understanding.

"Father is important to us, so Chris and I will be in London for Christmas," she said gently, having already booked the flight after her last phone conversation with her mother. She'd also spoken to Chris about the necessity of seeing their father. Their visit might be their last time to see their father alive. "My father, well, you know, don't you?"

The unspoken realization didn't need to be said.

"Yes, I know. My mother told me. I'm so sorry. I know how important this trip is for you. You and Chris." Kas clasped her hand in his across the table. "Can we get past this, Thena? My stupidity? Can we move on?"

She smiled at her handsome boyfriend looking so contrite. A part of her couldn't help but wonder what their makeup sex would be like later that night, but she quickly quashed that thought. Silly to let her mind drift in that direction but she had missed him. Longed for him at night.

"I think so. Only if you can truly forgive me."

The look on Kas's face expressed nothing but gratitude and relief. He raised her clasped hand and kissed the heel of her palm, held it against his lips. She felt the warm moisture of his mouth against her skin and could imagine the taste and smell of his manly skin under her hungry mouth.

"What can I say?" he murmured gently. "I love you."

"I love you, too," she added softly.

God help her. God help them both.

But there it was. Like it or lump it.

He looked so relieved that she instantly forgave his days of aloof silence. But she knew any future proposal of marriage was, as they said in the business world, off the table.

As her mother would say, *Va bene.*

He took a seat at the bar, hunched over the draft beer the bartender had just placed in front of him. The bartender gave him a look, like he'd sensed the tall man, wearing the tweed sport coat, hunched over on the bar stool was not your typical civilian coming in for a drink.

No big deal. He was just another customer aching for booze after a tiring day.

After a long swallow, he swiveled around in his seat, surveyed the bar area, then the restaurant section. Over there, at a bistro table, the girl sat. Looked like she was schmoozing with the guy, the Skoros guy, looking intense but cozy. He stared for a long moment, dared her to raise her eyes and look over at him. If she were a real psychic, she would've sensed him, known who he was, even looked a little afraid.

Wouldn't she?

Or was she just a fraud? Had Number Three just screwed up and been blabbing to a woman he was trying to impress? Betraying them and their cause to a pretty piece of ass, who for some crazy reason wanted to impress the cops? Maybe get her face on TV?

The notorious psychic who cracked the homeless homicide case in San Francisco and got famous?

Would Number Three have been so stupid? What would be their connection? She was way out of Number Three's league.

Anyway you looked at it, the girl might have to go.

As Athena smiled at Kas over her lifted wine glass, in her mind's eye appeared that same gold badge.

Her heart began to race, her stomach *dropped.*

He's here. He knows what I told the two detectives yesterday and he's worried.

Sipping, she glanced over at the bar. There he was, his back to her, one of the three killers. And there was nothing she could do or dare do without giving herself away.

She had to let him think she was a fraud or a con artist. For her sake and for Kas's.

As Kas finished his meal, his half-lidded gaze at her was unmistakably lusty.

"Let's go up," he suggested.

Her pensive expression morphing into a smile, she said, "Yes, let's."

Five minutes later, after signing the bill to his running account, Kas took her hand and they left the restaurant. Waiting for their elevator, Athena felt the killer's stare, like a hot poker burning a hole in her back.

Just like she'd had an obligation to protect little Alex, she now had an obligation to protect Kas. And she felt it with every cell of her body.

CHAPTER TWENTY-FIVE

The night was lovely with lovemaking, alternating between gentle and ardent to mad and wild with passion.

Now, at eight o'clock in the morning by her cell phone's buzzing, she was blissfully stirring awake. She pressed the button to turn off the alarm and then rolled up beside his naked, sleeping body. She loved the hard curve of his bare back, the softer contours of his buttocks, the wide expanse of his long arms. Her feet grazed his calves.

Smiling, she laid her chin upon the back of his shoulder and whispered into his ear.

"Time to wake up." Deliberately, she moved against him, rubbing and warming his backside and the rest of his delicious length. "That's what my father always told me in the morning. Time to wake up and welcome the day." Had always called her a sleepyhead, a challenge in the morning.

Father. Kind, sweet Father. He'd set the bar high for all men to follow.

Kas's eyes slowly opened. He scrubbed his face with one hand and turned his head in her direction.

"I'll try to rise to the challenge," he rasped, "especially the rising I have in mind."

"Oh? What kind would that be?" she teased. When he raised his arms and turned over, she knew. In a flash, he proved to her just how much he'd risen to the occasion.

Amid smiles and giggles and vigorous thrusts, they reached climax quickly. Their release left them satisfied but still in the mood to talk.

"So you've forgiven me for my stupidity?"

She playfully let her long locks fall across his face so he would have to blow them off his nose.

"Didn't I show my forgiveness last night? Just now?"

Kas wound the lock of hair around two fingers and tucked it behind her ear.

"I should apologize every night for some gaffe I make so you can forgive me every night."

"But we'd have to make each other suffer with hurt feelings. The makeup sex isn't worth it, is it, luv?"

His mockery of a salacious smile amused her. "Oh, I dunno, sweetheart."

"Take my word, it's not," she retorted firmly. "But maybe this is what people who love each other do every so often, make each other suffer."

"We're not superhuman, Thena," he pointed out with a small, crooked smile, "which brings to mind, making me suffer with your absence. How long will you and Chris be gone for your Christmas visit? Two weeks, a month?"

She sat up, turning to more practical matters. "A month at least."

As Kas frowned and stared into space, she dashed off to take a shower. Upon her return, she dressed in her slash-knee, faded jeans, t-shirt and work apron, she tried to answer him honestly. Kas remained in bed, looking utterly exhausted and depressed.

"What about you, Thena?" he finally asked.

"I don't know. Chris has a month off from school, a semester change. I'm just not certain about me. It depends on Father's condition. If he doesn't improve, I'll stay in London. With Mother."

Kas took the news poorly although he tried to cover up his disappointment. He got up and headed for the shower in a silent funk.

She went into the adjacent bathroom and raised her voice

so he could hear her.

"Kas, I think Dale Dargent could take over readily. He's a good salesman in addition to being a knowledgeable artist and framer. I hope you don't mind. There's still three weeks before Chris and I leave. I'll bring Dale up to date on the accounts, the upcoming, one-man shows. The collectors' list for special events and auctions. He'll do the gallery credit."

He called back, "That's not what I'm worried about."

Athena sighed.

An hour later, she decided to give up on her latest attempt at a cityscape of San Francisco. Inspiration had flagged moments after she began the depiction of skyscrapers with her palette knife. Instead, consuming her attention was a desire to capture the various portrayals of love. Newly inspired and flushed with the warmth of recalling their night of makeup lovemaking, she started a new canvas. Gessoed it, and then covered it completely in a dark gray color except for a penciled outline of two naked bodies, drawn from her memories of last night. After the acrylic paint dried completely, she began again, this time with light, flesh colors.

What followed was an abstract of skin tones and soft contours, a hazy montage of naked, intertwined limbs. The liquid warmth of physical desire, she tried to capture as she added darker tones for shading and depth. She had attempted the "sfumato" technique, the kind of painting technique made famous by Leonardo Da Vinci. There were no hard edges or outlines, just softy, fuzzy, subtle edges of flesh. The Mona Lisa was an example of this technique. Another technique she'd tried and found some success with, the thin layering of paint that tended to reflect ethereal light. The flesh tones in her painting shone with luminosity.

Stepping back six hours later, she was pleased with the

attempt. Her face warming at the thoughts of her and Kas's night together, she put down her brushes. The painting was good, stirring, sensual, an evocation of passion. Neither of their faces was revealed, just body curves in both warm and cool colors.

Seven hours had passed. So caught up in her task, she'd forgotten to eat. As she made herself a sandwich of turkey, baby spinach and mayonnaise on whole wheat bread, other thoughts intruded. Took a few bites of the sandwich, then put it down.

Lafayette Park, site of the latest homeless murder. Where was it? How close to Market was this park where the homeless slept in their bags and makeshift huts?

She ate another bite and gazed out of her living room window. A late afternoon sun was sinking behind the steel-and-glass canyons. Something compelled her to seek out this place. This Lafayette Park, and try to understand the reason for these murders.

Athena didn't want to care but she did. And now something urged her to go. Still, she fought the urge. It was too late now, and she had two phone calls to make.

Inspired by her latest creation, bubbling with excitement, she made the first call.

An hour later, she showered and changed into clean clothes, twill pants in a deep teal color and a V-neck sweater to match. Athena answered the door to Kas's signature knock. He smiled and held up a bag.

"Chinese tonight. Is that okay?"

"Oh yes, indeed. I'm starved. Didn't eat much all day."

"Why not?" Then his smile turned ironic as he glanced over at her work site. "Ah, of course. Got carried away." He set the bag down on her small kitchen counter. The two bottles of beer in his other hand, he promptly opened and handed her one, then clicked bottles. He downed half of his in a couple of gulps.

"Thirsty, much?" she teased.

"Celebrating. Finally agreed with the Specks on a price for designing those luxury condos. They came down over two-hundred thousand when I agreed to hire them for our next residential tower in Silicon Valley."

"Well, bully for you, you clever boy." She took a swig of the cold, bracing beer. "I have something to show you and a celebration of sorts of my own."

They kissed perfunctorily before she led him into her workspace in the living room. The thirty-six inch by forty-eight-inch canvas she'd completed an hour before sat on its large wooden easel, drying.

"What do you think?" she asked him.

Kas walked up to it, squinted and then backed up until he was almost ten feet away, then backed up another five feet until his elbows pressed against the floor-to-ceiling glass windows lining one wall of her living room. Outside, as dusk descended, lights came on and twinkled. Inside, Kas's dark blue eyes sparkled. She knew he was impressed.

"Is that us?"

"Yes. The way we were last night, it inspired me."

"Wow," he murmured in a gush of breath. "I want that in my bedroom. Over the bed."

She giggled. "I'll give you a giclee print. I'm keeping the original."

He continued to stare at the painting. "You mean . . ."

"Yes, I'm going to have Golden State Printers make artist proof prints on canvas of this one. The giclees I've told you about. Two hundred and fifty AP's. Artist Prints. Another two hundred and fifty Studio Prints. These will sell, one to two thousand a pop. I'll offer them in the Stargazer Gallery and I'm having the printers send some directly to a Milan art agent my mother knows and to the London gallery I've exhibited with. Also, the Visions Gallery in D.C. that Martin Larsen runs. I've put a rush on them, and the printer agreed. I also contacted the agent in London I had before and sent him a cellphone photo of it. He agreed to distribute this one and two more of the same subject matter in various provincial galleries all over the UK. I need to sell these giclee prints because I've paid the printers a deposit up front."

Kas turned to her finally, his brow creased. "You mean . . ."

Athena approached him and rested her head on his shoulder.

"Yes, if I sell them all . . . well, it will mean a steady income over the next two to three years. And a broader recognition of my name and work, perhaps. Of course, I'll have to embellish each print with my own hand, sign each one after each print is finished. A run of five hundred is no small matter."

"But you feel this painting is worth it?" He glanced down at her before settling his gaze upon the finished work of art. "I mean, I'm no judge of art but this is good, really good. And I'm not saying this just because those are my buttocks on display." He paused and shot her a dubious smile. "That's my ass, isn't it?"

She laughed. "And mine. So you do like it then? You think it'll sell?"

"Ha, like hot cakes!" He wrapped his arms around her and hugged her tightly. "How much for a print, did you say?"

"I don't know," she said, "depends on what the agent thinks is the market value. More, indeed, than the cost of making each print. I'm hoping, a minimum thousand each. Anyway, I shall take it to the printer tomorrow. They have a facility in Mission Bay. I'll go by taxi. SUV taxi, considering the size."

Another squeeze by Kas. "I'm very proud of you, Thena."

She smiled. That's all she needed to hear.

CHAPTER TWENTY-SIX

Two days later, after concluding her business with Golden State Printers, Athena found her thoughts drifting back to the homeless murder case. Questions crowded her mind and so, finally giving in to that urge to piece the puzzle together, she left the gallery in Dale Dargent's capable hands at five p.m.

She paid the cab driver and looked around. A couple of blocks away, they'd passed the Cable Car Turnstile at Polk and California. Standing now at the corner of Gough and Sacramento Streets, as the cab pulled away, she surveyed the homeless encampment already filling up most of the park's grassy area. There were also tents under the oak and sycamore trees flanking the grass.

A cool breeze wafted across the hill, briny from the bay waters but mixed with exhaust from passing cars. Reflexively, she tugged tightly on the tie belt of her coat. As she crossed the street to the park side, another smell arose. A stench from unwashed bodies and clothing, from human feces and urine. In response, she covered her nose and mouth with her hand. She looked down at her shoes, her right sneaker narrowly missing a mound of human poop. Reflexively, her fingers pinched her nostrils shut and she screwed up her face. Reminding herself to be careful where she stepped, she looked about and saw mounds on the grass, at the bottom of one tree. The preferred toilet of these *sidewalk sleepers*, as one radio host called them. Even on the concrete walkways there were dark mounds of human excrement.

So now that she was here at Lafayette Park, what was she hoping to find in this revolting place? Besides the disgusting human detritus littering the small park. Makeshift tents of dirty cloth and cardboard gave the appearance of an urban camp in some kind of post-apocalyptic dystopia. It disturbed her on so many levels, mentally, emotionally, physically.

How can people live like this?

Villalobos and his team had combed over the crime scene, as evidenced by the yellow crime scene tape that still encircled the tree area where the man was killed. The latest victim, number fifteen. Two small sycamores stood at the southeast corner, where the victim had been sleeping. Caught in a strong headhold, he could do nothing as the blade sliced across his neck. He bled out in minutes, unable to call for help. A sad end to a veteran who had survived the Middle East conflict.

She still wondered why she was there.

What did she hope to learn?

Why did she even care? No one she knew was homeless.

Did she even give a tuppence for these people?

Maybe that was the problem. The people with the power to help were so removed emotionally, they didn't seem to care.

Or was she naïve? Was the problem more complex than she could comprehend?

Lieutenant Inspector Villalobos was sitting at his computer, examining the fifteenth murder book, the police investigation report on the fifteenth victim. The other fourteen books were stacked on his desk, having been read and re-read that day. Looking for any clue, other than the three differences in methodology, repeated every three victims, there was nothing to indicate three perps.

There was no evidence, pure and simple, except the girl's

off-hand, unverified, inadmissible testimony.

A knock at his open door made him look up. Wycott and Vecchio entered his office after he waved a hand. They'd been assigned to pore over the police databases to try to find a link to the perp with the dark blond hair. The ME's tech had analyzed the stray strand of hair and compared the DNA to the vic's hair. The result: two different men.

As usual, they reported their findings and conclusions one by one, the eldest of the two always leading the youngest on the team. Vecchio slumped on a chair facing his desk.

"I just don't see it, Lieutenant. Nothing on the national or state databases showed up. Even the prison databases. Lots of dark blond-haired murderers who gave up their slobber, but they're all incarcerated."

Wycott, the Cal grad, continued to stand. "We now surmise he's got military training, at least the killer of vic numbers three, six, nine, twelve and fifteen did. A military vet with a big axe to grind. All killed with the same kind of precise neck slash, deep and exact. Right through both carotids. A super strong military vet who probably works out. I checked the Air Force and Navy databases for dishonorable discharges, or brig inmates to see if DNA swabs were taken. They were but no matches. I'll check Army and Army Reserve tomorrow. Maybe some gyms in the city."

Villalobos nodded. "Good idea, might lead somewhere." He looked at Vecchio, who was frowning and scratching his dark, trimmed beard. "Something bugging you, Frank?"

"I just don't see any evidence that there are three doers. Just that psychic's word, which of course is meaningless in a court of law. We can't assume she's right about anything. Three perps in cahoots with each other? Doesn't make sense."

Wycott appeared to concur. "Frank's right. Could be, our killer is this guy with dark blond hair. A lone killer. No one else. Or it could be randomly transferred trace from another homeless character. There's absolutely no evidence of three perps, just one twisted, enraged mind who's clever enough to leave a clean crime scene. Changes his weapons to throw us off, or likes variety, likes the game. Who knows? Obviously has a personal grudge against the poor, drug addicts, mentally ill. Maybe blames them for society's ills. Maybe has a personal history, got beaten up by a bunch one time, so he's out for revenge. A one-man vendetta. That's our theory, anyway. I can check past battery cases if you want me to, loo."

Villalobos shook his head. "Naw, too much of a long shot. Too broad, too many battery cases in this city. What do you have, Frank?"

Vecchio replied, "All we got from that one eye-witness at Dolores Park, it's a man, taller than medium height, maybe five-ten to six-two. That's probably sixty to seventy percent of the city's male population. And the witness was in a drug-induced stupor at the time, although he sobered up after we pumped him with three cups of strong black coffee and five donuts. A criminal defense attorney would eat him alive on the witness stand."

For a long moment of silence, Villalobos stared at the stack of fifteen report folders and shook his head. He hated to fail but he'd run out of ideas. That girl in the art gallery, that Athena Butler, was their only hope. But depending on a so-called psychic was really scraping the bottom of the barrel.

"Well, Len, spend another hour on the databases. Frank, go back to Lafayette Park. Ask around the residents there. Maybe someone saw something but didn't tell the uniforms on the first round of interviews. Probably a waste of time, but we got nothing else. Seems like we're always running just to catch up."

When both men left his office, the detective looked again at the stack of murder books. Downright demoralizing. Then he recalled what the girl had told him and Wycott the last time they'd spoken to her at the art gallery.

The superhero movie posters on the wall. A bar with affordable drinks, where off-duty local cops, firefighters and EMT techs hung out. Pete's Place.

A hangout for the perp? A lot of vets turn to law enforcement after they leave the military. Or the place could be a dead-drop site for the three perps? If there were multiple killers. A way to communicate incognito. What a far-fetched idea, that was, but that's what the girl said. He almost laughed. Instead, his open mouth turned into a grimace.

He swore aloud.

Well, why the hell not turn over every god-damned rock? He might just find a viper under one. Desperation was a bedfellow of the ridiculous, was it not?

Every god-damned rock. But he sure as hell wasn't going to let Wycott and Vecchio know about it. He'd never hear the end of it.

An hour later, he was sitting at the bar at Pete's Place. He'd known the bartender, an affable, taller than average Filipino American, for years. His name was Henry, but he went by Hank. Skinny as ever, with glossy black hair and an easy smile, Hank recognized him immediately. Villalobos had been a regular at a bar where Hank worked at years ago, before he'd quit the booze and gone sober. His wife had threatened to leave him if he didn't.

So he'd heard about Hank buying Pete's Place but had avoided the bar until now. Not a boozer himself, he preferred to go home to his wife and three kids at the end of a long day. But tonight he'd make an exception.

There weren't too many customers at this time of day. Most shifts hadn't ended yet, so Hank seemed to have time on his hands.

When Hank greeted him, Villalobos ordered a beer and

encouraged him to stay and chat.

"How's business, Hank? Heard from Len Wycott you bought the place from Pete Stanislowski. Good move."

"The business, not the hotel," Hank laughed. "Kept the name, though, 'cause people know it that way. How's Homicide treating you, Inspector Villalobos?"

Hank spoke his name with a Spanish accent, like the psychic girl did. Not Anglicized, like most people, indicating that Hank spoke Spanish. As the bartender spoke, he began to wash and dry glasses. The squirrelly man didn't like to waste time.

"Nah, not good lately," said the detective. "Sometimes I think the killers in this city are getting smarter. Learning how to evade detection with all these CSI and cop shows on TV."

Hank snorted. They joked and chatted awhile, and then Villalobos dove in.

"You haven't noticed anything strange around here, have you? I mean, guys coming in, doing dead drops?"

"Dead drops? What's that?"

In response, the lieutenant lowered his voice and leaned slightly over the bar.

"It's when two people who don't want to be seen together but want to communicate with each other. They leave something like a note that can't be seen by the average person. It's like a pre-assigned place and time to leave something for the other person he wants to communicate with."

Hank stopped what he was doing, looked down at his feet, thought in earnest. His gaze rose and settled on the far end of the bar, where a stack of coasters sat.

"Those coasters over there? That's the only thing I can think of. Come over here, Inspector."

Villalobos followed him to the other end of the long, curved, twenty-foot mahogany bar. Hank indicated the stack of cardboard, matt-printed coasters, packed neatly against the wall. He handed the stack of twenty or so round coasters to the police inspector.

"Well, I'm not on duty all the time. Take two nights off a week, so I'm not so sure. But I was here once when these two guys come in, always sit at the far end here, always pick up the whole stack of these coasters. The first one comes in about an hour before the second one. But both guys shuffle through the coasters. Kinda strange, huh? They don't take the top one like most people do. They shuffle through them like a deck of cards, y'know? I thought it strange but harmless. They don't steal them, just handle them. I mean, what do I care how they touch the coasters? I get them free with the kegs and cases of bottles."

The inspector's heart was pounding by now, so he took a seat on the far-right stool and picked up the tall stack of cardboard drink coasters. With effort, he kept his facial expression friendly, amused, anything but how his insides were lighting up with excitement.

"What do these two guys do then?"

"They order drinks, look through the coasters, choose one. Funny, huh? Like they can't drink until they've found their favorite coaster to set the beer on. Like someone with OCD?"

"Do you recognize them, know their names?"

Hank shook his head, looking confused.

"No, one guy I've never seen before. Other one's an EMT. I know because another guy asked him one day about the ambulance that broke down on the way to the hospital. You heard about that, right? It was on the TV news."

"What does he look like, this EMT?"

"Hmm, white guy, maybe thirties, fair-skinned, fair-haired."

Villalobos schooled himself to stay calm. "Blond hair? On the tall side?"

"Yeah, dark blond hair. The other one."

"Other one? So you're certain there were two men who came in and did the same thing, sort through the coasters?"

"Yeah, Lieutenant. Two. At least that one time when I was here. I've never seen them in here before. Just the past month, come to think of it. I've been here for over a year." When the inspector remained silent, the bartender went on, "Go ahead, look at the coasters. I haven't changed them these past two to three months. No need to. No one has stolen any. I've got a big stack on both ends and a big stack in the middle of the bar. No one else sorts through the stacks, just those two guys. That one time I was here."

Hank drifted away when another customer approached the bar. Without hesitation, Villalobos picked up the stack, looked at each one, front and back. Most of them bore the same graphics. One side sported a beer logo, the brands of the various beers and ales that the bar carried. The back side was usually blank. On the back of one coaster near the bottom of the stack, however, there were small drawings and tinier numbers. One set of Roman numerals one, two and three. Small drawings in blue-inked pen, arrows pointing right, meaning what? *Next* or *Continue*? Villalobos was guessing at the meanings of these doodles, but they intrigued him.

He let his mind throw out conjectures. Why the hell not? This was a guessing game, anyway. A line with a half-circle and rays, possibly a tiny sunset? A fancy six-pointed star. The Nazis' symbol of Jewishness? He frowned. None of the murder victims had been linked to Judaism. This star was different. There were flourishes inside the star, like fleur-de-lis loops. He'd seen that symbol before. Where? Code of some kind, a pre-agreed upon code?

Strange looking and distinctive. Where had he seen that kind of ornate six-pointed star before?

Steganography? He never told anyone at work, but his hobby was WW II, reading every book he could get his hands on about the Second World War. Spycraft. The codes, ciphers, the German Enigma code that the Brits at Bletchley Park finally cracked, thanks to Alan Turing's number-rotating machine. The writing of code in plain sight was called stegnography. Didn't the ancient Greeks invent this system of ciphers? If his memory served him, that would be correct.

But history in general was his hobby. Crusader history. The Templar Knights, in particular. They'd helped finance the Crusades, fought to vanquish the Muslims from the Byzantine holy land. Constantinople, the site of the Christian church in what was then called Byzantium.

One of their symbols was a six-pointed star with ornate loops within each point. The symbol of the Crusader Knights!

Well, son-uva-bitch.

He took his cell phone camera and photographed the stack of coasters with the coded coaster standing up alongside, its back exposed to the camera. Then, a close up shot of the coded coaster. After that, a longer view of the bar with Hank behind it. He put the coaster into a glassine evidence bag, one of several he always carried in his sports jacket pocket.

Fingerprints? Wouldn't that be lucky?

He had to smile. The habits of a homicide investigator. Always looking for the hidden, esoteric clue to solving the mystery.

Hank returned.

The detective asked him, "Mind if I take this coaster? Might be evidence in this serial killer case?"

"The homeless case? I read about it all the time in the papers, hear it on TV late at night. Sure, take it. Take them all."

"Just this one. Hank, the other guy, the second one, you've seen handle these coasters, always sitting on this side of the bar?"

"Yeah?"

"Do you recall what he looked like?" Villalobos asked.

Hank looked down again at his feet, then up at the detective. He scrunched up his face as if remembering was taxing.

"Well, I don't want to get anyone in trouble based on a maybe faulty memory." He shook his head. "The only thing I recall, it was a really busy night, three of us behind the bar that night. Things hopping, a big game on the screens, noisy as hell, drinks flying off the bar. So my memory might be faulty."

"Anything," the inspector prodded, "might be useful."

Hank hesitated before speaking, then launched in. "Handsome guy, y'know, but not movie-star handsome. Dark complexion, maybe biracial like me. But not too dark. On the tall side, a little husky, maybe in his forties. Dark hair, worn short but not a buzz cut, y'know. I was working here two nights in a row. I remember 'cause I was getting tired by the second busy night. First night, the dark-haired guy, then the blond guy comes in later that same night. That was this month, just a week ago. Friday and Saturday night. Right after Thanksgiving."

Around the time frame of the last homeless murder, the detective noted.

"How tall was he, the dark-haired guy? Did people seem to know this guy?"

"Hmm, taller than me. Maybe shorter than the blond-haired guy. Did people know him? I couldn't say. He wore a dark brown, leather jacket, like a bomber style. Had short dark whiskers. Like I said, it was a really busy night."

"Whiskers? No beard?" the detective asked. "Any distinguishing facial features? Tattoos?"

Hank frowned in thought. "I didn't see any tats. His face-no, can't remember his face except for the whiskers. He ordered two beers on draft, fiddled around with the coasters, and then left. That's all I can tell ya, Inspector. Sorry I can't remember more."

"What about the blond guy?"

"Taller than six feet, skinny, not bad looking. Wore his hair kinda long but no ponytail. I might've seen him before, but I couldn't be sure. Sorry."

The detective thanked him and sat back. For the first time on this case, Villalobos was beginning to feel like maybe the luck of the perps had run out. Number three was most likely the perp of the most recent murder. But who was the dark-haired guy Hank just described? Hell, he'd just described over ninety percent of the men in San Francisco in that age range."

He scowled into his glass of beer.

So, were there two killers or three, like the girl said. And were the two coaster-shuffling guys Number One and Two? Were there actually just two killers working closely together as a team? Giving each other these dead drops on beer coasters? Did they change their watering hole every week, every month? Hank had noticed the guys sorting through the coasters only this past month. The man was a good observer of his patrons, including those with off-beat behavior.

Maybe Villalobos was jumping to false conclusions, but he'd already concluded that one of the two or three killers might be the blond haired EMT tech. He'd have the lab narrow their search.

So why three MOs? To throw off the cops?

On his way out of Pete's Place, he gave Hank his professional card and asked him to phone him the next time any man visited the bar and went through the coasters like a deck of cards.

Despite the worried look on Hank's face, the man nodded and said, "Sure thing, Inspector."

Villalobos sat in his car for a while, assessing the situation. "Sonuvabitch," he muttered over and over.

The girl said there were three killers. Hank might have witnessed the covert communication of two of them. Or two men were the only killers.

The girl was wrong. There were only two killers. So why were there Roman numerals one, two and three on the coaster? Were they just denoting the victims that week?

"Sonuvabitch," he said in both wonder and dismay. His head began to pound with a headache.

CHAPTER TWENTY-SEVEN

A s Athena stood uncertainly to the side of the yellow
crime scene tape, two cops in dark blue uniforms saun-
tered her way. She'd noticed them strolling around the park,
passing each tent and hovel, pausing to look at each of the
men and women crouched or lying there. One woman in rags
was bent over a small hibachi, grilling something. Athena
could smell the smoke from where she stood. Two shapeless
men hovered nearby, waiting for their dinner, perhaps.

The clanging of cable cars could be heard, too, and the
noise of nearby traffic. She wondered how people could camp
outside in such conditions, especially under the blankets of
chilly fog every night. Looking around, she noted the billow-
ing fog rolling over the coastal hills and city rooftops. Already, the Golden Gate Bridge in the distance was nearly
obliterated by a dense cloud of fog. Just the top orange spires
could be seen.

Down here in the lowland park, the cool mists were just
beginning to swirl above their heads. She spotted a standing,
fiberglass port-a-potty in the far corner of the park, once a
bright blue but now looking as dismal and dirty as the park's
inhabitants.

*So why all the human rubbish? Why defecate on the grass and
sidewalk if there's a toilet nearby? Do these people not care? Don't
these people care that they're spreading diseases that way?*

The two uniformed cops approached her, looking intent on
a face-to-face confrontation. Athena took a deep breath, had
to remind herself that cops in America were armed, not like

the bobbies on patrol in London. She hadn't prepared in advance a reason for being there.

The uniformed female cop grinned in a friendly manner and greeted her.

"Can we see some I.D., miss?"

"Of course," she said. Out of her jeans jacket pocket, she took out her British passport, which she always carried with her, and showed it to the woman. While the two cops studied it, Athena noted the gold badges pinned to their left, upper shirt pockets. Despite the cool weather, neither cop was wearing a jacket, not even a windbreaker. Probably accustomed to the cold breezes and chilly fog, Athena thought.

"What're you doing here, miss?" the female cop asked, handing her passport back. "You obviously don't live here. Are you a tourist?"

An idea struck her. Why not tell the bloody, sodding truth?

"I do live here. I'm an artist, a painter of cityscapes . . . and other things. I work for the Stargazer Art Gallery, just looking for new ideas. New ways to portray the city."

The male cop gave a cynical laugh. They were both in their late twenties, growing up fast under these less than pleasant circumstances, Athena surmised.

"So you want to paint the city's homeless? What a crock! Think I've heard it all now."

The female cop was smiling, too, an ironic smile.

"You find this homeless encampment beautiful? Uplifting? Inspiring?"

Athena knew she'd be the butt of their jokes back at the station house but didn't care.

"No, just interesting. In a tragic way."

The people at the park began to come alive and move. A food truck had just pulled up to the curb on the far side, Laguna Street according to the street sign, and had honked its arrival.

The male cop smirked. "Like roaches at a Tenderloin flea-bag. They can't get enough of the free stuff. Free food, free plot of land to dump their crap. Then they go panhandle or do blow jobs to get money for drugs, booze." He glanced at his partner. "We need to move over there before a fight breaks out."

The female cop, a Private Smythe, according to the name plate on her shirt pocket, elbowed her partner in the side. As if reminding him that Athena was a foreigner and they should watch what they said.

"It's Free Taco Night at Lafayette Park. Better move on, miss. We'll get a pack of 'em arriving for the food truck."

"Who pays for the food?"

Private Smythe shrugged. "The city, who else."

Private Burgess, the male cop, piped in, "The city taxpayers, y'mean. The city's Board of Supervisors don't pay and don't care. They think of themselves as Saint Francis, catering to the poor. Why do you think this city's named San Francisco?"

"You're British," said Smythe, "so do the Brits do this for their homeless? Send food trucks around to feed them? Send mobile health clinics and mobile vets to check on them and their pets? Give them port-a-potties which they seldom use?"

Athena had to think. It had been awhile since she'd been back home in London, but she occasionally read a copy of The Daily Mail online.

"No, there are some shelters the homeless go to, but it's been over two years since I've been home. You seem to have a lot more homeless in the streets. Better weather, I reckon."

"At least seventeen thousand, at last year's count. In Los Angeles, it's worse," the male cop added. "A fifteen percent increase over last year."

"Why Los Angeles?" Athena had to ask.

Smythe and Burgess both smiled.

"Warmer down there, much warmer," Smythe was quick to answer.

Athena recalled Kas telling her that, even on a warm summer day in San Francisco, the temperature dropped to the forties and fifties when the fog rolled in.

She nodded to the common sense of it all.

The female cop glanced at her partner as they played out their obvious game of one-up-manship of parsing out facts to the foreigner. Obviously, they were soured by their assignment, as if Athena could blame them.

"See, I told you. We don't have enough shelters for all the homeless who come here. The shelters we have are just for the families and mothers with children. Guess the city'll have to build more. But y'know, many of them'll refuse to go in a shelter."

"Why?" asked Athena.

"They won't want to abide by the rules," said Private Burgess, "rules like no drugs, no booze."

Smythe surveyed the ragged crowd around the food truck. "Shame. Locals and tourists used to come to this park. Not anymore. Now it's a smelly dump."

Burgess added, "The state of California has a twenty-one billion-dollar surplus this year but can't afford shelters for the homeless. Or mental hospitals to warehouse 'em. Go figure." Burgess's eyes shifted away to something or someone behind her and his posture immediately straightened. "Better move on, miss. It's getting dark."

Athena nodded and turned around to leave. Her heart did a flop and she felt like she was going to faint. As if in warning, her Flow channel had yawed open and wide, smacking her mind with a flood of visions and information, leaving her breathless and gasping.

Facing her in the waning light of dusk, his hands sweeping aside his sports jacket to reveal his city-issued pistol on one side and the gold badge attached to his belt on the other, was one of the killers.

She knew it even before her eyes met his.

CHAPTER TWENTY-EIGHT

She took in the man's face, his general countenance, the dark, trimmed beard threaded with gray, the hard, steely dark eyes, his bushy eyebrows.

Not a shadow of guilt crossed his face. And yet, he'd killed at least five homeless people in cold blood. The other two killers had murdered a total of ten between them. Picked at random, except for the first two. Not in self-defense but cold-blooded, premeditated murder.

"Sergeant, she was just leaving," Smythe hurriedly said.

"Did she touch anything around the crime scene?" the homicide inspector asked. His voice was deep, throaty and gruff.

"No, we came up to her as soon as we saw her," assured the female cop.

"Good, now continue your duties. I'll stay with the crime scene. Wanta take a second look."

The two uniformed cops nodded to Athena before moving briskly over to the food truck. Already, people were pushing each other to cut in line.

Involuntarily, Athena kept her eyes averted but continued to read his thoughts. His venomous rage made her freeze in her shoes. This blighter was a cold-blooded murderer. She told herself, she mustn't give herself away. This man was dangerous.

She schooled her expression, kept her features calm and as relaxed as she could. But the knowledge of this man's potential power fueled a physical reaction that she had little control over. Sweat pooled under her arms, her pulse raced and pounded in her ears. Even her hands shook a trifle. Quickly, she dug them into her jacket pockets.

Bollocks!

Don't panic. Brits don't panic. Bloody hell! Stay calm and carry on.

The ol' British motto of Queen and Country.

So useless at this point. Or was it?

Though this police sergeant knew who she was, he thought there was a strong chance she was a fraud. It was that doubt in his mind that she had to foster. In order to downplay her own threat to him.

"Do you work with Inspector Villalobos, sir? He told me about Lafayette Park," she forced herself to say.

His dark eyes leveled back on her, a smirk curled one side of his mouth. He stood with his legs slightly apart, as if he were ready to pull out his pistol and aim it at her. She knew she had to stay calm and play the ditzy blonde, for he was going to test her.

"So, Miss Butler, is it? I've heard about you, but this is our first time meeting, isn't it? Yes, I'm on the lieutenant's team. And you've insinuated yourself into an ongoing homicide investigation involving a serial killer. Any reason why you should want to explore the latest crime scene?"

"No, sir. I-I was just curious, sir. I don't want to disappoint Inspector Villalobos when he asks for my help. He told me about the latest murder here at Lafayette Park."

"But he didn't ask you to come here, did he? I could arrest you for tampering with a crime scene's evidence, for obstructing justice, any number of offenses."

"I'm sorry, sir. I was just curious, I didn't touch anything."

"Is this what you do for attention, Miss Butler? You pretend to be a psychic to help the cops? You want to get on TV as a famous, crime solving psychic? Rake in the bucks?"

Athena looked down at her feet and said nothing, pasting

174

on her face a look of embarrassment.

"How did you come up with your . . . your information? The stuff you fed Villalobos and Wycott the other day about the bar? The strand of hair?"

"I don't know. Sometimes I just guess."

He harrumphed loudly. "Just lucky guesses, huh? You sure have those two guys buffaloed. Not me. I saw right through you from the start. Handling that dirty jacket, pretending to see visions. A crock of bullshit!"

She pretended to eat humble pie, playing the misguided, attention-seeking twit, looking down at her shoes in embarrassment.

"I don't mean any harm by it. My cousin does readings and she says it's a good rack—I mean, business. Inspector . . ."

"Vecchio. Surprised you don't already know my name." The big man let go of his jacket on the side of his holstered pistol, having decided she was harmless enough. "Time you found yourself another hobby, Miss Butler. Or another city. I know where you live, where you work. You might find this city a happier place to apply your artistic skills if you stick to art. I wouldn't meddle in police business if I were you. Are you hearing me, Miss Butler?"

"Yes, sir, loudly and clearly."

"Visas can be cancelled, you know. Yes, I know you're British and on a work visa. I know some folks at ICE." Immigration and Customs Enforcement. "Feds who'd be happy to pull your visa if I informed them you were practicing fraud in our—well, not so fair any longer—city. They could be persuaded to deport you. Wouldn't it be a shame if the rich Mr. Skoros lost his gallery manager and girlfriend? A good looking, rich guy like him wouldn't take any time at all to find a replacement for you, would he?"

She said nothing, continued to eat crow. His intimidating presence cowed her, true enough, but his prolonged stance in front of her was feeding her more information from the Flow. For the first time, she could see his motives, his suppressed rage, but also his cunning intelligence.

Still, her hands couldn't stop trembling. Perspiration ran down her back, even down the back of her knees. Her head buzzed with anxiety.

"I'm sorry, sir. May I go now?"

A long moment passed while he assessed her sincerity.

"Go on, then. Don't let me see you at the Hall of Justice again or I'll expose you for the fraud you are."

"Yes, sir."

Athena moved to the corner of the park and waited to flag down a cab. Meanwhile, she could feel the killer's eyes bore into her back. Was she convincing enough, she wondered?

A yellow cab screeched to a stop, unaccustomed to patrons signaling for a ride from the homeless encampment. She hurried inside and didn't look back.

Bugger!

She now knew nearly everything about the fifteen homeless murders, how and why they began. But what could she do with the information?

Nothing!

Vecchio would know as soon as she told Villalobos everything the Flow channel had just flooded her with. Besides, what could he do with her inadmissible testimony — the word of a psychic — against the word of a trusted, experienced homicide detective?

She saw no way around it. It was something she had to give up on, admit defeat, let the killers off with impunity.

The lack of justice rubbed her raw, like salt in a new wound. The pain left her breathless. She sat back in the cab, fighting a welling up of hot tears.

CHAPTER TWENTY-NINE

Entering the marbled lobby of the Stargazer Tower, she paused at the day manager's desk. Mr. Andrews was more than a desk clerk. He ran security for the entire building and made certain anyone who entered without a secured elevator pass would not stay very long. The night manager was just as competent and security minded. Curiosity seekers abounded but outstayed their welcome after five minutes of loitering in the lobby. They either went directly to the Stargazer Grill or they were invited to leave.

Mr. Andrews was wearing his usual uniform, a black suit, white shirt and black tie. A tiny transceiver included an ear bud and shoulder attachment, a voice away from the uniformed, private security team that patrolled the tower day and night. His black hair was cut in the military butch style, and even his bearing bore the hallmarks of an ex-military man. Athena knew he'd risen to the rank of sergeant in the Marine Corps.

"You're back, Miss Butler. Mr. Skoros has been looking for you."

"I see. Thank you, Mr. Andrews. Mr. Dargent took over in the gallery, so I could go exploring."

The lobby sparkled with a giant Christmas tree, all twinkling multi-colored lights and oversized glittery bulbs. Underneath the tree sat huge gift boxes wrapped in gold and silver foil and sporting satiny red and green ribbons and bows. Green garlands with giant silver and gold bows made festoons of the mezzanine staircase railing on the right. The door to the downstairs Grill sparkled with a cheerful Christmas wreath and evergreen garlands with twinkling lights.

Athena had often admired the decorations, but they made her feel homesick. Not tonight, though. Tonight, she was too preoccupied by other concerns.

"Mr. Skoros said to tell you if I saw you, he's back in his condo. He asked me to remind you about dinner reservations at Provence?"

She'd completely forgotten about her evening dinner date with Kas. *Blimey!*

"Indeed, thanks. Uh, Mr. Andrews, if any police detectives come to see me, please don't allow them up in the elevator. Call me and I'll come down, all right? I'd rather see them in a public place, down here in the lobby."

The security chief shot her a strange look but readily assented.

"Of course, Miss Butler. That's our standard policy, anyway."

"Of course, I'd forgotten. Please call me Athena."

"Okay, Athena. I'll make sure the night manager knows to do this, also."

"Thank you."

Riding up in the elevator to her twenty-first-floor condo, thanks to Kas's generosity, she wrestled with the question that now nagged her.

Should she tell Kas about her encounter at Lafayette Park with the killer, Inspector Frank Vecchio?

No. Probably not a good idea.

Standing at her southeast facing living room window that overlooked one of the city entrances to the Bay Bridge, Athena continued to wrestle with her dilemma. The myriad of lights below and at eye level appeared as blurs, for her mind lingered elsewhere, churning with pros and cons.

Should she worry Kas with the veiled threat from Inspector Vecchio, one of the three coldblooded murderers of the city's homeless denizens? Was she horrified by the Flow's revelation? Could the Flow's message be wrong?

Not really, she decided. Vecchio wouldn't be the first cop in American history to be a criminal. In London, her father had known a friendly neighborhood bobbie on the street beat in Kensington, who also ran a secret brothel on the side. In Lyon, France, one of the Chief Inspectors of the Gendarmerie had run a money laundering scheme for years before he was finally caught. No, Vecchio wouldn't be the first corrupt cop in history. But a coldblooded murderer? She sighed audibly. People had a way of rationalizing their immoral acts, justifying all manner of cruelty and evil doings, didn't they?

No, Kas, a former Sheriff's deputy, wouldn't be shocked. That was not the issue. Her reluctance rested on her fear that he would be upset with her. He'd warned her not to get involved with this murder case, not that he knew one of the detectives attached to the case would turn out to be one of the criminal perpetrators.

His concerns, she knew, after their dangerous confrontation with that twisted killer in D.C., were closer to home. Kas simply didn't want anyone he cared about to be hurt. Again, the threat was real, not just for her but for Kas and Chris. Even the Skoros family would be affected if anything were to happen to another son of theirs. Losing one out of four was terrible enough. The family had been good to her, kinder and more accepting than she probably deserved.

A soft rap on her front door aroused her from her troubled thoughts.

When she opened the door, Kas rushed in, smiling, hugging and lifting her into a twirl. A whiff of nice masculine cologne assailed her, along with a sniff of scented soap. He'd come not from his office downstairs but from a shower in his condo.

He wore a lightweight, cobalt-blue sweater, the same color as his eyes, and clean, snug jeans. The outfit emphasized his broad shoulders and the way he filled out his jeans, front and back. And the effect of his sudden presence overwhelmed Athena with a rush of love and desire. Her very toes tingled with arousal.

She kissed him heartily, deeply, pushing out of her mind the ugly confrontation at Lafayette Park. When they pulled slightly away, Kas's eyes looked glassy, unfocused.

"Well, I was hungry . . . I had French in mind down at Provence. But maybe we can catch a quick dinner and come back up here. Or have them send up a couple of steaks from the Grill."

He was being gallant for she could smell herself, the result of sweating like a pig during her faceoff with Vecchio. Her clothes still carried the acrid smells of the homeless encampment.

"I really need a shower, myself. You smell yummy, luv. I love your cologne."

"Only the best for you, sweetie."

"But Kas, dressing up and going for French, I truly don't need."

With effort, he smiled and held up a forefinger, pulled out his cell phone. Then he ordered two dinners of medium rare filet mignon, baked potatoes with all the trimmings, and side Caesar salads. To be delivered to Athena's condo in . . .

He looked over at her. "Forty minutes?" She nodded, grinning widely.

"I wouldn't mind company in my shower," she said.

Kas's dark eyebrows poked upwards. He shot her a crooked smile. "No, make it sixty minutes. Oh, and a bottle of your best pinot noir."

After he rang off, they seized each other.

A little over an hour later, they were digging into their dinners. Both wearing terrycloth robes, one pair of which hung in each of their condos' bathrooms. They clicked their bulbous wine glasses.

"Cheers," she said. Their vigorous lovemaking had left her very relaxed, contented, feeling almost boneless.

"Saluti!" Kas was pointedly practicing Italian in his plan to impress her mother for Christmas. He could stay away from the Stargazer only a week, and while discounting her reminders of the flight cost of such a short visit, he was typically throwing himself into the idea. Athena had already made reservations for the three of them on the same flight. Two weeks away. She could hardly wait!

"You speak a little Spanish so Italian will come easy for you. We should make a tour of Italy some day." Athena spoke French, Italian, Spanish and a smattering of German, and encouraged him in his endeavor to learn another language. In actuality, she was happy that he wanted to visit her parents and she suspected that he was gearing up to ask her father for her hand in marriage.

In any event, having Kas with them for Christmas would be welcomed by everyone concerned. Her mother liked him, and Athena wanted her father to meet him, too.

Only while placing her utensils on her plate did the day's unnerving events return to Athena's mind. She shoved them away, not wanting to ruin the evening. However, Kas had his own agenda. He put his plate aside on her small kitchen table and pulled out his cell phone.

"Thena, I heard back from Deputy Tom Buckley in Grass Valley. He ran that partial license plate from that dark blue pickup and came up with four possibilities, all residents of Placer County. He also got addresses. Then he went around and took photos of the front of these places. One's a house, here, I'll show you. He sent pictures. By the way, he hasn't made an official complaint on my behalf. I told him to hold off on that, don't want to get the Skoros name involved. This guy could have a gang, could be desperate, who knows? I don't want to endanger my folks."

Athena nodded. She understood completely how delicate of an investigation Kas had undertaken.

He held up his cell phone. It took her a moment to focus on the topic at hand, the skinny, bearded man who tried to kidnap little Alex that Saturday night at the Cornish Christmas Fair in Grass Valley.

"This is a house in a golf course resort. Doubt the owner would be the asshole we're looking for . . ." He shrugged. "But you never know. These two are rural driveways leading to somewhat older, rundown, wooden cabins." He swiped his forefinger to another photo. "This is a shorter driveway leading to a small horse farm, about ten acres. The deputy used a telephoto lens to take a closeup of the house, like he did with the other two. House is clapboard, kept up, paint looks fairly recent, chain link fence all around the property."

She sipped the last of her wine while squinting at the photos on his cell phone.

"Are you getting anything?" he asked.

She shook her head. Kas frowned, his dark eyebrows furrowing deeply, his forehead creased.

"Are you sure, Thena? Look again."

Her Flow channel had closed while she allowed her senses to bathe in Kas's warm pool of love. The wine, as alcohol tended to do, had kept her channel closed as well.

"All right." For added measure, she drank a little from her glass of water. Then took his phone and swiped aside each transmitted photo. One, she dwelled on as a buzzing began in her ears. "This small horse farm with the nice house?"

She paused to take a large swallow from her water glass to

dilute the effects of the wine even more, then closed her eyes.

The Flow channel opened a little, like a visual representation of a space module's four-part, airlock door slowly parting.

She waited patiently, her eyes still closed, knowing full well these supernatural insights could not be hurried. Finally, while Kas waited silently, the Flow increased.

"This nice house on the small horse farm," she began, "that man with the beard doesn't live here. He sometimes works for the man who lives there. That night, the rotter with the beard borrowed the man's old truck. The kidnapper tries to be careful when he's on the hunt, so he uses a borrowed or stolen car. The little girl, she was taken, too. Maybe a while ago?" She saw something unspeakable and blinked open her eyes. Helplessly, she gasped aloud. "Oh, god, poor child."

Athena looked up to see Kas's eyes riveted on her face, recognizing the disgust and rage she saw there. She hesitated to say more but the little girl's fearful eyes came back to haunt her. That little girl, that child, she wants to be saved, too. Moreover, Athena had to admit that she wanted that bearded man stopped and punished as badly as Kas.

"The bloody bugger lives nearby." She let out a loud groan. "Oh god, he's been kidnapping children for years, trafficking them for money. That little girl . . ."

Kas gave her a long, hard look. "Are you sure, Thena? These are really serious allegations. We can't afford to go after the wrong guy."

She sighed. The average person had a hard time accepting her visions, even someone close to her who knew her and loved her.

"Yes, I'm sure. Ring up the man who owns that old pickup truck. Talk to him first."

Kas slapped his hand down hard on the table, making the plates and glasses jump.

"I'm not going to call him. I'm going this weekend, stop that bastard any way I can."

"I want to go with you," she said.

"No, you're not. I don't want you near that asshole. No doubt his place is like a fortress, loaded with guns, maybe booby-trapped." Kas's blue eyes drilled into hers. "Besides, you have that showing on Saturday."

She widened her eyes at the reminder. How could she forget such an important event? Dale Dargent, her part-time gallery manager, had a one-man show of his Lucite sculptures and she'd promised to host it for him. She just couldn't let him down.

"Kas, please. Let's go on Sunday. Together. I want to help you find that horrible man."

Athena held her breath while Kas looked aside, a thousand-mile stare masking his thoughts. Her Flow channel had closed for the time being, evidence of her mental and physical exhaustion.

Finally, his angry blue eyes turned back and pinned hers. Simultaneously, he covered one of her hands with his.

"Okay, we may need your help. This won't be a walk in the park, getting the evidence for a search warrant. We'll need physical evidence. Right now, the person who owns that pickup is our only connection. He's a person of interest, that's all."

"And if we can't get it? The evidence, I mean. What happens then?"

His handsome face crumpled but, in a flash, hardened again.

"No such thing as can't. Just, how can I?"

She knew he wouldn't give up.

And neither would she.

One failure was enough!

CHAPTER THIRTY

The Skoros Loomis estate was quiet, all the vehicles belonging to Kas's parents parked away in the five-car garage. One Placer County Sheriff's white SUV was parked in the long, spacious driveway but the deputy, Tom Buckley, wasn't in it. Lorena Skoros, however, greeted them at the door and ushered Kas and Athena in. Looking comfortable in pale green woolen pants and matching top, she hugged them both, then held a finger to her lips as she smiled. Her smooth, short pageboy cut, kept dark brown, framed her lined but attractive face. Faint circles under her eyes belied her fatigue.

"Both males in the house are asleep, so let's not wake them up. It's my only chance on Sunday to read."

"Both males?" Kas asked, carrying in his and Athena's overnight suitcases.

"Your father and little Alex. I just put the boy down for a nap. I've had him since Friday night. Nikki will be back to pick him up later tonight."

Kas nodded. Of course. His parents took turns with Alex's mother, Nikki Skoros, driving down to Stockton to pick up the child every weekend and bring him to Loomis, or take him back to Stockton. Since taking over as COO of Skoros Enterprises, Kas joined them in Loomis whenever he could. Everyone in the family agreed that Kas would stand in for his deceased brother, Alex, as much as humanly possible.

Two years ago, he'd married Alex's pregnant fiancée in order to give the child the Skoros name, claim him as one of their own, and to help Nikki and the Theopoulis family prevent a scandal. As far as Kas was concerned, his obligation to Nikki, not little Alex, was over. An annulment, which satisfied the Orthodox beliefs of Philip Skoros and Abe Theopoulis, ensued a year later. Not ideal but the solution had prevented a scandal and had given the baby the Skoros name.

And with it, came obligations and access.

"Like I told you, Mom, we're here for just a few days. We're hoping to help the Sheriff identify that kidnapper."

"That horrible man . . ." Lorena Skoros already knew what had transpired that night and what they now were planning to do. "You must be careful. He does have an arsenal of guns, you know."

"Yes, Mom, I suspected as much. Where's Tom? Deputy Buckley? That's his squad car, isn't it?"

She nodded. "Just don't tell your father. His heart couldn't take it."

They followed her through the tiled entry way. Directly past the living room, dining room, and open kitchen and family room, through the double French doors leading to the back terrace, its floor set with gray pavers. Big black, ceramic pots of white and yellow day lilies and shaded rhododendrons lined the spacious terrace.

There, sat Deputy Tom Buckley, sipping an iced tea, waiting for them to show up. Temporarily off duty, he wore civies, faded blue jeans, a red and blue plaid flannel shirt, dark boots. And held in his hand a white, Western-style deputy's hat. His light brown hair spiked up in a butch cut, adding to his youthful appearance. Quickly, he stood and greeted Kas and Athena. Lorena turned to go back into the house.

"Mom, don't you want to sit in and," Kas began.

"Not necessary, son. Athena knows as much as I do. Trust her."

Athena smiled in gratitude while she, Kas and the deputy took their seats at the black-painted, wrought iron table. A tray on the table held a bucket of ice, a pitcher of tea and two tall glasses. A second tray held sandwiches, cut in triangles without the crust.

Kas grinned. "Thanks, Mom. You're always a step ahead of the rest of us."

Lorena smiled, disappearing inside with a soft click of the French door. Right away, Deputy Tom Buckley, apparently missing the implications of their brief mother-son exchange, got to the gist of things.

"Well, y'know, Kas, there's a wrinkle. Grass Valley, where the alleged kidnapping attempt took place, is Nevada County, not Placer County. I spoke to Sheriff Farnsworth there and he's willing to give us some leeway, but he wants one of his detectives to accompany us wherever we go. At all times. It's a county jurisdiction issue, of course, but that's not the only thing."

Kas impatiently drummed his fingers on the table, already realizing that, Athena noted. They'd discussed this issue on the drive up to the Sierra Nevada foothills.

"No problem. When I was a deputy with Placer County, we worked with the Sheriff's office in Nevada County all the time. We often shared Search and Rescue equipment, the helos especially. What else?"

Deputy Tom Buckley's boyish freckles stood out in the sunlight, making him appear the age of a high schooler. His full cheeks reddened a little with embarrassment before taking a large swallow of iced tea.

"The guy who owns the old pickup, the one with the small horse farm on Oso Road, he's Sheriff Farnsworth's son-in-law. So, he doesn't want any yahoos going in there with guns drawn, especially when we doubt he's behind this attempted kidnapping. The son-in-law doesn't wear a beard, either. And he wasn't at the Cornish Christmas Fair that night, either. According to his and his wife's testimony, he took his wife, the sheriff's daughter, down the hill to a movie in Auburn. One of those super-hero movies that just came out. I confirmed all of this. The sheriff has cooperated fully. His son-in-law and daughter, too."

Athena knew that Deputy Buckley was unaware of her and Lorena's gifts of clairvoyance, that her visions of the bearded man did not point to the son-in-law's guilt or involvement in the kidnapping attempt. She glanced over at Kas. His eyes met hers as he shook his head slightly. He wanted their secrets to remain just that, secret. Mainly for the sake of Kas's parents. He didn't want them involved in this manhunt in any way.

"That's okay, Tom. We just want to find out who used his truck that night, if that someone was the guy with the beard. And if the sheriff's son-in-law might know anything about the guy." Deputy Buckley heaved a big sigh of relief.

"Okay, good, just wanted you to know I've done some checking and made clear to Sheriff Farnsworth we weren't vigilantes riding in with blazing guns." He wiped his forehead with a plaid sleeve before continuing, "He said his truck was parked next to the old garage in back, where he always parks it. Before they left for the movies and it was there after they got back. Nothing had been tampered with, that he could tell."

Kas smiled at young Buckley but Athena could tell it was all show. He patted the deputy on the shoulder.

"Thanks for doing this, Tom. Much appreciated. Finish your tea and let's go talk to Sheriff Farnsworth's son-in-law. Can Farnsworth's detective meet us there? I know it's a Sunday."

"It's okay. It's all set up. In the spirit of our two offices working together, y'know. The new Placer County Sheriff, Holbrook, is cooperating, too. He assigned me to investigate with the Nevada County detective. His name is Jesus

Orlando. Did you know him?"

Kas's eyes lit up with recognition. "Sure, I know him. We were in Search and Rescue together for a while. Then Orlando went on to criminal investigations."

"That's why he said he trusts you to do what's right."

"Yeah, we called him Jay. He hated his name, said everyone expected him to be holier than thou. A funny guy. I'm happy to be working with him."

Deputy Buckley relaxed even more. "We vouched for you with Sheriff Farnsworth. We told him you were no hotheaded vigilante. He also knows who the Skoroses are. You're probably the richest family in the county."

Kas took on a shuttered look. "Well, I don't know about that. It's not relevant, anyway. We're just out to stop a child trafficker. I'll assure Sheriff Farnsworth's son-in-law that he's not involved in this attempted kidnapping." A pregnant pause followed. "But I bet he knows the bastard who is."

Shooting a significant look over at Athena, Kas's smile wavered a moment, but held for the young deputy's sake.

"Do you mind if my girlfriend comes along? For the ride?"

Deputy Tom's light blue eyes met Athena's, almost shyly. "No, don't mind at all. It's a nice ride from here, up Interstate Eighty and over Forty-nine."

Athena spoke for the first time. "Forty-nine? Named after the Gold Rush Forty-Niners?"

Deputy Tom chuckled. "Yep, you know our local history. We football fans like to think it's named after our favorite NFL team but hey, history counts, too. Yeah, the area is full of Gold Rush history."

"I've heard that the Cornish and Welsh miners settled in the area. We'll have to stop and pick up some Cornish pasties. For dinner tonight, Kas."

Deputy smiled and seemed to relax. Kas played along with her coy, innocent act, exchanging a long look with her.

"Sure, after we talk to the sheriff's son-in-law, we'll go for those pasties. You'll like the nice ride in the mountains."

Despite her returning smile, Athena already knew the day was going to be anything but a *nice ride.*

* * * **

Frank Vecchio waited in a bar on Bryant, down the street from the Hall of Justice. His mind circled around on the homeless homicide case, as the squad room at the Hall of Justice was calling it. He preferred to call it Destroying the Dregs of Society, but that moniker, he kept to himself. Although it was a Sunday and his day off, he'd been called in by the lieutenant. There'd been a break in the case.

He swore to himself, nursing his second beer since he was officially off-duty, waiting until three o'clock when Villalobos said to meet in the squad room.

The whole elimination campaign had started with an encrypted website that he'd happened across one night after accidentally bumping into his drug addicted whore-of-a-mother. He'd been running down a potential witness at an underpass encampment in the Sunset District. Emerging out of a cardboard shanty, her addled brain hadn't shown a glimmer of recognition for her only son, whom she'd abandoned when he was twelve. Their father having ditched them long before, the bitch had chosen her cokehead boyfriend over her own son and daughter, Katie, who was eight years old at the time. After being placed in two separate foster families, Frank had lost touch with his sweet, dark-eyed sister. A sister he'd adored, who'd grown up shy and withdrawn, frightened of everyone and everything. He never did learn the name of the family who'd adopted her.

Twelve years old and he'd lost everything.

That fateful night he'd recognized his whore-of-a-mother.

Despite her gaunt and disheveled appearance and the baggy, dirty clothes she wore, he recognized her. The jolt had sent him staggering almost to his knees.

Two weeks after his campaign to clean up the streets of San Francisco started, he'd had the pleasure of plunging the hypodermic needle filled with full potency fentanyl into the heart of the selfish bitch who'd once been his mother. The powerful anesthesia drug, he'd procured from his girlfriend at the time. A surgical nurse who'd had a problem with speed and needed a drug to knock her out at night.

Why injections of fentanyl? It seemed poetic justice. You crave the needle, you get the needle. Four bottles of the stuff had done the other jobs, had carried him over eight weeks. One, four, seven, ten, thirteen. That's all they were to him, just numbers. Five scumbags over eight weeks. Fifteen total, thanks to his like-minded comrades.

Number seven was the most satisfying.

Now he'd run out of fentanyl. He'd broken up with the nurse and, besides, it was too risky to approach her again. He'd told the girlfriend that the fentanyl was needed for his sleep apnea and she'd never questioned him. He knew she'd never rat on him, anyway, for she'd broken the law, herself. The three different *modus operandi* had never been leaked to the press, so the nurse and public were clueless to what had dispatched those homeless scumbags off to Neverland.

Was it time to call it quits? Or just time to switch methods? An untraceable pistol with a silencer from the Evidence Storeroom would do the job just as well but that was risky. Another method that was quick and quiet would do the trick, but he'd lost the incentive. The whole point of it had been to dispatch the whore without leaving a trace back to him. He'd thanked his lucky stars for taking the last name of the foster family who'd ended up adopting him.

Their targets, every one of those dirtbags, deserved what

they got, each one ruining not only his or her life but other lives as well. All of them too selfish to care. Meanwhile turning the city into a shitty toilet. And the risk had grown too high to continue.

A clamor of noise arose from his television set. A touchdown from the rival team across the Bay. Another interrupted day off with the roar of football and the haze of beer. His satisfaction with their crusade, venting his long-held rage and need for vengeance, justified what they had done. They'd done society a favor no one else had the guts to do.

Well, it was no longer satisfying. This soul-deep contentment that came with purpose and intention—a grand cause—had faded. And nothing had taken its place.

Not yet. One of his colleagues in the Homicide squad, almost as burned out as Vecchio, had passed on a tip. The guy's son worked for a high-tech company in the city, whose CEO and founder, Mr. Big-shot Billionaire, was looking for a personal security director who knew how to be . . . discreet. The pay was more than twice what he earned as a homicide inspector. Was now the time to bail? Start a new career path?

But still find a way to continue a campaign that the local politicians were too chicken shit to solve?

His cell phone buzzed. Len Wycott's deep voice rose with unconcealed excitement.

"Len, what's up? You there already?"

"Got here early, y'know, anxious to find out what's new. Just got the word from the lieutenant. That button the ME found in the folds of that last vic, the Gulf War vet, we got a fingerprint off it. It's not the vic's. Might be the perp's. If so, combined with the perp's dark blond hair and a new tip, we might have a prime suspect. At the very least, a person of interest."

Vecchio's heartbeat leaped into warp speed. He strained to keep his voice steady, even purposely slurring his words to show his nonchalance.

"Yeah? Did you run the prints through AFIS?" The national database of fingerprints held everyone's prints who worked for any local, state or federal government in addition to every person who'd been arrested, booked and held in police custody.

"Nothing yet, so the perp might be clean. Haven't checked the military or civilian government workers, law enforcement, firefighters, First Responders. Yet. That'll be next. Loo got a tip to look at EMT techs. Thinks one of the killers might be an ambulance tech. Anyway, we should have something by tomorrow, Tuesday at the latest."

"Great news," he gushed, his pulse pounding in his throat. *Fuck, fuck, fuck!*

"Lieutenant says he has something else, something tangible. He'll show us. Something with a code on it. He thinks it's a communication device between the two killers."

"Two killers? Not just one?"

"Loo thinks there are at least two. That psychic girl said three, but he thinks she might be off by one."

"Okay, see ya in ten." He rang off, then grabbed his burner phone.

Time to make a move.

Number Three had to go. Too bad but he'd gotten careless. If the cops jammed him up, he'd squeal like a stuck pig. Even though Number Three had never met him directly, or Number Two, or knew their real names, they might be identified through their dead-drop venues. That had always been a risk but a minor one. So Vecchio thought while he was setting up the whole dead-drop system.

He was Number One, had started the whole crusade. He'd been careful not to come in direct contact with either Two or Three.

Or was it possible that Number Three did what Vecchio had done, had returned to their designated dead-drop bar of the month on those assigned nights to see who would sit at the far-right end of the bar and shuffle through the coasters? Nothing was fail safe when coordinating crimes. Their other dead-drop venues had similar weaknesses.

That's how he had identified Numbers Two and Three, himself. How he'd exchanged burner phone numbers with Number Two over their encrypted website. Only Two had the burner phone number for Number Three. Names and personal items were never used with each other. A contingency fall back means of getting in touch in case of a screw up.

Tomorrow was the first day of December. Their new dead-drop venue was the bar at the Drake Hotel on Powell Street. Same day, same times. Mondays at seven pm for Number One, Number Two an hour later, eight pm. Number Three would come at nine pm. For two months, it had worked like a Swiss clock. The remainder of the week, each one would choose his own victim, his own night and time of execution, his own homeless hangout, his own vic. Three executions a week, randomly chosen by three unknown assailants.

No, better than a Swiss clock. Like a damned fine spy network. A network for curing society's ills, one miserable scumbag at a time.

In this instance, though, their agreed channels of communication would take too long. Villalobos could have the EMT tech in custody before Wednesday. Now Vecchio had to use the burner phone with Number Two. Time to off the screw up, Number Three. Too fucking bad.

Definitely, time to call it quits for now.

Vecchio punched the numbers on his burner cell phone. At least thirty seconds passed before a gruff male voice answered. Another second passed before Vecchio's Voice Changer app clicked on. One more second before he began to speak. Decisively and without hesitation.

"Number Three has identified us, sent me photos of us to

my cell phone, photos he took in the bar. Did you get them, too?"

A long pause. "No."

Vecchio texted Number Two a hazy but recognizable photo of Number Two sitting in the bar at Pete's, the stack of coasters in his hands. Two muttered a curse, which prompted Vecchio to continue.

"The asshole wants money to keep quiet. Also, I heard from my cop source that homicide cops will identify Number Three by Wednesday morning. He got careless and left behind physical evidence. A fingerprint and a strand of hair. He must be eliminated. I gotta go out of town on business for the next week. Can you do it?"

When Number Two consented to do the job, further instructions followed, then Vecchio cut the connection. Number Three, after showing up at their designated bar for December, would be followed home. Then eliminated.

If Number Two didn't follow through, as per their pledge, he too would be eliminated.

There would be no balking from Number Two.

Their campaign would end for now.

Vecchio pondered over the future of their crusade. *Who knows? Maybe we've inspired others to carry on our work.*

CHAPTER THIRTY-ONE

A n hour later, Deputy Tom followed the long, black-topped driveway past a fenced pasture where about a dozen cows grazed. On the other side of the driveway, a black bull grazed behind a tall, cyclone fence. It looked up, its dark eyes tracking their progress until the bull, its fears allayed by the non-threatening movements of these human trespassers, returned to its midday meal.

"Sheriff Farnsworth said Jeremy Thomas, the son-in-law, he's a civic engineer for Placer County. So I've run into him at City Hall a few times. He knows me and Detective Orlando and has agreed to answer our questions. By the way, these cows you see, he's trying to raise livestock on the side. Mostly for his wife and kids. The sheriff's daughter is an animal lover and grew up with 'em. Their two kids help out."

"How much land?" Kas asked as the SUV pulled up in front of a two-story house, its architectural style a combo of California farmhouse and country French manse.

"Twenty acres, according to the sheriff. They bought it five years ago, before all the land around here started to skyrocket in value. Looks like Detective Orlando's already here."

On the wide front porch stood two men and a woman. The Hispanic man, Detective Jesus *Jay* Orlando, appeared a little older than Kas, mid to late-thirties, and was dressed casually in jeans and long-sleeved shirt. So much for an off-duty Sunday. Nevertheless, he greeted Tom and Kas with a hearty smile. Introductions were made all around.

Neither Deputy Tom nor the detective were wearing their

issued pistols, so Athena assumed their guns were in their cars. The sheriff's daughter was an attractive, auburn-haired woman in her forties, dressed in a navy-blue, stretchy exercise outfit. She looked like she'd just gotten off her exercycle. Wearing faded jeans and a black t-shirt, the tall, husky man by her side appeared a little older. He was fair skinned, blue eyed and bald, having shaved all his hair, Athena knew, because he'd found himself at forty-eight with just a tonsure of light brown hair. Better bald than looking like a middle-aged monk was his conclusion.

Immediately after Kas introduced Athena as his girlfriend, the collective tension relaxed. Detective Orlando and Kas shared a few stories from their days together as Search and Rescue deputies. While the ice was broken by the casual chit-chat, Athena noted that the visitors were not invited inside.

Sheriff Farnsworth's daughter, Denise Thomas explained, "I'm sorry but we are scheduled to meet Jeremy's parents in the city" — meaning San Francisco — "by five o'clock and we still have to get ready and drive the two hours to pick them up at their hotel."

Her husband Jeremy added, "Yeah, so can we make this quick?"

"Sure, no problem," said Deputy Tom. "We know, Mr. and Mrs. Thomas —"

"Call us Jeremy and Denise, please," offered the wife. She turned the open front door and addressed the two teenagers standing just inside the doorway, obviously curious.

"Start getting dressed, Jake, Bobby. We leave in thirty minutes."

Athena realized that Tom Buckley was taking the lead in questioning the Thomases. Kas and Detective Orlando were hanging back purposely to give the young deputy some latitude and independence.

"That night of the Cornish Christmas festival in downtown

Grass Valley, you were at the movies." The Thomases both nodded but remained silent. "But we know that your pickup truck was used and the person driving it attempted to kidnap Mr. Skoros's two-year-old nephew, who was with his girl-friend—Miss Butler here—at the time. Mr. Skoros and Miss Butler chased after the man, a tall, skinny Caucasian man who wore a bushy beard, and had a girl about seven or eight with him. According to their testimony, the bearded man let go of the little boy and took off in your truck with that little girl. They were able to see the rear license plate. The bearded man was driving your truck. One of three vehicles you own."

Jeremy Thomas rubbed a hand over his stubbled chin. He looked like he'd put in a morning with the cows.

"Well, for the life of me, I don't know how he got my truck for the night of the Cornish festival. I've never given him the key to it, never given him permission to use it. He's our neighbor, lives down Oso Road about a mile, does work for me occasionally like muck out the barn—we have two horses. I've hired him for odd jobs around here, turn the soil with my tractor, make minor fence repairs, that kind of thing. His name's Scooter, or so he says. It's most likely a nickname." He turned to his wife, who was staring down at her tennis shoes.

Tom Buckley frowned and exchanged glances with Detective Orlando and Kas. It was obvious the whole story wasn't being told. When Athena opened the Flow channel to the woman's thoughts, a very different scenario had taken place.

She spoke up. "What do you know about this guy, Mrs. Thomas? This neighbor of yours?"

Detective Orlando, Deputy Buckley and Kas turned around to look at her. She wasn't supposed to say anything.

"Not much. He calls himself Scooter, like Jere said. Says he's from Oregon, or maybe Washington state. Not a great worker but my husband needs help from time to time. He said he couldn't get more than part-time work, temporary stuff."

Athena watched her slide her eyes over to her husband, then back to her shoes. The woman had been hiding something from her husband. A moment passed before she looked up, surveyed everyone standing before her on the porch.

"He's very poor and thin. I saw his daughter once, a cute little girl but dressed in rags and . . . unkempt. He said his wife died a year ago and things were rough. We felt sorry for him, so we hired him for little chores around here, things that my boys are too busy to do, what with sports and schoolwork."

"What did you loan him?" Athena persisted.

"Nothing." The woman folded her arms across her chest.

"Anything you're not telling us?" Tom persisted, drilling her with a cold stare.

She sighed loudly, over dramatically, Athena thought. The woman was gearing up to justify her deceptive behavior as she flung her arms in the air.

"Well, Jeremy's not going to like this."

"What?" her husband said, his brows furrowing. He turned to face her. "What's going on?"

Finally, the truth, Athena mused, glancing over at Kas and Deputy Tom, glad that the young deputy was so tenacious.

"I felt sorry for the man. He's so thin. Bad teeth, too. I know he doesn't have much money. His daughter always looks so depressed, so sad. He told me the day before the Cornish festival that his truck had broken down and he didn't have the money to fix it. So I told him where to find the spare key. Jeremy always keeps it in a magnetic doo-jiggy under the front, left wheel well. That's not our main truck. I have a car and Jere has a newer truck, so I didn't see the harm in letting him use it." She looked up at her tall husband, who was shaking his head and glaring down at her.

"So I guess he took it to the festival. Probably bought groceries, too. Gave his daughter a treat. I truly didn't see the harm in it. Are you certain that he tried to kidnap your nephew, Mr. Skoros?"

His arms akimbo, his facial expression crimped with impatience at the woman's naivete, Kas recalled the horror of that night, the abject fear, and broke in.

"Absolutely certain, Mrs. Thomas. And that daughter of his, we believe, is one of his kidnap victims. Both Detective Orlando and Deputy Buckley have done due diligence. The school which that child would be going to, doesn't have a girl of her description, living on Oso Road or hereabouts, attending the first or second grade class. Deputy Buckley has learned, based on his supposition that this Scooter lives near you and somehow got permission to use your old pickup, that no child on Oso Road or nearby off Highway Forty-nine was enrolled at the nearest elementary school this year. A couple of boys from this vicinity but no girls."

The Thomases looked at each other, their mouth open in shock.

"The girl—a kidnap victim?" Denise managed to gasp. "That poor child?"

Deputy Tom interjected, "Using the FBI's national database for missing children, we did find a girl of that age and description missing from Bend, Oregon. Taken three months ago as she was walking home from school."

Jeremy Thomas closed his mouth and stared at his wife. "Didn't he say he was from Oregon? As far as I know, he's renting that place up the road from here. I've never been there." His wife squirmed under his frosty stare. "Have you, Denise? Have you been to his place?"

The woman gasped again, both palms flying to cover her mouth, her gaze darting down to her shoes again. "I took him a pot of stew one time. I felt sorry for him and his dau—that little girl. She wasn't there so I assumed she was at school."

"What does his place look like, Mrs. Thomas?" asked Tom

Buckley.

After taking her hands from in front of her mouth, she held both to her cheeks, as if to control her shock.

"Let's see, this was a couple of weeks ago, but I told him then about the truck's key, where to find it if we weren't home when he came to use it, if he ever needed it." She shook her head and glanced up at her husband, whose countenance had turned cold with censor. He was not an easily forgiving man, Athena knew.

"There's a driveway through the trees, about half the length of ours. The house is old, just a ramshackle ol' thing, paint's peeling off. Exterior boards are warped. There's an old barn in back, looks in better condition than the house."

"Did you go inside either the house or barn?"

"No, I just handed him the pot of stew when he came down the steps to the grassy area in front of the house. More weeds than grass. From the looks of things, he doesn't do much yard work around the place. Come to think of it, he's a handyman of sorts so you'd think he would maintain things. At least, paint the house."

Detective Orlando broke in at this moment. "Did he leave the front door open? Were you able to see into the house at all?"

Denise Thomas considered his question. "Now that I think about it, yes, the front door was open. I saw a television screen, a big screen divided into squares. I thought it kinda strange, that he could afford a big screen TV like that."

"Fencing?" Orlando continued, "Is there a fence surrounding the property?"

Next, her hands constantly twitching, Mrs. Thomas put a fist up to her mouth and stared back at the plain clothes detective. Her eyes were big with concern.

"Some wooden fencing, not well taken care of, the part I could see, anyway. Let me see," she paused to calm herself down, "I drove past a cyclone fence and a metal gate. The gate was open because I called him to tell him I was coming with the stew. His place is surrounded by lots of trees, overgrown brush. A big oak to the side of the barn."

"Acreage, would you guess?" When she shrugged her shoulders, Orlando turned to Jeremy.

"I don't know exactly, three, maybe five acres at the most. It's a small piece of property."

"Do we know who owns the place, Jeremy?"

"One of the Barton brothers I grew up with, but he moved down to Southern California somewhere. A year or two ago. Guess he decided to keep it but rent it out. That's what Scooter — this guy — said, he was renting the place. Craig Barton owns the place next to that one, to the right. It belonged to his father, but he tore the old place down, said he was going to eventually build a new home there for him and his family. But he hasn't done that yet."

"Anything else about the property occupied by this Scooter guy that sticks in your mind, Mrs. Thomas? See any guns?"

She shook her head and cast a guilty, sidelong glance at her husband.

Deputy Tom thanked them for their time and added one more thing before he, Kas, Detective Orlando and Athena left the Thomases' front porch.

Detective Orlando turned back to the Thomases. "If he shows up in the next day or so, don't tell him we talked to you. You and your kids might be in danger if he feels threatened, so maintain your distance. Better yet, when you leave town tonight for the city, think about staying overnight there."

The foursome left the gaping couple and gathered in a huddle by Tom Buckley's SUV, which was parked beside Orlando's sedan.

While the three men were strategizing their next move,

Athena stood still and gazed into the distance, facing in a northwesterly direction. Kas noticed her stillness and faraway stare. He motioned for Detective Orlando and Deputy Tom to hush, and then followed up quickly with a half apologetic explanation.

"Jay, Tom, believe me. What I'm about to tell you is the bald-faced truth. Athena is clairvoyant. She can see things we can't see, and I think she's getting something."

Speechless, both law enforcement officers turned Athena's way. They looked from Kas to Athena, back to Kas. Bewilderment etched their faces.

Athena continued to face away, seeing something that she knew none of the three men could see. But she had no choice but to reveal what she saw, for their very lives depended on it. And the life of a child.

"There are surveillance cameras on the trees lining the driveway, at least four. All along the fence line, there are motion sensors that turn lights and cameras on. The barn behind the house is close to the northern fence line. That's where he keeps the girl when he's not . . . well, abusing her. He has a lot of guns, handguns, rifles with scopes. And he's looking for another child, getting frustrated, has started hanging around schools in the area. Elementary schools. He likes the young ones because they're easier to catch and control. Easier to lure away using the girl. He never lives in one place for very long. The money he gets, he lives off the money he gets from his buyer."

Her voice cracked as she related what she saw and sensed, the tone building in strength, then sagging with sorrow.

Kas walked up behind her, gently placed his hands on her shoulders. "Does his buyer live nearby?" he asked softly, as if he were reluctant to interrupt her visions.

The two other men stood stunned and silent.

"Is there a town in the mountains called Truck?"

"Yes, Truckee, little over an hour from here, between here and Reno, Nevada," Kas replied, almost inaudibly.

"Near Nevada? The buyer is coming soon. I don't know when. But he's expecting at least two small children under ten years old. The buyer . . . the child trafficker, I mean . . . he pays the bearded guy ten-thousand dollars for each child. He has a special van with cages inside. A black panel van, no windows or they're painted over." She paused and scowled. "He drugs them, takes the kidnapped kids over to Nevada. From there, they disappear," she whispered, her voice catching, "like sparrows in the night."

Orlando and Buckley stared at her, their awestruck silence hanging in the air like a heavy, moisture-laden cloud.

Kas asked softly, "How many kids?"

When Athena turned around to face Kas, her cheeks were wet with shed tears.

"Two girls. In the barn. In cages."

Kas enfolded her in his arms and held her, as though his embrace could prevent her heart from breaking.

"People can be so horrible," she murmured against his big, broad shoulder. He muttered back to her, "Yes, yes, they can. Some, not all. But this bastard beats them all."

When they drew apart, Kas took a step back and looked at the two men behind him. Their mouths agape, they remained silent.

"Jay, Tom, I think we need to change our strategy."

CHAPTER THIRTY-TWO

"We need the FBI," said Kas. Jay, the Nevada County detective, and Deputy Tom both nodded in unison.

Jay Orlando was the first to speak. The detective's deep frown registered with Athena.

"What's going on here, Kas?"

Athena stayed Kas's explanation by jumping in, herself.

"Detective, I've been clairvoyant since the age of nine. I get visions, impressions, information through my special . . . uh, mental channel." All she could do was gaze back into the detective's face and pry open her Flow channel. The horrifying images she'd received had caused her, disgust swamping her, to slam the channel shut. Yet, persuading this man to believe her was essential to freeing those little girls and stopping this child trafficker.

Deputy Tom interceded, "Kas's mother is psychic, too. The whole county knows it. She gives readings—"

Kas's surprised look swept over the two men. "I had no idea people knew . . ."

"Oh yeah, everyone I've spoken to knows about your mother's special gifts, how she used her psychic ability to make y'all rich." The young deputy smiled benignly, turning his stare on Athena. "So is your girlfriend like your mother, Kas? From the same group of women?" He shrugged. "Hey, people talk, the word gets around."

Kas frowned, obviously not liking the deputy's revelation. "More or less, from the same ancient Greek bloodline. The soothsayers of Mount Olympus."

Detective Jay interrupted, rasping a loud chortle, his hands rising impatiently to his chest.

"Whether she is, or she isn't, Deputy Buckley, the FBI won't get involved with the word of a . . . a, y'know, psychic. I'm sorry but they'll need hard evidence, at the very least a photo of the little girl this guy claims is his daughter. With a photo that matches the Oregon child, they'll come in like gangbusters."

"Detective Orlando," ventured Athena, catching his glance and returning his stare, "I'm sorry your elder brother has pancreatic cancer. He was just diagnosed and told your wife last night. You wouldn't talk to him, but you need to bury your grudge and reconnect with him."

Jaw dropping, Orlando took a step backwards. "Did you talk to my wife?"

Very quietly, she replied, "I didn't have to."

A long, uncomfortable moment passed. Kas studied the ground before clasping her hand in his and smiling at her. She relaxed a bit, hoping that she hadn't offended the detective. The family had just learned of the brother's diagnosis last night, and they were still reeling from the news even though Orlando and his brother hadn't been on speaking terms for years over a never paid back loan.

The detective, a very private man, Athena knew, needed to process her revelation but at the same time, was guided by his professionalism.

Orlando wiped a hand roughly over his mouth.

"Don't know if you're playing a trick or not, young lady, but I know Kas here and I trust him. We'll go ahead and try to get some evidence. Nevada County law enforcement will lead the way on this stakeout. I'll run point on this, but Deputy Buckley here can help. The Placer County Sheriff's already okayed his liaison with us and you two civies. If the child is the Oregon girl, the FBI will take over jurisdiction. If she's his abused or neglected daughter, then it's a case for Child Protective Services. If the former is true and the child trafficker is coming soon from Truckee, they'll want to catch both the kidnapper and the middleman. This buyer could be the head of a big Northern California trafficking ring, for all we know." He ran a hand through his thick, black hair. "Or we're going to look like fools to the FBI but maybe save a child from her negligent father."

Tom Buckley lifted his face to the nearest tree and scratched his chin. "Either way, it's a win-win, right? We need that little girl's photo. Her ID is vital."

Kas, his right arm wrapped around Athena's back, had brought her back within the circle of men. He glanced down at her before addressing the detective and the deputy.

"I've got an idea. Tonight, get him outside, get him distracted and rattled, lure him away from his surveillance monitors. Then someone slip into the barn and photograph the girl."

Athena was aghast. "I could see that the single barn door on the side, the one he uses, has a big padlock, and a surveillance camera. The other big door is a garage door and I think it's always closed. It's remote controlled. Even if we could get in, why would we leave her there? We can't just take her photo and leave. If he feels threatened, he could panic and kill her."

Kas showed his assent. "True, we have to take her with us. We can't leave her there. Athena, could you see if she's gagged, tied up?"

She shook her head. "No, I couldn't see. I just felt her presence in the barn. In some kind of cage. The human fear crashed upon me in waves."

Her figure of speech made Deputy Tom grimace, but he soon recovered and began to tick off the items for a possible solution. "Okay, we take thick, steel bolt cutters, watch out for booby traps, take a dog if necessary. Make him think a feral dog is trespassing, turning on the motion sensors. I'll take Riley, my Lab. He's well trained, barks on command. The suspect goes and investigates ... armed, of course. Someone frees the child while he's checking out the light above one of the sensors along the perimeter fence. Even if she turns out to be his real daughter, the scumbag's facing child abuse at the very least. If she's the kidnap victim from Oregon, we'll lean on him and get the buyer from Truckee. But we've gotta make sure he doesn't have a chance to warn the guy off. We have to jam cell phone frequencies."

Detective Orlando nodded soberly. "Do it tonight and I'll provide backup along the perimeter from Nevada County deputies. At the very least, it's a possible child abuse situation, reported by a neighbor with first-hand knowledge of the little girl. Don't worry about the Thomases, they'll provide witness. Today, I'll go back to the office and contact the FBI's Sacramento field office and get Missing Persons involved. What do you think, Deputy Buckley? We can't send in investigators who'll spook the guy beforehand. I think we keep with the civilians here until they can identify the girl."

Tom Buckley agreed and outlined a plan that sounded feasible, if not more than a little dangerous. Kas added a few suggestions based on Athena's insights, and the three men set up a time to meet back at the Thomas property. That would be their rendezvous point.

At last, Kas shook hands with Jay and watched as he warily shook hands with Athena. They watched him drive away before climbing into Tom's SUV. Tom drove in a northwest direction up Oso Road but stopped a couple of yards before the entrance into Scooter's driveway. A minute or two passed while the three looked over the front of the property facing Oso Road. The SUV was parked at a dead end in the road, the adjacent property being uninhabited, raw land. According to

Jeremy Thomas, this raw land was owned by one of the absentee Bartons.

They surveyed the property from Tom's SUV. Scrub pine and oak trees comprised the largest trees in the area, followed by unhealthy looking, leaning cotton trees and huge, leafy sugar maple trees. The brush on the ground was yellow and dry from the summer drought. They could see the fence line on the north side, a straight line from the asphalt roadway. Indeed, Athena saw, a metal cyclone fence.

Kas had a proposal. "Tom, if you distract the guy along the south fence with the sensor light, I'll take the cutters and break into the barn. I can see a corner of the barn from here, just the part closest to the northern perimeter fence line." Kas looked over at Tom. "My father's gardener has a bolt cutter for emergencies. I'll take that."

Athena's attention riveted immediately on the two men.

"It'll take two of us to get her out of there, Kas," she said, "And the second child. I'm coming, too."

Kas shot her an ironic smile. "Oh no, you're not. He has guns, Thena."

"Please let me help. I'll know things before you will."

His smile turned into a wry grin, he added, "If the whole operation blows up in our faces, we'll be hit with trespassing charges, breaking and entering, arrested and jailed. Have you ever spent time in jail, Thena? Want to lose your visa?"

Athena shook her head from the back seat but caught Deputy Tom's glance in the rearview mirror. He was smiling with barely suppressed amusement.

"Don't worry, I'll be just as culpable," Tom said, "I'm risking my badge and so is Jay. But hey, I'll vouch for you in court, Kas? So will Detective Orlando."

Catching his teasing tone, Kas played along. "I don't know. Last time the Forty-Niners beat the A's in that playoff game, Jay lost a cool fifty to me. Don't think he's ever forgiven me for rooting against his favorite team."

The deputy shot the two men a sneer, playing along. "Yah, maybe he'll throw you to the wolves." His laugh died to a grunt. "We've just gotta make a smart plan. Use radios to stay in touch. If we're lucky, it'll work."

Athena was not amused by their show of male bravado. "Jail doesn't concern me as much as getting our heads blown off with the guy's shotgun."

Kas reached back and tapped her knee. "Don't come along, then."

She huffed out a breath. "What do you Americans say, wild horses couldn't stop me?"

CHAPTER THIRTY-THREE

At the Skoroses' Loomis mansion, Kas approached the dining table as he held the hand of a very excited and talkative little Alex. Letting go of his uncle's hand, the two-year-old boy clasped Athena's.

"I wanna sit next to you, Thena. Gamma said I can. Can't I, Gamma?"

Lorena Skoros clearly wanted to indulge her youngest grandchild. "Of course, tonight is special because Athena is our guest."

The four adults and child took their seats, the two grandparents at either end of the shortened dining room table. At its full length, at festive family gatherings, the table could seat fourteen. Tonight's Sunday dinner was a small casual affair but made special because of Athena's infrequent presence. After all, most weekends she was tending to gallery business, selling art, making contacts with local artists.

Athena noticed the toddler's frequent furtive glances at her, her dark blue cotton shirt, a V-neck which revealed her gold chain and medallion of the Goddess Athena. She caught Kas's grin over the little boy's head, and as they ate their roast beef, carrots and new potatoes, she helped cut up the boy's cutlet into smaller bite-size portions.

"Gamma told me you made that picture," the boy said. One little hand pointed in the general direction of the painting of Alex Skoros hanging over the mantel in the large adjoining living room.

She smiled down at little Alex's cherubic face. "I did."

The toddler, using a child-size fork, speared a small piece of beef, stuck it in his mouth, gravy dripping over his pretty lips and down his chin. Like his biological father, his chin bore a slight cleft.

"I have two fathers," announced the little boy. He pointed in the direction of the portrait over the mantel and then to Kas. "Daddy is here with me. My other daddy is in Heaven. I see him in pictures."

Behind her eyes, tears gathered but she willed them away as she nodded to the child. "Yes, you have two. Most children have only one . . . if they're lucky."

The toddler nodded and smiled up at her, then at Kas.

Kas's grin wavered, then rebounded. "Alex, did you know, Athena painted my portrait, too?" He hooked a thumb over his shoulder. "The one hanging on the other wall. That's me."

Busy chewing, the boy nodded vigorously. "I know, Daddy." His eyes grew big as his mind switched to another topic. "I like to paint . . . with my fingers. And sometimes I paint with a brush."

"Ah yes, Athena's seen one of your masterpieces. It's on my fridge."

"Can I come and see it?"

Kas grinned. "My condo in San Francisco? Sure, someday I'll bring you up there and Athena and I will take you on a boat ride in the bay. There's a boat that looks like a big, yellow duck. It's called an amphibious boat because it runs on the ground and in the water. Would you like that, Alex? Ride the duck boat with us?"

His dark eyes growing big, the toddler nodded so heartily with his whole head, that Athena wondered if he'd put a crick in his neck. Everyone at the table chuckled, even the usually somber, octogenarian Phillip Skoros. Lorena Skoros, the precognitive matriarch, settled a long look in Athena's direction before glancing away. Her countenance was unreadable, purposely so for Athena's benefit. Whatever she saw, she didn't look predisposed to revealing.

While enjoying her time with Kas's family, Athena kept her Flow channel closed, not even certain why she did so. To respect their privacy was one reason, most assuredly. The other reason?

The child was adorable, so handsome in a sweet, little boy way that he reminded her of Kas's brother, Alex, the good-looking charmer and ladies' man. Nevertheless, she had to admit to herself her fear of getting too close to the child, becoming too invested emotionally.

Why was that? Was she ready to become a wife, a stepmother? She was soon to be twenty-four. A lot of women, she realized, were married and had children by that age.

What was she really afraid of, she wondered frankly to herself? Bloody hell if she knew.

She could see the secrets of strangers but often she found her own mind and emotions a mystery.

Before long, dinner was over. The cook and kitchen help cleared the table while she joined Kas and his father for an aperitif of oozo in the living room. Grandma Lorena readied herself to hustle little Alex upstairs for a bedtime bath-the boy's mother not arriving to pick up Alex until the next day, after all. Athena was relieved not to face Kas's ex-wife, the beautiful Nikki Theopoulis Skoros. She occasionally wondered if the woman ever lusted secretly after her stand-in ex-husband. Any lingering, secret attraction between Nikki and Kas was something she'd never picked up on. Not from Kas, anyway.

The little boy made the rounds of hugs and kisses, dallying with Kas and Athena for a second hug and kiss from each of them before skipping up the stairs, holding onto *gamma*.

The banked fire warmed them as they settled on the sofa in front of the ornately wood-sculpted fireplace. Now retired but still the Skoros Group's Chairman of the Board, Phillip placed the gilded metal screen on the marble hearth before slouching down in his plush easy chair near the fire. The elderly man had grown bony and frail in the intervening two-and-a-half years since she'd first visited the Loomis estate. His once luxuriant white hair had thinned, his skin paler and more crepey, his posture hunched over. Even so, in his dark eyes, she could detect the will to carry on at all cost, proud of his accomplishments and his legacy, loving life as he did, loving his family above all.

She couldn't help but wonder if her father was fighting the good fight as well. Her throat filled with emotion as she thought of Trevor Butler, the staid and steadfast English gentleman, always proper and reserved, always well-dressed whether in tweeds or tuxedo, his dark blond hair precisely parted on the side. The oozo burned her throat and made her eyes tear up, emotion suddenly swamping her. In that moment, she missed him and her mother more than at any other time in the past year.

Soon. In less than two weeks, she'd be boarding a jet for a badly needed Christmas reunion for her and Chris. God willing, she'd arrive in time to will her father back to good health.

"Another, son?" Phillip asked Kas, holding up the flask of clear, liquid fire. Kas's father claimed that a shot of oozo every night helped him sleep as soundly as a baby.

Kas smiled and stood up. "No thanks, Pop. I'm taking Athena to the movies tonight and I don't want to fall asleep in the middle of them." He looked pointedly at Athena after glancing at his watch. "It's time to go." To his father, "Don't wait up for us. It'll be late." He bent down and kissed his father on both cheeks in the Greek way. "Tell Mom goodnight for us. See you in the morning."

Outside, as they climbed into Kas's SUV, wearing their winter parkas and mountain boots over jeans and sweaters,

Athena couldn't resist teasing him. "Do you normally lie to your father?"

Kas grunted. "If I'd told him what we were about to do, he'd insist on coming along. Besides, Mom knows, and she won't tell him, either. She doesn't like it, but she knows we must stop this creep. And no, she didn't tell me the outcome, either." He checked the back seat, where he'd put the steel-toothed metal cutter, then patted first his ankle, then his jeans pocket. "Okay, let's do this."

Her pulse began to pound even as Kas pulled out of the driveway. She knew he'd strapped a gun holster to his right ankle. He sometimes carried spare bullets in a pants pocket.

No turning back now, she told herself.

CHAPTER THIRTY-FOUR

Behind the Thomases' two-story house, hidden from view of Oso Road, Deputy Tom set up Command Control post A, as he called it. Kas parked his SUV alongside of the deputy's white with green striped patrol vehicle. Back in uniform, Tom had brought the Sheriff department's transceiver ear buds for both Kas and Athena, showing them how to wear them. From the radio on his shoulder and belt, he'd stay in constant communication with them. On his hood perched a small drone with an array of instrumentation and antennae attached. This drone was the flying frequency jammer that Deputy Tom had operated before and had told them about. His intent was to jam the electronic signals from the motion-light sensors along the southern fence. Inside the SUV's cargo hold, his golden Labrador slouched, waiting for his owner's call.

"I'll radio you when to approach the barn—and let's hope that's where the girl is. If she's in the house, it's all bets off."

"No, I saw her in the barn in that cage," Athena reassured him. "She's already eaten from a plate he brought her or tried to eat. A sandwich and a glass of milk. She could hardly stomach it." She'd seen two girls in two separate cages, she was sure of it.

By now, her pulse was galloping, just like the adrenalin rush she got when she tried to stop the attack at the British Embassy in D.C. over two years before. The memory flooded her mind, but she pushed it away, needing to focus on the operation at hand. "I tried to send the older girl a telepathic message," she added, "you know, to stay calm, we were coming to rescue her."

Deputy Tom studied her for a moment. "Did it work?"

"No, I don't think so. She's too frightened, too shut down. She may have been drugged."

Kas said, "It's over a mile away. Do you want us to approach from this direction?"

"No, I'll work the drone from here. Jam up the sensors and surveillance cameras on the south side of the property, draw him out in this direction away from the house and barn. You two slip into the barn through the northern fence line. That's where Jay and his deputies will be. If the scumbag's away from those monitors that you say he's got." He looked directly at Athena. "If he's watching the monitors, the motion sensor lights and cameras won't go on, the screens will stay dark. Maybe he'll go out to investigate. Or maybe he does an hourly patrol. If he does, he'll most likely be armed. The point is to draw his attention away from the monitors and out to the southern fence line. That'll buy you some time."

"Okay. And the other command post?" Kas asked.

"On the Barton property, next to the perp's northern fence. They're already set up there, two squad vehicles from Nevada County, Detective Orlando's sedan. He and two deputies are ready to go, radio'd up and armed. Sheriff Farnsworth's okayed this but only if you two civilians aren't armed. You'd face serious charges in addition to trespassing and B and E, if you're armed."

Kas nodded. "Okay by me." He patted his own jacket pockets, lifted the back to show no pistol in the back waistband of his jeans. Athena held up her hands, palms outward. Those gestures seemed to satisfy the deputy.

"Remember, Kas, only in self-defense. If this all pans out and the creep's guilty as hell, no problem. Even if he's just abusing his own kid, we can't use armed force. In effect, you'll be trespassing."

Kas and Athena fingered their ear buds to make sure they were secure, tested the reception while Deputy Tom turned away, cupped his hands over his shoulder attached mic and whispered a few words.

"Testing, testing . . ."

"Copy that, Tom." Kas looked over at Athena, who nodded after testing her ear bud.

Tom opened the SUV's hatch and let his dog out. The Lab obediently nestled to the deputy's side, looking up for cues. When the man launched the jammer drone and started walking in the direction of the Thomases' fence line, the dog stayed by his side. "Okay, just go down Oso Road and take the Barton driveway to Command post B."

"Good luck," Kas called out, pushing two thumbs up.

"You, too," Tom fired back. They watched him as the two figures receded in the distance.

Dusk had settled in, casting longer shadows around the Thomases' house and outbuildings. The sky bled with pinks and oranges before morphing to purples and blues, the tall trees surrounding them turning dark gray, then black, merging with the growing darkness of the ground and shrubbery. The woods were eerily quiet as if the birds sensed trouble was brewing.

"Let's go," Kas told Athena, "unless you want to stay. You can monitor the situation from here, Thena, radio us if you see or sense something. You don't have to come with me."

He clasped her shoulder and looked into her eyes, aware of her mounting anxiety and fear. Undulating off his body, a scent of sweat mixed with Kas's own brand of musk and citrus assailed her heightened sense of smell. Despite the cold, evening temperature, perspiration ran down her back in rivulets, her forehead and temples damp as well. They both were as bloody anxious as they could be, no denying that.

For a moment, she hesitated, but only for a moment. She shook her head.

"No, I'm all in. Let's stop this blighter, shall we?"

In reply, he pressed his lips against hers before abruptly pulling away.

"Okay, let's take him down."

They drove in Kas's SUV out of the Thomases' driveway, down Oso Road until a half mile before two separate driveways appeared at the dead end of the road. Kas cut the headlights, reduced his speed to a crawl and turned into the driveway on his right, flanked by a split-rail fence along the front. Into the Barton property, he steered, following a winding dirt road until three dark masses loomed before them. The two Nevada County squad cars and Detective Orlando's sedan fanned out at angles in a dirt clearing, though at first hidden behind tall, thick brush and granite boulders. The darkness of night had descended fully as Kas and Athena silently emerged from the SUV.

To their right, a copse of tall trees surrounded an open glade, where it was apparent a cabin had once stood. The cold air was still and silent, the only sound a slight ruffling of treetops in a high breeze. Earthy smells, thick and musty, filled her with a new awareness of nature, reminding her that they'd left the city and suburbia far behind. This was as country as it got in this Nevada County mountain area. Having grown up in London and a variety of European cities, she felt overwhelmed. This little corner of Sierra Nevada Mountains was more wilderness than she'd ever experienced before in her life.

Her eyes adjusted to the black shapes around them until three individuals could be seen, two in light tan uniforms partially covered by black jackets bearing the Nevada County Sheriff's logo. The two deputies held rifles with night-vision scopes, sidearms in holsters as well. Detective Orlando, dressed in casual street clothes and a dark wool coat, gestured to Kas and Athena to approach. Holding a portable mic in his hand, he appeared to be waiting for Deputy Tom's jamming drone to do its job along the other side of the property.

From the property border Athena could see, about fifty yards away beyond the protective, granite ramparts where they stood, an aluminum cyclone fence. On nearby trees, she knew there were sensors and cameras which she and Kas couldn't see in the darkness.

The detective brought the two into their huddle.

"Just got the word an hour ago, a kid, a four-year-old girl, disappeared from the front yard of her grandparents' house in Nevada City. The family's frantic, searching all over for her, think she disappeared while they were cooking dinner. That would make it three to four hours ago. If she's not found in the next five to ten minutes, we'll assume this creep's maybe got her, either in the house or barn. Like Miss Butler said. Another complication, Kas, in addition to the cyclone fence. You'll have to cut through it. It's too high to climb over."

Athena felt their disappointment like a heavy weight. The anxiety of Kas and the three other men had risen exponentially.

Jay Orlando handed Kas infra-red binoculars. "Look over by the side of the barn. How many sensors and cameras do you see?"

While Kas focused the heavy, hand-held apparatus, scanning the tree line by the barn, she turned inward and opened her Flow channel. What she saw made her gasp but Kas spoke first.

"Two, no, three motion sensors with cameras attached. Jeez, let's hope that drone works on the other side. He's gotta be distracted, gotta leave those monitors, move outside to that southern fence line."

When Kas handed the infra-red binoculars back to Jay, he was scowling. He turned to Athena.

"You have to stay here with the deputies. This is far more dangerous than I thought it'd be."

"Kas, I saw the other little girl. Smaller, younger. She's asleep, drugged, in another cage. No, the rotter, he's got them in kennels, big-dog kennels, locked up. Both children are lying down, both drugged from the food they ate. We'll have to carry them out."

The Nevada County Sheriff's detective cursed under his breath. "Yet, we have no visual proof. Just her word. That's the problem."

One of the two deputies watching the house on the far side of the barn while lying on his stomach on top of the tallest granite boulder, another set of infra-red binoculars in his hands, turned to them and whispered, "Not the only problem, Detective. A car just pulled up, parked in front of the house. A van. The suspect is visible, too. He's outside in front and he's carrying a shotgun. A man is getting out of the van, a pistol in his hand. The two men are greeting each other, looks like. Now they're on the move, heading south."

"It's now or never," said the detective to Kas and Athena. He told the two deputies, "Mike, you head to the fence behind the two civies. Chet, you veer off towards the house, keep watch to see if the two guys come back to the house. Stay in contact. Both deputies, stay on this side of the fence until we get verification on the girl."

He swiveled to Kas and Athena. "Text me a photo as soon as you get it. I need visual proof. I've got a photo of the Oregon girl to compare it with."

Kas hefted the steel cutters on his shoulder and stood up. A large flashlight, he seized in his other hand. Athena held up her cell phone, the detective's phone number already set in her contacts directory.

"I figure," the detective added, "you have five to ten minutes max. Good luck!"

Kas stepped out from behind the granite boulders and led the way, making a footpath in the underbrush with his long legs and big boots. Athena faced the light from her cell phone downward to the rough ground in front of him, spilling enough light so neither of them would trip and fall.

She followed Kas close behind, her heart beating wildly. The passing of seconds sounded like the drumbeat of a hard rock band in her head.

No turning back.

CHAPTER THIRTY-FIVE

After a minute or so, they arrived at the cyclone fence. Two lights blinked on, flooding them with two circles of illumination. Seconds later, they heard two dull thuds followed by crackling glass that showered the ground on either side of them. One of Orlando's deputies must've shot out the motion sensor bulbs with a suppressed rifle. Suddenly enveloped in darkness, Athena held up her cellphone light to guide Kas as he raised his steel cutters.

Kas went to work on the fence with his cutters. All the while, he cursed under his breath as he made a long vertical cut-long enough for the two of them to hunch over and squeeze through. Then he cut two horizontal ones, one above and one below. Each snap of the blades sounded like it reverberated through the woods.

Athena held her breath and glanced over at the shabby, wooden house. A dog's barking was a faint but distinct sound in the southern distance as Kas laid the cutter down and, armed with leather gloves, tugged on the metal. Finally, seemingly too many minutes later, he pried open a portion of the fence wide enough for them to step through. Bending it back as far as he could, he picked up the steel cutters and stepped through. Athena followed, careful not to snag her clothes on the jagged metal and fixing her eyes on the thick combination lock on the barn door not twenty yards away. The dog's barks had stopped. Kas paused for a moment, looked to the south but continued.

"Through the fence. Now cutting the lock on the barn," he

said for the benefit of the detective and his men.

"Four minutes. Gotta move faster," was Detective Orlando's reply in her earbud.

Pungent, earthy smells assailed her as they approached the barn door. She fought the urge to pinch her nostrils shut. Kas immediately went to work, grunting as he finally snapped open the lock's handle.

"God almighty, I need to spend time at the gym," he muttered.

He opened the barn door and strangled back a gag. She took in the same unmistakable, acrid odor, human feces and urine wafting from several tin buckets along the wall. Vomit mixed with other musty dirt and straw smells. Pointing to the two large dog kennels to their right along the same wall as the slop buckets, she finally gave in and covered her nose and mouth with her left hand.

Two more motion sensors concealed in the corners by the opened barn door blinked on their lights.

Athena pointed and gasped while Kas made a low, growling noise. Two cages, equal in size and each able to accommodate a very large dog, had closed doors in front. Neither door was locked but two combination locks lay on the cement floor between the two cages. Apparently, the rotter had expected the buyer to show up tonight to inspect the merchandise and hadn't bothered to lock up the cages. She and Kas bent down in front of each cage.

"They're asleep," Kas murmured.

"No, drugged," she said, "We must pull them out of the cage so I can take their photos. We'll have to carry them. I can get the little one but the bigger girl, you'll have to take."

Kas nodded as Athena shone her cellphone light on the cage that held the older girl. Since her head was facing them, he opened the cage door and tugged on her shoulders until she was completely out of the cage and lying on the dirty cement floor, dressed in a filthy, ragged tee shirt and jeans.

"Ohh," he moaned, "poor child." On his knees, he cuddled the girl's head in his lap and swept aside stringy, oily locks of hair from her face. "She's still breathing, thank god. Take the photo, quickly."

Athena squatted down and snapped the flash photo. The child, the same little girl who had lured Alex away from her that night at the Cornish Christmas Fair, didn't stir. Her head lolled back on Kas's lap before she rolled forward onto the cement floor. He stood up and hoisted her over his left shoulder.

Athena sent the photo to Detective Orlando and texted, "Same girl that night, Cornish fair. Second child here, younger. Sending photo now."

Squatting in front of the second cage, she snapped a photo of the second child and texted them to Orlando.

"Waiting for verification on the Oregon girl. Smaller one, looks like the one taken locally, about the same age," came through over the earbud transceiver.

"Hurry," Kas issued by her side. She pocketed her cell phone and placed her arms under the smaller child.

The earbud crackled with a second of static. "The suspect and the other man headed towards the barn. Get out of there . . . now!"

With effort, Athena was able to swing the child into both her arms and stand up. She shone the cell phone light Kas's way.

Kas was already at the opened barn door, about to step through. A tall, black figure outlined in the darkness blocked his way. He froze in place, then began to back up.

A beam of intense light blinded her.

"Put the kids down and your fuckin' hands up!"

CHAPTER THIRTY-SIX

"Put the kids down," yelled one of the dark figures behind the garish circle of light.

"Don't fire, you'll hit our assets."

"Shit, no."

Athena couldn't move or speak. In horror, she watched Kas bend over and gently place the older girl on the barn's filthy cement floor.

"Let's take this outside," he said, his voice sounding hollow and dispassionate.

"You heard, lady, put the kid down and come outside."

"Kas?" she ventured. In the harsh glare of the man's LED flashlight, she saw Kas hold his hands by his head and nod.

Trembling a little, she put the little girl down on the floor and raised her hands, too.

"Outside," barked the shorter of the two men. Passing by him, she saw his dark beard and unkempt hair, realizing this was the man who'd attempted to kidnap Alex. He was cradling a shotgun within the crook of his elbow. The taller man, of stocky build and massive shoulders, pointed a long-barreled revolver at Kas. Trying to get her internal quivers under control, she followed Kas through the opened doorway and stood by him. She took her cues from his silent but tense demeanor. Remembering the small pistol he always carried in an ankle holster, she tried not to glance down. He'd never have time to reach down and get it out.

"Hey, peel yer eyes at this looker. Not bad, huh? Why not get rid of her by adding her to your shipment? How much would she pull in?"

"Buyers want 'em young but I've got a damned sheik or two that might like 'er. Mebbe I'll try her out, see if she's worth five-thousand?"

"Sure, save a bullet. Why the fuck not."

Such callousness, Athena thought. These blighters cared nothing about human life. She swore she'd die before she let this sodding wanker touch her.

At the point of their gun barrels, she and Kas were ushered to the cyclone fence. The bigger man, apparently the middle-man in the trafficking ring, swept a flashlight over the hole in the fence.

"Perimeter lights are out here, too?" he asked his supplier.

"Fucking A!" the bearded kidnapper swore, "My costs just went higher, dude." He jabbed Kas's shoulder with the barrel end of his shotgun. "You did this, asshole? And broke my sensors?" When Kas said nothing in return, the bearded man hit him in the back hard with the butt of his gun. Kas stumbled forward, hit the fence face first but managed to grab a finger-hold on the cyclone metal. "Answer me, you fuckin' moron!"

Athena screamed. The bearded man turned to her. "Shut the fuck up, bitch!"

Kas straightened up, and cast a hate filled look back at the two traffickers. "You bet I did all that," he replied coolly, "and I'll do more before I let you assholes get away."

Both rotters laughed out loud. While the bigger man swung his flashlight up and down the fence line, he said, "You two come alone? Or d'ya have an army on the other side?"

They laughed even louder when Kas said, "Nope, just us."

"So what do we do with these fuckin' crazy do-gooders?" the bearded man asked. "How d'ja find me out?"

The bigger man waved his revolver in Kas's direction. "Never mind. Just shoot'im and bury'im, the motherfucker.

I'll take the girl and the kids. You mop up, what I'm payin' ya for. Right?"

The bearded kidnapper swung his shotgun's muzzle to his right. "Over there's an empty lot. That's why I liked this place. No one's there to hear the kids in the barn. Probably parked their car over there. Lots of places to dig and bury."

The bigger man pointed his revolver at the back of Kas's head. "Empty lot, huh? Okay, keep the guy in yer sights while I tie up the broad. I'll take 'er with me in the shipment. I'll tame 'er good 'nough so she'll be beggin' me to suck a rag-head's dick." He belched out a deep chortle and the bearded man chuckled. "She can keep the kids in control 'til I can get rid of 'er. Got more comin' from other counties."

"And this fucker?"

"Take care of 'im, bury 'im in that empty lot, then get the motherfucker's car and drive it somewhere so it can't be tracked back here." He signaled for Kas to step through the opening in the fence. Kas let go of the fence and bent over, his hands still up. Carefully, he started to pick his way through the jagged opening.

Athena's earbud crackled. "Verified. Go after them," ordered Detective Orlando to his deputies, hidden among the brush and debris by the barn.

What followed happened so fast that Athena had no time to react. In the darkness of the woods, Kas seemed to lose his balance as he pitched forward, twisted around, raised his arm and fired his pistol. The popping sound was small, but his aim was spot-on, good enough to drop the smaller, bearded man in a heap. His shotgun fell by his side on the dirt. She gaped at the man's prone body, the dirt that scattered from his weight hitting the ground. A dark spot on his chest leaked blood.

The taller man lunged forward towards the hole in the fence, his revolver raised, aiming at Kas. She crouched down and readied herself to fling her whole body at the man's back when Orlando's two deputies emerged from the woods, their military-grade, semi-automatic rifles pointed at the kidnapper's chest.

"Drop it or we drop you!"

The man swung his gun around in the direction of one of the deputies, his finger on the trigger. Amid the deafening blast that followed, the man jerked backwards, his revolver blasting forth straight up in the night air, rending the quiet night like a lightning strike. The man fell at her feet and for one awful moment, as the revolver went flying to the side, Athena gazed down at his twisting body. He was still alive, wounded and bleeding.

No time to think! Or feel relieved or sick to her stomach. Kas picked his way through the hole in the fence, the pistol in his right hand still smoking. She ran to him and crushed him in a fierce embrace. He held her for a moment, heaving with relief.

"Let's get those little girls!"

"Omigod, yes!"

She dug out her cellphone light and flashed it before them as they ran to the barn. One of the two deputies used his military-grade flashlight to light up the scene outside of the barn. Their radios crackled loudly in the night air. She could hear Tom Buckley shouting, his dog's barks growing louder as they approached.

"Two families are going to celebrate tonight," Kas exclaimed. "Mine, too. There's one bad guy my son'll never have to worry about."

Athena had known from the start that this was personal for Kas, but her relief was personal, too. And reaffirming, for her clairvoyant gift had helped save these children and would save others as well. Not for the first time, she felt truly grateful for being one of the descendants of the Delphi bloodline.

Orlando appeared behind them and flicked on the barn's overhead lightbulb from a wall switch.

"I've called an ambulance and backup from the Sheriff's office. The one you shot, Kas, probably won't survive. The other perp, maybe. It was justifiable self-defense, so don't worry. The deputies and I heard everything." Orlando looked from Kas to Athena, back to Kas. He was breathing hard, his excitement palpable and nearly matching their own adrenalin rush. "Anyway, an FBI team from Sacramento will be here in thirty minutes to take over the case."

He looked over the two little girls that Kas and Athena had lifted into their arms. The older one moved one skinny, filthy arm around Kas's neck. The younger one was still out cold, but Athena could feel the pulse in her tiny neck and the little girl's breath against her cheek.

"I think she'll be okay. She's breathing steadily but she'll need something to counteract the drug. Chloroform, I think. Or something in her food." Sure enough, on a wooden shelf above the slop buckets stood a brown bottle and wad of gauzy cloth. Athena pointed to it.

Orlando nodded and said, "Probably used when he took her. I think we've just cracked open a local child-trafficking ring. Where this leads, who knows, but it could be statewide. I'm going to recommend special commendations for you both."

"Not necessary, Detective Orlando, but if it helps to renew my work visa . . ." she said weakly. The shock began to wear off and she found her arms and legs quiver.

Orlando smiled at her. "Kas, any time you want to return to deputy duty, let me know."

Kas gave a small, mirthless laugh. "Ha, not likely, sir."

Athena ignored the detective as Orlando took a long, speculative study of her while they left the barn. She knew what he was wondering.

No matter. They did what they came to do.

A bench in front of the barn, made of an upturned half-log, beckoned them for a sit down. Emotionally wrung out, Kas and Athena sat, held the two children in their laps and waited for the ambulance to show up.

Kas looked down at the child in his arms. "This could've been Alex." His voice broke and he glanced away into the darkness. She gazed wearily over at him.

"You took a big chance, Kas. What you did—"

"What we did. I was trained, that's all. But your information was vital." He looked over at her and smiled.

A glance down at the sleeping little girl on her lap gratified her to tears, which smarted behind her eyes.

"All right, but what we did was worth more than all the tea and sympathy in the world."

Kas's voice was rough with emotion when he said, "I think we're a good team, you and me."

"Yes, we are. We are a good team," she said.

"But let's not push our luck. Too many close calls . . ."

He left unfinished what they were both thinking. She stared at the profile of his handsome face and made a decision.

No, more a frightening leap than a decision.

CHAPTER THIRTY-SEVEN

"**D**id you have a relaxing weekend?" asked Dale Dargent, in the Stargazer Gallery.

Athena was standing behind the counter, totaling the weekend receipts, including Dale's Saturday exhibit's sales. It was Tuesday morning and she and Kas had just returned to the city the night before, after having endured hours of interviews all day Monday with the Nevada County Sheriff's Office as well as the FBI's Sacramento field office agents. Having satisfied everyone involved in the inquiry and having witnessed the successful return of the two little girls to their families, they signed statements and then they'd been allowed to leave.

Detective Jay Orlando continued giving Kas updates on the case, including the child-trafficking ringleader whom Kas had shot. The suspect was in recovery in a Nevada County hospital, under the close watch of Sheriff's deputies. The other suspect, the bearded kidnapper, was dead, having been killed by Orlando's deputies that horrible night. Beyond that, there were no news except Orlando's hope that the ringleader would cut a deal and expose the entire Northern California operation.

Since the gallery weekend had overflowed with customers, according to her cheerful assistant manager, and Monday was a closed shop, she and Dale Dargent had some catching up to do.

She smiled at him while he hung and straightened her acrylic nude. Already matted and framed, it held center spot on one wall. He angled the nearby track lights just so. The painting would come down in a week and be taken to Golden State Printers to be photographed and processed into five hundred giclee prints on canvas.

"I wouldn't call it relaxing, no. But very productive, I must say." She hadn't revealed her and Kas's exploits in Grass Valley, or her clairvoyance to Dale. Nor would she. "You did well, Dale. The receipts are double what they were all last week. And your sculptures, did you think you would practically sell out?"

Her assistant manager was in very good spirits. He'd sold eight of his ten Lucite sculptures. All willowy women in Twenties' style dresses, hats and cropped hairdos, a copy of once popular Art Deco sculptures but a good copy, nonetheless. Not her cup of tea but blimey, who could always assess correctly the eclectic taste of Americans? Not her, anyway.

"Not hardly but one of the Academy of Art professors bought two of them. Going to give them as Christmas gifts," she said. "The others, a few men bought them for their wives but mostly they appealed to women of a certain age."

"I see. Do you have another subject in mind or will you stick to Art Deco flappers for your next sculptures?"

"Don't know yet. Waiting to get inspired." He touched one corner of her framed painting, then stood back. "This is really hot. The giclees are going to sell like—"

"Like hot cakes?" She looked up at his blushing face. "That's what Kas says."

"I was going to say, like good scotch on a cold winter's day." He put a hand to his chin, a habitual contemplative gesture of his. "Actually, the subject matter inspires me. Maybe my next sculptures will cater to the gay crowd. Lots of us here in the city, you know."

She waited for him to continue. Having known almost immediately that Dale was gay, she'd realized that he still had none of the stereotypical mannerisms that some gay men displayed. However, it had been doubly clear from the start that he wasn't attracted to her sexually. Which was probably why Kas liked him so much. No threat there.

"Your painting is a real turn-on, the fleshy limbs, the curves, the suggestion of desire and pleasure."

She smiled. "Yes, I was inspired that day." *What a thing to say!* She felt her cheeks. *A little warm there?* "I just hope my giclee prints sell here and abroad. I'm investing a fair amount of money in ordering them. I started a second nude, maybe part of a series. I tried the cityscapes, but just couldn't feel it."

Dale was nodding his head with vigor. "Yes, I know exactly what you mean. I have a new boyfriend. He's a software engineer, doesn't understand art but thinks having an artist for a boyfriend is awesome. Avant-garde, y'know. So I ran the idea by him last night after he saw your nude. I made some drawings for a couple of sculptures. Lucite sculptures painted between the layers like my flappers, but this time of nude men, embracing, like a spiral twining of nude male limbs. What d'ya think, Athena? Is it too out there?"

"I say, carry on. I hope you can make one before I leave in a week. I'd love to see a prototype."

She and Dale chatted for a while as she entered the receipts for the gallery's lucrative weekend into her digital spreadsheet. A bell jingled at the street door and Dale stuck his head out of the back room, where he was framing a few paintings he'd sold that weekend. A wave of her hand told him that she could help the new customer, but Dale persisted on coming to the front. As she stayed behind the counter, working on the computer's spreadsheet, the customer, a well-dressed, perfectly coiffed man in a pinstriped suit, strolled around the gallery.

Glancing up, she noticed the black, stretch limousine that appeared to be waiting for him at the curb, noted his youthful, tanned face and slim build, his glossy chestnut brown hair, swept back from his forehead. Another well-heeled business-man, she concluded. So many in this city, it was impossible to count them. Not a techie, though, but a man who ran a successful business of some kind.

Dale was acting as though bloody King George V, himself, had just walked in. He was fawning all over the man, almost bowing his head with every word the man uttered. She was curious, but just a jot. Not enough to open her Flow channel, anyway. Another man, his chauffeur, she guessed, dressed in a black suit and tie, entered the shop and looked around. Just browsing, he told her.

Athena shut down the computer. "Dale, I'm finished here, taking a break. See you in an hour. Ring me if you need something." She shot Dale a pointed look, to which her assistant barely acknowledged.

Surprisingly, the well-dressed man approached her and said, "Miss Butler, it's you I'd like to talk to."

She exchanged a glance with Dale, whose eyes were popping out of his head, and extended her hand. "Mister . . ."

"Mr. Zuckerman," he offered, shaking her hand. "I've heard so much about your gallery, the exquisite art you've gathered here, I knew I had to pay a call."

Now more than a trifle curious, she opened her Flow channel just enough to allow through a transmission of his immediate thoughts.

He's lying. It's me he's heard about. And he's got a plan.

She let go of his hand. *Who would've told him about me?* A heartbeat later. *Inspector Villalobos? No, not Villalobos.*

"Thank you," she managed, "The Stargazer Gallery has been gaining a reputation, I suppose. We had a good turnout this weekend. My assistant, Mr. Dargent, sold most of his Lucite pieces. He's a talented sculptor."

The man let go of her hand and scanned the large room. His eyes settled on the two Lucite sculptures on a table, then roamed over Athena's nude painting. Zuckerman stood before it, his eyes roaming all over it.

"I'd like to buy that original. Of the two nudes."

"It's not for sale, Mr. Zuckerman, but thank you for the offer. It's a nice example of romantic expressionism. Giclee prints of it are —"

"I buy only originals for my collection. It's very well done, wonderful colors and shapes. I would make a nice offer if you changed your mind. A quarter of a million?" He grinned like a fox, Athena thought.

For a long moment, her breath caught in her throat, she hesitated. *Blimey! That would buy a lot of trips back and forth to England and Italy.*

"No, I'm sorry. I need the original for my giclee prints."

The man shrugged. "Well then, hold it for me and I'll buy it afterwards. Just name your price. For now, I'll buy the two Lucites. I know just the ladies who'd appreciate them at Christmastime."

"Your offer is quite generous, Mr. Zuckerman. Let me think about it over Christmas break. I'll be going home for a while but I shall let you know upon my return. If that's acceptable to you."

Zuckerman nodded slowly, then offered a credit card which she ran while Dale wrapped up the two Lucite sculptures, as carefully as if they were Michelangelo treasures from the Uffizi Gallery in Florence. He deposited them in a gold foil box and affixed the gallery's label on top, all the while his hands trembling a bit.

From Dale's reaction, the buyer must have been both famous and ultra-wealthy, but for the life of her, Athena couldn't place him. Her Flow channel had not revealed any more than a vague kind of threat. Not his name or business connection. The man's thoughts were opaque as he signed his credit card transaction with a flourish and an unrecognizable signature.

As he turned to go, his chauffeur, who had been strolling about the southeastern corner of the gallery, ostensibly perusing the cityscapes by Ian Chen, whipped around in his employer's direction and appeared to be pocketing something. He hurriedly went to open the entrance door. Before leaving, Mr. Zuckerman paused, looked back at her, nodding in his solemn way. He said nothing in parting.

"Thank you, Mr. Zuckerman, for your patronage," she told him, "Do visit again."

"I will." He was in his limo and taking off by the time Dale broke out of his reverie and excitedly sidled up to her.

"Athena, do you know who *that* was?" She shook her head.

"Elon Zuckerman is one of the richest men in America. Certainly the richest in Silicon Valley. He founded Apollo, the computer company about twenty years ago. Now he's into everything else."

Her jaw dropped. "Not possible, he's too young."

"Early forties, I think. Started Apollo when he was twenty. Was a billionaire by twenty-five." A breathless Dale went over to a plush chair, sat down and fanned his face. In two seconds flat, he was on his cellphone, excited and speaking so fast, his words were tripping over themselves.

"Guess, Enrico, who just bought two of my Lucite sculptures? Yes, the last two from the launch. You'll never guess in a million years . . ."

Amused by Dale's frenzied fan's reaction, she gathered her coat and purse. "Back after lunch, Dale," she called out with a brief wave.

An hour later, she telephoned her mother to ask about her father. He was recovering from his arterial scrubbing, or quadruple angioplasty, at hospital in London. The ordeal had rendered him so worn out, his natural immunities so low, the surgeon wanted to keep him in hospital for another week. After which, he'd be sent home for recuperation and rest. The

Foreign Office had given him a medical leave. For how long, her parents didn't know. Athena sensed, as did Lorena Skoros, his condition was more serious than her parents had let on.

"Mum, since Father will be home by the time we arrive, we shall go straightaway from Heathrow to the flat."

They spoke for a while about Chris and his progress at Stanford University. Although unable to play on the soccer team for the first month while his arm healed, he was now playing guard and enjoying the team's camaraderie. He'd made friends and, as far as she knew, his grades were good. He was dropping hints about changing his major from International Relations to Computer Science.

"He's caught the Silicon Valley fever, Mum, all the excitement of innovation and being on the cutting edge of technology and such," Athena offered.

"Well, *cara mia*, he is in the middle of it, isn't he?" added her mother. "Although your father will be disappointed to hear it. He so wanted Chris to follow him into the Foreign Service." A moment's pause. "We shall not tell your father about this, Athena. Tell Chris not to mention his change of major while he's here. Indeed, your father has enough to deal with at the present."

A minute later, Athena broached the subject that was in the back of her mind.

"Mum, is there a reason why the head of a Silicon Valley computer company would be interested in the Delphi bloodline?"

"A computer company? No, not that I can think of, Athena. Why, has someone approached you?"

"No, not really. I was just wondering. Would you meditate on this question when you have a free moment, Mum?"

"Yes, of course, my darling."

"Give Father our love. We'll see you next Monday.

Arriving at Heathrow, an ungodly hour, I'm afraid, seven AM."

"I'll send your Uncle Terence to the airport to fetch you."

"No need, Mum. We'll take the Tube to Kensington, or a cab."

After they rang off, Athena returned to the gallery. Kas was in meetings all day, including a lunch meeting with his general contractor.

"Okay, your turn for lunch, Dale," she told her assistant manager.

He was still on his cellphone, spreading the word of his sales to one of the wealthiest and most influential men in the world. "Yes, Mom, can you believe it?"

His cellphone was still glued to his ear as he hustled out of the gallery through the hotel door, on his way to the Stargazer Grill. Athena had to laugh and shake her head.

Not a minute later, Athena heard a faint buzzing in her ears. She didn't hear it as much as she sensed it.

Glancing around, she gradually raised her head. Something was on the gallery ceiling that hadn't been there before. She couldn't see it but felt its presence. In her Flow vision, a miniscule green light in whatever-it-was blinked on and off. It was black, the same color as the twenty-foot high, acoustic-tiled ceiling. She wished she had high-powered binoculars with her. What the bloody hell was it?

A surveillance camera? There were already security cameras scattered around the gallery in all the ceiling corners.

Ahh. Zuckerman's chauffeur. But why? And what exactly is it?

An hour later, she and Dale were watching one of the Tower's maintenance men climb up an extension ladder. Mac was a thirty-something general mechanic wearing gray coveralls and a tool belt around his waist. He shone an LED flashlight up and around the entire ceiling.

"Oh, there's something, I see it now," he said, his raspy

voice carrying down to them. "About the size of my thumb-nail."

"What is it?" Dale asked.

"I'll be damned, it just flew away. Now it's on the other side of that ceiling truss. A big fly or a moth. Can you see it?"

Dale glanced at her. "I can't, can you?"

She couldn't tell him that she sensed it, not saw it.

"Yes, I can."

"You've got better eyesight than me," Dale exclaimed.

Using the ladder's rollers and the ceiling trusses for balance and support, Mac moved the ladder over a foot. He pulled a spray can out of his tool belt. A spray of white paint, which he often used for quick coverups on dry wall, coated the tiny object. Going dead, it issued a *pfft* sound, and then dropped off the ceiling and landed on the gallery floor. Athena picked it up with a paper towel and examined it after rubbing off some of the paint. Dale came in for a closer look while Mac descended, looking pleased but curious.

"Huh, it looks like a moth," she said, knocking it against the hard granite top of her work counter. "It has a hard-plastic shell and these tiny wings, some kind of nylon mesh, maybe. What do you call a mechanical thing that's designed to look like a living creature?"

"I don't know," Dale replied, frowning.

"A cyborg," Mac answered. "People make them in Silicon Valley. Usually for secret surveillance, military spying. Let me see it, Miss Butler."

"Of course, a cyborg." Frowning, she handed it to the man.

He turned the tiny object this way and that. "Must have a long-term battery. Here, look at this." He rubbed off more of the spray paint with a clean rag. "Yep, it's a camera lens, maybe wide angle. And the button below looks like a mic of some kind. Really high quality. A surveillance cyborg? Did you know about this? Obviously not," he said, answering his own question.

Athena looked around at the Tower's four security cameras, situated at the four corners of the large gallery's main room. Their black, bulbous lens were easily visible. As far as she knew, the back-framing room had a security camera as well. The adjacent bathroom did not.

"Of course not. This camera wasn't authorized. But, just to be certain, I'll call Kas—I mean, Mr. Skoros."

Mac glanced over at Dale and smiled. Of course, everyone who worked in the Stargazer Tower was aware of her and Kas's personal relationship.

She gave Kas's cellphone a ring. On his immediate answer, she summed up what they had found. She listened a few seconds, then rang off.

"He'll be down later to look at it. And no, it wasn't authorized."

"Well, I'll leave you to it. Got some wall repairs in one of the hotel rooms to do."

"Thanks, Mac." Athena smiled and offered a crackers and cheese snack, which she kept on a tray for customers. He helped himself to a snack and a glass of lemon infused, iced water from the jug standing nearby, and then went back to work, collapsing his extension ladder and carrying it out of the rear-side door.

When he was gone, Athena turned to face Dale, who was turning the mechanical device over to study its underbelly.

"Tell me, Dale, why would Zuckerman's chauffeur launch this . . . this thing?"

Her assistant looked up, astonished. "You think it was Zuckerman's chauffeur? Zuckerman, himself, who had this done?"

"Yes, I do. I don't think, I know. The man was standing in that corner, his back to us. At first, I thought he was caught up in Chen's paintings. No, it was him and therefore, by

Zuckerman's order."

Dale shook his head. "I don't know. Does he think the gallery's doing so well, that he wants to check out what we're doing right, what we're doing that's working? I don't know, maybe he wants to start his own gallery? He's known to be a serious collector of art, you know. What do you think?"

Athena shrugged, pretending to be just as clueless as Dale was. But she knew that Zuckerman had learned about her somehow, from Inspector Frank Vecchio.

Didn't he think she was a charlatan? Hadn't she convinced him? What would be Vecchio's connection to Elon Zuckerman, anyway?

"Well, who knows?" she said, "Kas says he'll have maintenance check around for any more of these cyborgs. He's having them check the main lobby, the elevators, his office."

"Hey, could these cyborgs be industrial spies?" Dale offered.

Hmmm. She remained silent and shrugged again. Just then, a customer entered the Stargazer Gallery and Dale drifted away.

Athena held the tiny object in her hand. Someone assigned to manipulate this cyborg had turned it off the minute the sprayed paint had covered the lens. And now they knew she was on to them.

The realization hit her.

She'd passed a kind of test.

Zuckerman's test. The cyborg was designed to be nearly invisible and yet, she'd sensed its presence straight away.

The man now had proof of her clairvoyance.

But why would he care?

CHAPTER THIRTY-EIGHT

Inspector Sergeant Wycott entered Villalobos's office with barely a brief knock. His lieutenant looked up with an exasperated frown on his face.

"Sorry, loo, but this is important."

Inspector Lieutenant Villalobos dropped his pen, sat back and folded his hands together. He hated being disturbed in the middle of reading case reports. Since last week, two more murders and four suicides had taken place but not one of them was related to the homeless murder case in any way. He assumed-and hoped-that the homeless killers had gone on a hiatus of sorts.

"Okay, let's hear it." Trying to sound as benevolent as he could be.

The young black detective approached his superior's desk and took a seat at one of the metal chairs facing it.

"The murder vic in Noe Valley from this weekend. Remember, you told me to have the hair of all dark blond-haired vics analyzed and compared to that dark-blond hair found on the homeless vic last month. The young vet."

"Ye-ah," drew out Villalobos's reply. Wycott had an annoying habit of speaking slowly when excited, as though the person being spoken to was hard of hearing. Or suffered from memory loss.

"Well, it matches."

Villalobos sprang up in his chair, a swivel rocker that nearly bounced him forward. "What? I thought that Noe Valley vic shot himself in the right temple. The gun was found on

243

the right side of his body. How does that square with a left-handed murderer? It was established by the ME, the perp sliced the homeless vet's neck from right to left. He was left-handed."

Wycott smiled. "It doesn't square, loo. Also, the partial prints from that homeless vic's button, we matched to this new vic's left forefinger. Our suicide is a homicide, so it's been thrown back to us by the captain. One of our homeless murderers was killed, himself. How much d'ya want to bet, by the other killer? Or by one of them, if there were more than two. Was he getting ready to blab, jump ship, rat them out, disappear?"

Inspector Frank Vecchio suddenly appeared at the open doorway, looking expectant.

"Come in, Vecchio, we're having a party," groused Villa-lobos. His second detective took the second chair in front of his desk.

"I heard the news. Sounds like what we thought was a solved series of homicides is now open to question. Right?"

"Right." Villalobos recalled Athena Butler's last words to him, something about there being three killers, not two. The bartender he'd spoken to remembered two men who'd sat at the bar in the last seat on the far-right end of the bar and had fiddled around with the coasters. He'd let his two detectives have a look at the coaster he'd taken from that bar, only to find out from the forensics lab that the fingerprints were so smudged, not even one fingerprint was retrievable.

"So where does that leave us, Lieutenant?" Vecchio asked.

Villalobos studied the two men, the older one and the younger one. No other homeless in the city had been discovered murdered. The ones found dead in the past two weeks had died of drug overdoses or from natural causes. After all, the weather had turned cold to freezing since the onset of December. The frosty fog that blanketed the city at night and that took hours in the morning to recede added to the homeless plight.

"It's obvious. The blond vic wasn't the only homeless killer out there."

Vecchio hunched over. "Have we explored other possibilities, that this latest vic may have taken a hit, like a drug deal gone bad? Or some other reason? A jealous husband or boyfriend?"

The lieutenant steepled his hands in front of his face, raked them up and down his chin, lost in thought.

"Alright, Vecchio, you explore that angle. Check into this guy's life. He was a vet honorably discharged, an EMT tech, a first responder. What would set him off on a mission to murder the homeless?" He looked at Wycott, knew his agility with computers. "Wycott, you explore his murder from the other side. He had two computers in his home, obviously computer literate. Why two? Was he trying to hide something on one of them? Get one of our illustrious techs to help you out. Do some, what do you guys call it, deep diving?"

"What about you, Lieutenant? What angle are you taking?" Vecchio asked as both underlings stood up.

"Right now, the only angle I'm taking is slogging through these murder books. The homeless case isn't our only one, y'know. If we can't get results, we might have to shelf it until . . ."

"Until?" Wycott queried, his expression crestfallen.

Villalobos took up his pen and glanced over the stack of reports. "Until another poor homeless sap gets it." He looked up as Wycott and Vecchio exited. "Close the damn door, Vecchio."

With the door shut firmly, he waited until both men had vanished from sight. Then he picked up the cellphone lying on the desk, went to *contacts*. He placed a call.

"Miss Butler, can I have a meeting with you? No, not here

at the Hall of Justice . . . somewhere near you . . . how about the lobby bar of the Hyatt Regency? It's on Drumm Street, just north of Market . . . very close to the Stargazer Tower . . . Good, you've been there? Yes, you can bring your friend, Mr. Skoros . . . Of course, I'll make sure I'm not followed . . ."

When he put down the cellphone, he frowned. Was he a superstitious fool, just like his cousin, Juan Pablo? Believing in the supernatural or ESP and all that psychic phenomena crap? Maybe, but everything she'd said so far had given him almost enough clues to solve this case.

Almost.

But almost wasn't good enough.

Chapter Thirty-nine

Darkness had fallen by the time Villalobos exited the Hall of Justice building but streetlights illuminated his figure. He crossed the street to the Hall's parking lot, his slow, hunched over gait telling Vecchio that his superior, a man bending under the weight of his homicide cases, was too old at fifty-eight for the job. He, at forty-five and with nerves of steel, should have been in charge this past year.

Still, Vecchio had heard rumors that Villalobos was being looked at to replace their captain once he retired the end of January. If that was true, then Vecchio, next in seniority, would be bumped up to lieutenant inspector in charge of homicide. An increase in pay and power. But not even close to the lucrative offer he'd gotten just that very day. Would now be the sensible time to leave police work? He had twenty years under his belt, commendations, no reprimands. And no one suspecting him of masterminding the homeless murders. Why not chuck the whole damned thing and find greener pastures? He'd done what he'd set out to do. Get revenge on the whore that brought him into this lousy world.

So why was he stalking the loo? Something was off, he knew. Sensing that his boss was on to something involving the homeless case, Vecchio had clocked out, gone home to catch a bite to eat and change clothes. And the car. He was driving his second car, a five-year-old nondescript black sedan. Unlike his crimson red sports car that he usually drove to work. The black sedan was one that Wycott and the lieutenant had never seen. Tended to blend into the night.

247

He was wearing a high-collared, black raincoat over casual clothes — a black sweater and black slacks — leather gloves and a black fedora, couched low over his forehead. The white wig, sporting long hair down to his shoulders, was the best disguise of all. His face in shadows, the outstanding, memorable feature was the white hair and black fedora. Always give possible witnesses something to remember.

He called Villalobos's home number. A woman answered. The man's wife, he knew as an acquaintance, the two now adult kids having left home for college years ago. He disguised his voice as well as he could through the handkerchief he held over his mouth.

"Hello, Mrs. Villalobos, this is the Night Watch Commander over at Justice. Your husband left without leaving an address where he could be reached and two of his detectives were expecting a meeting with him, at some watering hole nearby. He's not answering his cell phone so . . ."

He listened while the wife consulted her phone.

"Yes, he called to say he'd be a little late for dinner. Meeting a confidential informant, he said. Yes, here it is. The Hyatt Regency Hotel, the lobby bar."

"Thanks, very helpful."

"That's not like him, not answering his phone. Have him call me, would you, please, if you get in touch with him."

"The two detectives are embarrassed that they didn't write the address down, forgot about the meeting and just now remembered. We'd appreciate it if you wouldn't mention it to him. Thanks."

He shut down the call, kept his car's lights off and waited for Villalobos's distinctively styled, ninety's sedan to pull out of the Hall of Justice's parking lot. Now that Vecchio knew where the man was going, he'd take a different route and park around the corner from the hotel on Drumm Street.

Whoever Villalobos was meeting, he suspected it had

something to do with the homeless case. A case that hit too close to home.

The lobby bar was filled with low, excited chatter, people shopping for Christmas gifts stopping to refuel themselves, business folk in the financial district exchanging stock market tips, sightseers from out of town perusing one of the city's hot spots. A piano tinkled from the raised dais to the side of the bar located in the middle of the lobby. A pretty, maroon-gowned, red-haired woman gathered in front of the piano to sing another mid-century tune, catering to the largely Sinatra, Dean Martin, Sammy Davis crowd present at the moment. The huge, decorated and glittering Christmas tree behind them acted as a cheerful backdrop to the performers.

Above them rose at least ten tiers of open hotel corridors, a popular hallmark of the Hyatt Regency. From the balconies overlooking the lobby, twinkling garlands draped, adding to the holiday ambience. Athena kept glancing up at the fes-tively decorated tiers, feeling warmed and excited about the Christmas season. It was her favorite time of year, no matter where she was. The season seemed to bring out the best in people.

Not Kas that night, evidently.

Across the bistro table from Athena, a perturbed Kas Skoros slouched over his favorite cocktail, a bourbon-and-seven in a cut-glass highball tumbler.

"Why didn't you tell me you were meeting that detective?" His frown didn't mar his handsome face but did highlight the fatigue she saw in it. The extra line in his broad forehead, the crinkles under his eyes, the shadowy smudges. The nonstop, all day meetings had taken their toll and she sympathized with him and how hard he worked.

"I'm sorry, Kas. I just didn't think you'd want to come if

you knew the detective had called me and asked for this meeting." She perked her ears to the lovely alto sound emanating from the red-haired singer. "Oh, listen. She's singing one of my mother's favorite songs. 'I've got you under my skin, I've got you deep in the heart of me . . .'" She clicked her glass of chardonnay with his raised tumbler. "You know, the songwriter chose the perfect words. Kas, that's how I feel about you. You're under my skin, you're deep in the heart of me."

Kas looked surprised. She seldom expressed sentimental or maudlin feelings. A frown replaced his astonishment.

"Ah, flattery as a diversion? A peace offering? What's with my staunch British girlfriend?"

She pursed her lips. "You think I'm a cold fish? After last night? And the night before?"

He finally grinned in return, his frosty mood melting. "Never a cold fish. You just hold your emotions close in. You don't wear your heart on your sleeve."

"Like some women who throw around the word 'love' like they're saying, I love pizza? I can't be that kind of woman, you know that."

He took her hand in his, the one that hadn't touched his icy drink. His palm was warm and made her skin tingle. In fact, every time he touched her in some way, she felt herself tingle. Was this love? Lust? Deep friendship? A combination?

"I know, Thena. When you say it, I know you mean it."

"I do mean it. You're deep in the heart of me. You're my Leonides."

"Who . . . oh, that Greek bodyguard?"

"Macedonian soldier turned temple priestess bodyguard, yes. That Leonides. I've dreamed of him and her, my very, very ancient ancestor. Your mother has, too. They both live in us. We're their descendants."

With his other hand, he lifted his glass and took a sip. "Well, I don't know about that. If I am this guy's reincarnation, two-thousand years later, you can blame my father for the most part. He's the Greek in the family. Well, maybe a little on my mother's side since she's one-quarter Greek." He grinned, his good mood returning. "Far be it from me to question the wisdom and actions of my Greek ancestors. If you say I'm his reincarnation or genetic descendant, I won't argue. There are worse things I could've been, I suppose." He chuckled. "It might be romantic nonsense but who am I to question the sanity of a dearly loved precog and the clairvoyant woman I'm mad about?"

Athena teased, "You're right, luv. Don't question our sanity, just accept your fate."

Their snack food was delivered to their table. A small tray of four beef sliders beckoned them. Kas fell upon the food like a starving man.

"Forgot lunch today, with all those meetings and getting the maintenance crew to search for flying cyborg moths. No others were found, by the way, but that really pisses me off. The nerve of that bastard, putting a mechanical spy in our building. So you think it was Zuckerman's chauffeur who placed it in the gallery? Why would a man like Zuckerman do such a thing? If he wants a corporate spy in the Stargazer Tower, he could bribe any of my staff. And Zuckerman's got the dough to bribe anybody."

Nervously, Athena fingered the seeded pearl choker at her neck. Her low-necked, green silk cocktail dress had been chosen to forestall Kas's annoyance, which she knew would follow as soon as she told him about her meeting with the detective. The dress was doing its job. His eyes flitted between her face and her décolletage, she noted with satisfaction. Poor chap, she certainly complicated his life with her clairvoyance. But didn't her gift also help him at times, like last weekend?

In any event, she was extremely happy and grateful that he was there to help her face all of her challenges. Not to mention the one she faced tonight.

After wolfing down two of the sliders, he sat back, wiped his mouth and sipped his drink. He eyed her suspiciously as she watched him intensely. He was shooting her his usual ironic smile.

"Do you mean it, Thena? That I'm deep in the heart of you?" he said. His deep blue eyes rested pointedly on her expanse of skin between the pearl choker and her bodice.

With difficulty, as emotion welled with her, she swallowed and ventured forth.

"Yes. After our adventure together in the Sierra Nevada foothills, saving those little girls, seeing how bold and brave you are . . . I realized I wouldn't find anyone else like you. And-and I think we're meant to be together, you and me . . . during this lifetime. Like Leonides and Porphyra in theirs."

Kas frowned as if trying to understand the true meaning behind her words.

"Are you saying that if . . . if I asked you to marry me again, you might . . . say yes?"

"Yes," she whispered.

"Excuse me, I didn't hear you." He angled his ear in her direction. "You would say what, exactly?"

"Oh, blimey, you're never going to forgive me for turning you down the first time." She giggled and leaned over the table and cradled his chin in her hand. Kas looked deeply into her eyes, his sculpted mouth set in a rigidly skeptical line.

"I am sincere, Kas. I said, yes, I will marry you. If you want to ask me again, that is. Though, god knows, I'm not even twenty-four, and I'm not a good wife prospect. I mean, I don't really cook, I'm a bloody, mad, self-absorbed artist and a crazy clairvoyant to boot-"

Her peripheral vision became aware of someone close by. Villalobos was standing by their table, unwrapping his plaid coat scarf. "Hope I'm not interrupting anything."

Caught by surprise, Athena pulled back and sat up straight, dropping her hand from Kas's face. He was the first to regain composure and was quick to invite the man to take the pub chair they'd saved for him. The detective looked at Kas, then Athena.

"I'm sorry, I think I just interrupted something important."

Kas laughed shortly. "You're the first to know, Inspector Villalobos. We've just gotten engaged, Athena and me. Guess that makes us both kinda crazy."

Athena laughed despite the seriousness of the meeting she knew would follow. She clicked her glass with Kas's. "We truly are certifiable."

Kas raised up, leaned over and kissed her on the lips. "Oh well, crazy in love."

The singer belted out, "You're really a part of me . . . I've got you under my skin . . ."

She and Kas smiled at the timing of the lyrics before the detective shed his wool balmacaan.

"I'm so sorry," Villalobos began, "maybe we can do this another time."

The detective's-stricken countenance evoked her sympathy. He'd come to see her for her clairvoyant guidance, she knew, and she would give it to him. And that would be that.

"No, please, give me what you brought, and I'll see if anything comes of it," she urged him. He looked taken aback, forgetting for a second that she already knew what he'd hoped would be an important source of insight. "But first, Inspector, tell me something. Did you tell anyone about me, about my clairvoyance?"

The man frowned. "No, just my two detectives on the homeless case. Oh, and my wife. She's a believer and she's also heard my cousin Juan Pablo talk about you. Why?"

Athena nodded. "I believe you. Does your wife work in Silicon Valley? For Apollo?"

The detective looked askance. "Heavens no, she's a high school history teacher here in the city. We live in South San Francisco."

"Somehow, people are finding out about me. One is beginning to intrude in my life . . . and he's not welcomed." She cast Kas a glance and saw him scowl as he realized she was referring to the cyborg's surveillance capabilities. "I'm sorry, let's get to the business at hand. I know you came to show me something."

Slowly, Villalobos removed a plastic evidence bag from an inside pocket of his balmacaan. It contained the drink coaster that had been doodled on. The coaster that held the code. The secret code that enabled the three killers to communicate with each other.

He took out blue latex gloves for her to put on, which she did. Kas munched on the third slider and watched as the process unfolded.

The inspector spoke quietly in almost a whisper. "Miss Butler, there are no fingerprints on this coaster, none that we could retrieve. But I believe this coaster was one of several used in the planning of those homeless homicides."

Athena nodded, then clamped her gloved fingers around the edge of the round coaster and closed her eyes. A vision slowly formed, accompanied by the internal thoughts and emotions of the men who had handled the coaster and drawn on it. For a few minutes, she allowed herself to feel the emotional stew of their rage, their scattered, fragmented thoughts. Inside each one's head, one by one, she still couldn't see their faces. Finally, she was ready to interpret the vision she saw, and the emotions transmitted to her.

"All three killers of those homeless people have touched this coaster. First, killer Number One, then Number Two, then Number Three. In these code drawings, Number One tells Number Two to go ahead as planned. Choose your own victim, time and place. That plan was already understood. Then if all goes well, the second killer tells Number Three in code that it's his turn, and so on."

"Three killers? We were convinced there were two. We think one of them was recently killed. The one with dark blond hair."

She nodded, her eyes still closed. "Yes, the younger one with dark blond hair. His mind is now blank. The last thing he felt was shock. A man came to his door and overpowered him, shot him in the head, left the gun. Number Two killed him, tried to make it look like a suicide. But he made a stupid mistake."

Villalobos broke in. "He didn't check to see if his victim was right-handed or left-handed. He shot him in the right temple, left the gun by his right side. Such a rookie mistake."

Athena started for a second at the detective's choice of words. But unknowingly, he was right. The killer of Number Three was definitely not the cop.

"Definitely not the cop," she muttered more to herself than the two men at the table. But she'd spoken more loudly than she intended.

"What do you mean, definitely not the cop?" Villalobos asked, his voice tense, edgy.

Athena widened her eyes and looked at Villalobos. Something else distracted her and she turned her head to survey the men at the circular bar on the other side of the stage, where the piano player and singer held the limelight. The tall Christmas tree blocked the left side of the round bar. Patrons at bar stools circled the bar as three bartenders scrambled around, filling drink orders.

"Oh bloody hell, he's here. I can sense him."

Villalobos stood up, as did Kas, gazing around them for signs of danger. They looked in the direction of the bar, where she had fixed her gaze. With her hands, Athena motioned them to sit down.

"No, please, don't call attention." She gave the detective her best, warning stare. "Just know, Inspector, that the third killer, Number One on the coaster, is the instigator of the group, he met them online in some encrypted chat room, urged the other two to join him in this killing spree. And that was to cover up his own crime. He killed someone close to him . . . no, not close." She gasped and covered her mouth as she recalled something from her vision. "He killed his own mother."

"His own mother?" the inspector asked, "Do you know this man's identity?"

"No," Athena lied. She exhaled and handed back the coaster and latex gloves to Villalobos. "But I know this much. His mother abandoned him when he was just a boy. Like most of the homeless, she started out with a family and she threw it all away." She shook her head sadly. "But he did all this to cover up his own crime, his hatred, his rage."

"Jesus," breathed Villalobos.

Even Kas was gawking at her. "Chrissakes, Thena, are you sure?"

"Yes. One of the three killers is a cop."

Kas repeated, stunned by her revelation. "One of the killer's a cop?"

Wiping a tear from her eye with one finger, she used her cloth napkin to swipe her nose.

"Yes, I'm sure. This is what I'm seeing in my Flow vision. But Inspector, he's too smart to leave behind evidence, too smart to screw up. He'll probably kill Number Two to make certain he never talks but he'll bide his time."

"One of the perp's a cop?" The detective's voice was so hoarse, so laden with shock that she barely heard him.

"Yes." Athena looked over at Kas, who continued to stare back at her. His eyes connected with hers and the unspoken understanding said it all. *Don't say it. Too dangerous.*

A full minute seemed to pass as the detective silently put away the latex gloves and the precious evidence bag, now holding the coaster again. Not enough to charge anyone with a crime, too little even to promote a viable theory for the D.A. to take seriously. His heart heavy with defeat, Villalobos thanked Athena for her time, apologized again for interrupting their engagement celebration.

"Oh, that's all right," she assured him.

He looked grim as he took his leave shortly afterwards.

Crestfallen, Athena went back to her wine. Kas seemed to understand the injustice of it all but uppermost in his mind, she knew, was the threat they would have faced if she'd named the killer.

"You know, sweetheart, if you name him, you'll open yourself to all kinds of legal troubles, put us in real danger. He could set us up in all kinds of ways, plant drugs in the Tower, close us down. Bribe the contractor to sabotage the building. God almighty, destroy my family, destroy you, destroy me. Let the cops do their job. If they can't find the evidence, the proof, well . . ."

Kas was pleading with her and she understood. She nodded, then slowly her spirits rose again as the singer sang *San Francisco* at full volume. Surrounding them, the crowd responded with a rousing rendition and sang along.

"San Francisco, open your Golden Gate . . . I'm coming home today, no more to roam . . ."

She and Kas joined in, and by the end of the song, they were happy and smiling again. The optimism of youth and the stirring lyrics of an iconic song had prevailed.

"I've got a ring in my condo with your name on it," Kas announced, "the same one I've been holding onto for the past three months. Want to see if you like it on your finger? If not, I'll exchange it for another one."

"Are you mad? I'm positive I'll love it."

She slid off her pub stool, went over and kissed him soundly. He called a waiter for the bill while looking at the tiered balconies rising above them on all sides, the festive air all around the hotel.

"Why don't we see about a room for the night?"

"Here? We're just blocks from the Stargazer. I like your bed."

"Okay, but we're taking a taxi back. You said the guy, the killer, was here. Walking back is not a good idea."

He helped her on with her coat and then shrugged into his own winter jacket. She cocked her head for a second. "No, he's left. He won't bother us. He was traumatized as a child, had a difficult father but as an adult, he chose revenge and murder. He may be a sociopath but he's not mad, not crazy. I can only hope he makes a mistake someday. The man is evil incarnate, but the kind of evil that's smart and cunning."

"Don't worry about it, Thena. You can't single handedly rid the world of all its evil. Especially when law enforcement and the legal and justice system haven't caught up with people like you, people with special abilities. They probably never will."

They left the hotel lobby bar, arm in arm, absorbing again the Christmas spirit that infused the air around them.

CHAPTER FORTY

Encrypted chat room. For haters of the homeless? Or as his wife called them, the hopeless. Inspector Villalobos called Sergeant Wycott as he waited for the valet to bring out his car. He was feeling rotten after hearing what that psychic girl had to say, but that was no excuse to give up on the case. She *had* provided a clue or two.

"Hey, Wycott, sorry to disturb you . . . your night off, I know. I got a lead on the homeless case. You and our IT Brainiac, what's his name? Scott Henry, yes. Tomorrow I want you and Scott to put your heads together, go searching for chat rooms that attract haters . . . yeah, cults, groups of people who hate the homeless, have a grudge against them . . . yeah, the dark web. Go search for a chat room that's encrypted . . . Scott might know where to look. If you find someone who sounds like a leader, who's inciting violence, look for the guy's IP, anything that might lead us to some possible perps. Also, do a background check of all the cops in the Homicide Division, where they grew up, their family situations, that sort of thing. I'll authorize it with H.R., don't worry. And don't say anything about this to anyone outside our team . . . just don't. I have my reasons."

A few more instructions and Villalobos punched out. A minute later, he paid the valet and got behind the wheel.

When Vecchio saw his boss's gloomy countenance as he headed out of the lobby towards the Hyatt Regency's porte-cochere, he hesitated at first. Did the loo feel he'd wasted his time with that scam artist of a psychic? Or did she give him something that made him believe in her, something to follow up on? He reviewed in his mind everything that had transpired between the detectives on the case and the psychic girl. Sure, she'd been lucky about the bar scene but that had been the extent of her useful clues. The dark blond hair strand was probably a lucky guess. And from the cozy looks swapped between her and that rich Skoros guy, there was no chance she was hooking up with Number Three. No information there, but the fool was about to be identified and leaned on. Number Three had to be taken care of, but Number Two had even fucked that up.

Time to eliminate that potential threat as well. Only Vecchio knew the identities of the other two killers, something he'd been very careful not to reveal. There was nothing to link him with Number Two, except a coaster at the Drake Hotel bar on Powell. He'd go there tomorrow and destroy it. Or better yet . . .

Maybe another man in the city was going to die of a sudden heart attack.

Ah, the magic of chloral hydrate . . .

His thoughts interrupted by the lieutenant's car pulling out onto Drumm, Vecchio started his car engine and slowly wove his way into the traffic flow.

Ten minutes later, it was apparent that the loo was heading home. It was too risky and pointless to try anything on the man. The department would just put more men on the homeless case since that was Villalobos's main assignment for the time being.

No, let it go away by itself. Soon, if the rumors are true, the loo will be too preoccupied as captain of homicide to waste time on the damned homeless case. It'll join all the other unsolved cold cases that fill the basement file cabinets.

The sky was cloudy, threatening rain, and the coastal fog had covered the city buildings like a shroud. Death seemed to stalk the place like a ghostly apparition. It's the damned, fucking city, he thought, it creeps into your skin like a chilling virus. Infects your brain, makes you afraid of your own shadow. Makes you want to lash out at the darkness.

Too much darkness in this city.

With effort, Vecchio's thoughts turned to sunny Silicon Valley, just forty-five miles to the south. He'd had an offer he couldn't refuse from the man, himself. After a series of strange interview questions, including if he knew any psychics, he'd mentioned Skoros's girlfriend as a joke, the man himself had shown an interest. A few days later, he'd gotten a return call and a job offer.

While sitting at the lobby bar, careful to keep his collar up and head down, the final call had come through. Apollo Enterprises wanted him for personal security chief. At a quarter-million a year, how could he look a gift horse in the mouth and say no?

His job was done. He'd done what he'd set out to do two months ago, executing the plan like an engineer designing and building the longest suspension bridge in the world.

Brilliantly executed, he thought. The problem with most murderers, he knew from experience, was they acted impulsively. They seldom plotted and planned. So their impatience screwed them up and they got caught. No big fucking mystery there.

Time to swing home. Home. Not much there. A tomcat. His two ex-wives, bitches both of them, were long gone. It was a miracle he'd held on to his ol' house in the Sunset District. But he was better off without the broads. Couldn't be trusted, anyway. Always disappointing, always lying. No kids. Hell, he wouldn't know how to be a father even if he had 'em. No good role models when he was growing up except for the clever villains in the movies. Those were *his* role models.

Darth Vader. *He* knew how to take care of business.

An idea struck him. Inspired, he drove down Market Street and swung by the Stargazer Tower, just as the girl and her boyfriend climbed out of a cab. Their arms around each other, their happy expressions made him want to puke. If the asshole she was fucking wasn't the son of a well-known, rich Bay Area developer, Vecchio would've felt compelled to take care of her, just for the hell of it. Who was she, anyway? Some English chick who'd gotten her claws into this damned fool? Pretending to be psychic?

What a crock!

He drove on past the Stargazer Tower and, the Ferry Building looming over him, took a right on the Embarcadero. Eighty-west would take him to Nineteenth Avenue and Holloway. Time to head home and catch a few winks. He'd let Apollo Enterprises know first thing in the morning that they had a new security chief. Maybe in that capacity, he'd be able to travel with the head honcho and still stay in touch with Wycott to make sure the homeless case ran cold and stayed cold.

Also, he'd have the power and wherewithal to keep an eye on that damned broad. With one swift movement, he whipped off the white wig and the fedora. He glanced at himself in the rear-view mirror, his dark, piercing eyes glittering in the dark car.

He smiled, pleased at his future prospects.

Chapter Forty-One

"**N**ever been here before," said Wycott, climbing out of the passenger's seat. He and his lieutenant scanned the area in front of the Robert Drake Hotel. The scene on Powell Street was chaotic. Blue uniformed cops had set up a perimeter, blocking foot and car traffic on both north and south sides of the hotel. Stanchions and yellow tape prevented the ultra-curious from invading the crime scene, another potential homicide from the nine-one-one call they got.

Villalobos set the *police on duty* sign on the dashboard of his car that was double-parked at an angle. Only the cable cars were allowed to continue their Hyde-to-Powell-to-Eddy Street route, the clanging bell of one being heard loud and clear as it passed by. It was the Sunday before Christmas and shoppers and sightseers crowded the area near Union Square, just a block south.

What a mess!

Since Vecchio abruptly resigned four days ago, he and Wycott had been pulling overtime and weekend duty until another sergeant-grade inspector could replace the man. His sudden resignation had, in Villalobos's mind, raised him to person of interest as the killer cop the psychic girl had mentioned that night at the Hyatt Regency bar. The fact that they had no proof of the man's involvement kept the unlikely prospect firmly entrenched in the back of his mind. Pure suspicion didn't make a prosecution case. No way was Villalobos going to jeopardize his career by making flimsy allegations against a fellow law enforcement officer.

He and Wycott entered the downstairs bar. The Robert Drake had been an old, established and prestigious hotel but had recently fallen on tough times. Although it was under new ownership and had undergone a complete renovation, the establishment never fully recovered its former glory days. Once one of the favorite watering holes of such famous, mid-century people as Joe DiMaggio, Tony Bennet, Joe Alioto, now the hotel was at best a three-star. However, the lieutenant couldn't help but whistle under his breath at the length of the polished mahogany bar, the fine oak paneled walls and gleaming brass fixtures.

Two uniforms parted and let the detectives through. The man's body lay on the floor next to the far-right end of the counter. Lying on his back in a supine position, he displayed the chalky skin of the dead. The two young bartenders sat at a table nearby, looking solemn, a bit frightened.

A uniformed cop spoke up, consulting his notes from a small, spiral notepad.

"Inspector, we have a witness," he said, indicating the younger of the two bartenders, a tall, skinny guy in his twenties, his light blond hair spiked all over his head.

"What else do you have?" Wycott asked the cop.

"Approximately, fifteen minutes ago this man, a regular customer by the name of Fidel Alvarez, was drinking a scotch and soda, talking to a man who'd just bumped into him. The man was tall and had long, white hair. Things got a little heated, according to Mike here, the bartender who waited on him, but the white-haired guy said he was sick and off he went, staggering to the men's room. Said he was going to throw up, so off he went. Mr. Alvarez let him go and went back to his drink. About five minutes later, he clutches his chest and keels over. And that's about it. Oh, here's the DB's wallet."

Villalobos thanked the cop as he squeezed on latex gloves,

took the wallet and turned to inspect the body, indicating that Wycott should interview the spiky-haired bartender.

Gazing at the man's open, dark eyes, the lieutenant concluded by his swarthy complexion, his short stature and black hair that he most likely was a Latino by heritage. A dribble of frothy spittle leaked from the corner of the man's mouth, which was open in surprise. The man looked too young to die from a sudden heart attack. He was lean and muscled, appeared in good health otherwise. The rigid grimace in his facial expression at the moment of unconsciousness indicated the man's shock over his sudden physical crisis.

Villalobos opened the man's wallet, looked at his driver's license, charge cards, one family photo, an old one from the frayed edges. Maybe he'd left his family behind in Mexico, who knew? Something else came loose. Another ID card, this one indicating his EMT license, assigned to Saint Agnes Memorial Hospital ambulance service. This man was a first responder, same as the homicide victim with dark blond hair. Suspect Number Three. The two men worked for the same ambulance service. Not hardly a coincidence, was it?

He turned to the bartender, now speaking in a subdued voice with Wycott.

"Have you moved his glass or the coaster under it?"

The young, spiky-haired bartender shook his head vigorously. "No, sir, detective. Didn't touch a thing. I've been trained not to in case of, well, in a case like this. I swear, I didn't put anything in his drink except scotch and soda."

Villalobos nodded his thanks, and with his gloved hands, deposited the one-third-full glass into a glassine evidence bag, using a special wire tie to close it. The poison was probably in the liquid. If not, the ME will find a puncture hole somewhere on the man's body.

He then picked up the coaster, upon which the glass had rested, and turned it over.

Bracing himself emotionally, he studied the penned doodles on the back. The right-pointed arrow before the sunset looking doodle, the Number Three with a circle around the "three" and a thick black line through it. Next to that was the sunset code. Above all the doodles, a small, decorative six-pointed star caught his attention.

Was this man the Number One killer or Number Two? Number Two killed with a silenced pistol, if he recalled correctly. Number One killed with an injection. There had been how many other homicides in the city since the last homeless one nearly a month ago? Eight, ten? Most of the victims killed by firearms.

He glanced down at the dead body of Fidel Alvarez. A small man would most likely use a firearm, wouldn't risk a physical confrontation with a potential vic.

His next query, so did Number Two shoot Number Three? And did Number One-if the psychic girl was correct and there were three killers involved in the homeless homicides-kill Number Two? Was this vic Number Two? Because this investigation was heading straight back to Number One?

The killer cop, as the girl had declared.

Villalobos deposited the coaster into another evidence bag before going over to the small, round table, where Wycott and the young bartender sat.

"Tell me in your own words what happened right before, during and after the confrontation with the white-haired man who claimed to be sick?"

Wycott's dark brown eyes registered surprise, but a look from his lieutenant kept him silent. The sergeant took notes, himself, while the bartender spoke.

An hour later, the two detectives met in Villalobos's office with the door closed.

"Any progress with our tech master, Scott Henry, on that

encrypted website, targeting the homeless?"

"Yes, we located a website, reported it to DHS and the FBI. Just rants and raves, no real threats, just talk like, someone should put them out of their misery, stuff like that. But the three trollers who exchanged rants on San Francisco homeless all had their IPs buried under foreign IPs, and the web was so tangled, it was pointless to continue. But those three trollers did talk about good bars to drink at. Was that a sign, you think, that they were planning their coded communications?"

The lieutenant tossed onto his desk the glassine bag with the drink coaster inside.

"Could be. I doubt we'll find any fingerprints on it except those belonging to the DB. The drink's being processed by the FBI forensics lab, the body by our very own ME. We'll know by tomorrow night whether he was poisoned by the drink or by an injection. Now, take a close look. See the same kind of markings that we saw on that other coaster I showed you. It's a code, of course, the six-pointed star."

Wycott studied it for a moment, then glanced away, a faraway look in his eyes. When he returned his gaze to his supervisor, he was frowning with confusion.

"I don't know, sir."

"The Templar Knights, the crusader knights from the middle ages. They accumulated a lot of wealth, built monasteries and churches all over Europe and what's now modern-day Turkey and the Greek Isles. They loaned other crusader money for their journeys to fight the Muslims."

"What on earth does that have to do with the homeless here in the city?" the younger detective asked, thoroughly perplexed. The younger detective ran a hand through his black, wiry hair. There was a spark of insight livening his expression.

"Hmm, the Templars were known for their dedication to a cause. They took oaths, something like silence until death, that sort of thing. From what I learned about them, kind of a hobby with me during college, they gave each other permission to be sacrificed if the group as a whole was threatened."

Grunting his approval, the lieutenant slumped back in his seat, appeased by Wycott's confirmation but still feeling discouraged.

"Well, it's a theory although a farfetched one. I wonder if there are other wannabe knights in the city taking up this cause, getting rid of the homeless on our streets." He slapped his hands on his desk. "What a nightmare of a case!"

"Yep, I guess," agreed Wycott, "it caused Vecchio to give it up."

Villalobos gave the younger detective a speculative look.

"You think this case was why he resigned?"

"Oh yeah, he told me more than once it was time for him to move on. All these homicides with no solutions. Guess it took all the steam out of him. Made him feel like giving up."

The lieutenant harrumphed. "Think you'll stick around for twenty years, sergeant? A college man like you?"

Wycott slowly shook his head. "To be honest, lieutenant, I don't know. My girlfriend wants me to use my master's and get a job teaching junior college. Pay's about the same and there's no risk in teaching history." The young African American stood up but paused at the doorway. "That girl, the one you think is psychic-do you think she'll continue to help us solve cases? I mean, she got us to the bars and the coded coasters, anyway. Got us on the right track, anyway, even if she couldn't identify the perps."

"Don't know," the detective said. He stood, also, placed the evidence bags into a labelled cardboard box and fixed the lid down tightly. "Here, put this on top of the other boxes."

Five cardboard boxes which held evidence and case notes lined the far wall of the lieutenant's office. Wycott lifted the homeless homicide box and placed it on top.

"I'm going home, lieutenant, it's been a long day. I'll have one of the uniforms take these boxes down to the basement tomorrow. Y'know, I didn't mind the overtime. The extra pay's not bad but I missed the playoffs. Good thing I set the recorder."

They bade each other good night. Before Villalobos turned off his office lights, he cast the homeless box a grim look. Did the psychic girl know who Number One was, but she wasn't telling? Maybe, maybe not. Was she even the clairvoyant she claimed to be? Who knew in this crazy world?

Too bad.

Chapter Forty-two

A thena paused in her packing to answer her cellphone. It was Dale, down in the gallery about to close shop.

"Athena, your giclee prints for the nude arrived. I'll frame one and hang it up alongside the first one. All fifty of the first order were delivered today. D'ya have a name for this one? The first one's titled, Bliss One. And the second nude?"

She smiled inwardly at all that her painting implied. "Just title it Bliss Two. So glad those prints arrived. Store them in back in case you're able to sell them."

"Just got orders for five prints, Bliss One. I think the other'll do well, too. The giclees are on order. Should be done in another week. They're a great pair, those two nudes. In case I don't see you, have a safe and wonderful trip. You, your brother and Mr. Skoros."

"Thanks, Dale, lovely of you to say that. And I must say, you've been absolutely splendid to work with."

They rang off just as she heard two knocks on her front door, then heard it open. Kas had a key to her condo just as she had a key to his.

"Back here," she called out.

Her now legitimate fiancé appeared at her side in a flash. His arms wrapped around her and he snuggled in close, his lips finding her neck.

"I'm all packed. My brother George is coming tomorrow to make sure the Tower's manager knows what to do while I'm gone. I told him it wasn't necessary, I trained Tim well, but you know George. Even Pop's coming. They're both curious to see how the new condos are coming along. I told them five'll be finished and ready to sell by the time I get back." He snuggled in closer. "By the time we both get back."

She glanced at her watch. Four o'clock. Chris should be arriving soon via an Uber driver and she'd just started her packing. Her huge suitcase was half full, causing her to feel panicked. Their red-eye, nonstop flight from SFO to Heathrow was leaving at eleven-thirty that night. Loosening his embrace, she turned around in his arms.

"Will you let me get on with it?" She gave him a deep kiss before unwinding herself.

"Okay," he said good naturedly, "what can I help you with?"

She pointed to three pairs of shoes on her bed. "Can you put them in those shoe bags? Thanks, luv."

The center diamond on her engagement ring caught a sunlight beam, flashed and drew her attention. Holding out her hand, admiring the ring and Kas's choice, she added, "Won't Chris and Father be surprised? Mum already knows. She always knows everything before it happens, no surprising her, darn it."

Kas laughed. "My mother, too. She's already told the rest of the family."

They worked side by side, Athena pointing to the stacks of pants, skirts and jumpers on the bed.

"Hand me that jumper, Kas," she said.

"Jumper?" Kas asked, looking around, confused.

"Sweater, I mean. That one over there, the red one with the Christmas Grinch on the front. I'll wear it on Christmas Day. We have a family contest for the ugliest or funniest."

"Glad I packed my reindeer one," he said, "haven't worn it in ages. Rudolf's nose lights up."

She looked at him fully. He looked wiped out. "You've been working so hard, Kas, you deserve a short vacation.

Don't you think? Don't feel guilty for a few weeks off."

"Two weeks, a short vacation? For my family, that's a long one. Especially now, with everything going on here during this crucial phase."

With alacrity, she cupped his face with both hands. "Crucial phase? Every phase in this building has been crucial. You deserve to take a break."

His deep blue eyes glittered warmly. "So glad you're on my side, Thena. My family, my father, brothers. They're all driven taskmasters. You know that. The family's very successful but it takes a toll."

"I believe you're right, so right." Her thoughts leaped to her own small family, now resettled in North Kensington. Her Flow channel had delivered ominous news to her this morning as she lay in bed, her mind gradually rising to full consciousness.

Her father was dying. She knew she wouldn't be back in two weeks. Maybe not even two months. Kas and Chris would return without her, but she would stay in London. She didn't want to dampen Kas's Christmas visit by telling him so soon.

Not until she absolutely had to.

"I want you to have a good time," she told him softly.

His smile warmed her completely. "I will, I promise you," he said. He took her hand, kissed the back of it, then added, "C'mon, let's try and close this thing. Then let's see if I can lift it."

An exaggerated huff and puff followed. When he finally settled it on the floor, its four sturdy wheels causing it stay upright, she exclaimed, "Ah, my wonderful Greek warrior."

He chuckled and shook his head.

"Warrior and lover," she amended proudly.

ABOUT THE AUTHOR

A retired high school English teacher, Donna loves to read, write, and travel with her husband, Joe. She's a member of Sisters in Crime and International Thriller Writers. A singer with a Sweet Adelines chorus, she intends to make another trip to London to sing at the Oxford Music Festival. An unabashed Anglophile, she admires the stoicism and humor of the British people. Also, she thanks her family for their encouragement, their contributions to and suggestions for this book: Joe, Leigh, Todd, Jacob, Charlie and Dionne.

www.ingramcontent.com/pod-product-compliance
Lightning Source LLC
Chambersburg PA
CBHW061554170626
46811CB00001B/200